T0288226

What the River Said

WHAT THE RIVER SAID

A Novel

Sandra Cavallo Miller

UNIVERSITY OF NEVADA PRESS *Reno & Las Vegas*

University of Nevada Press, Reno, Nevada 89557 USA
www.unpress.nevada.edu

LIBRARY OF CONGRESS CATALOGING-IN-PUBLICATION DATA
Names: Miller, Sandra Cavallo, author.
Title: What the river said : a novel / Sandra Cavallo Miller.
Description: Reno ; Las Vegas : University of Nevada Press, [2021] |
Summary: "In What the River Said: A Novel, the author's final book in
   her trilogy, is the story of a woman physician at the Grand Canyon
   Clinic undertaking the challenges of an unusual spate of heart attacks,
   heavy metal poisoning, and a missing friend, as she and her physician
   partner temporarily parent a troubled teenager. Their new alliances
   strengthen as the dark schemes of illicit drug sales become clear"—
   Provided by publisher.
Identifiers: LCCN 2020045086 (print) | LCCN 2020045087 (ebook) |
   ISBN 9781647790080 (hardcover) | ISBN 9781647790097 (ebook)
Subjects: LCSH: Women physicians—Fiction. | Interpersonal
   relations—Fiction. | Grand Canyon (Ariz.)—Fiction.
Classification: LCC PS3613.I55293 W45 2021 (print) | LCC PS3613.I55293 (ebook) |
   DDC 813/.6—dc23
LC record available at https://lccn.loc.gov/2020045086
LC ebook record available at https://lccn.loc.gov/2020045087

The paper used in this book is a recycled stock made from 30 percent post-consumer
waste materials, certified by FSC, and meets the requirements of American National
Standard for Information Sciences—Permanence of Paper for Printed Library
Materials, ANSI/NISO Z39.48-1992 (R2002). Binding materials were selected for
strength and durability.

First Printing
Manufactured in the United States of America

25 24 23 22 21   5 4 3 2 1

This book is a work of fiction. Names, characters, places, and incidents either are
products of the author's imagination or are used fictitiously. Any resemblance to
actual persons, living or dead, or events is entirely coincidental. While most of the
references to astronomy, geology, and medicine are accurate, certain geographic
or logistic details have been altered to accommodate the plot. And with scientific
knowledge being what it is, there is a considerable chance that something is altered
between the writing and the reading.

To Ted and Katie:
For all the times... You know what I mean.

What the River Said

1

For the last week, every November morning at the Grand Canyon dawned clear and cold. The night let go of its secrets as sunlight flared up over the rim and promised a bright, pleasant day. By noon, though, dark clouds blotted out the blue, clouds that rose and seethed, as if annoyed by so many humans enjoying the views. These were not typical scattered thunderheads that wandered over, dropping dizzy shadows and quick downpours. These storms besieged the sky, throwing hard rain like weapons and hurling spears of lightning into the earth. Tourists ran for shelter, and even old regulars who lived at the canyon for years felt apprehensive.

New signs were posted, warning about the dangers of lightning.

"Here we go again," muttered Dr. Abigail Wilmore, wincing as thunder exploded and shook the clinic.

Abby was about to examine a man with one of the worst diabetic foot ulcers she would ever see. Herman White, sixty years old going on seventy-five and a resident of his car for the last year, scuttled in just before the cloudburst, asking if a physician could look at his foot because it oozed more yellow fluid and pus than usual. While Abby felt some days that she had seen nearly everything, she also knew that the human body still had the capacity to astound her.

"I think my sugars are pretty good," said Herman, pulling off a stained linty sock. "I can tell because I've got more energy."

"You don't have a glucose meter?" Abby asked, rapidly typing into her laptop, trying to document his medical history before examining him. "When you use insulin, it's really important to know your sugars. A low blood sugar—you know, hypoglycemia—can kill you."

Thunder crashed and they both paused, staring at the frosted window where rain streamed like a waterfall down the glass.

Herman rubbed at his cheeks, bright with rosacea, and gave her a doleful smile. Pale hair straggled around his seamy face, the thin strands a washed-out gray, almost colorless. "I can't win, right? If my sugars are too high, diabetes will kill me. If my sugars go too low, insulin will kill me. High, low. Up, down. Who can take that kind of pressure? So I just threw out my glucose meter and I've been happier ever since. I was always out of batteries anyway."

Dolores Diaz tapped at the door and stuck her head inside, handing Abby a paper slip. She looks weary, Abby thought. The clinic nurse was one of Abby's favorite people, calm and competent. But they had been swamped this year with high patient volumes, and there was talk of hiring a second nurse, or at least an assistant.

"Well, something is working right," Abby said, glancing at the lab slip, a little surprised. "Your A1C is seven-point-five, which is pretty good." She would have guessed eight, or even higher. "So your diabetes is fairly well controlled."

"I think it's the walking I'm doing." He nodded and thumped his mounded belly. "Believe it or not, I've lost some weight."

Abby compressed her lips. Walking might be the worst thing he could do for a foot ulcer. Putting down her laptop, she picked up his brawny foot. His legs were thick, crusted and flaked with dry skin, like the bark of an old tree. She raised his foot higher and grimaced involuntarily at the yawning wound, a deep cavity burrowing into his sole at the base of his toes. The dark red crater consumed nearly a third of his foot. A dense white rind lined the perimeter, and a dank polluted odor seeped up to her nose.

"It's pretty bad, huh," he said apologetically, craning to look.

"Mr. White." Abby paused. "How much have you been walking on this? How much does it hurt?"

He laughed, a short grunt. "Not really walking that much. Do I look like someone in good shape? But I used to not walk at all. And it doesn't hurt, because I'm basically numb from the knees down. It's like walking on wads of cotton instead of feet."

"Well, I applaud your efforts, and I'm sure that's helped your sugars." Abby peered into the ragged depths of his foot, seeing only moist beefy tissue but knowing that, buried somewhere in there, the bones were exposed and infected. She gently lowered his leg. "When was the last time you saw a doctor for this?"

He sighed. "Almost a year. I went to the wound clinic for months back in Chicago, but nothing worked. They wanted to amputate, and I just panicked and left. I've been on the road ever since. I find odd little jobs, just enough to get by." He was passing through, no medical insurance, and he planned to leave the canyon that day as soon as the rain let up, headed for the sunny warmth of Phoenix and Tucson.

Abby felt defeated. "I'm pretty sure it's infected, and probably into the bones. I can give you some antibiotic pills, but I have to be honest—it won't be enough. It takes IV antibiotics to reach the bones, sometimes for weeks. Or even months. I can give you the name of a low-cost clinic in Phoenix, and maybe you can get some emergency coverage. Although that's tricky to arrange."

He started to pull on his sock, but she stopped him, taking out clean gauze and elastic bandages, wrapping his foot.

"You don't suppose I can avoid amputation?" he asked, dispirited now.

Abby shook her head and felt bad. He seemed nice, just overcome. His impulsive escape hadn't worked. "Truthfully? I doubt it. It's really severe. But don't depend on my opinion—you need to consult with a wound expert. Maybe there's more they can do. Have you tried hyperbaric oxygen?"

Herman stared at the floor and nodded. "Maybe you should give me the name of that clinic. But thanks for explaining everything."

Abby touched his arm in sympathy and asked him to wait while she arranged his paperwork and wrote a note for the underserved health center in downtown Phoenix. Walking down the hall, she peeked into the small office where Pepper sat bent over a computer. She started to say something, then decided not to interrupt him and moved on to the front desk, where Priscilla and Marcus were preparing charts and finalizing bills.

Marcus grinned and waved his fingers, but he was on the phone. His canary-yellow polo shirt, stretched over his wide stomach, made a bright splash in the dreary afternoon. Abby turned reluctantly to Priscilla.

Priscilla looked like an urban secretary. She wore a frilly, snug blouse, a deep V-neck that plunged between her breasts, down past where one would usually find a bra. Abby tried to imagine what might be underneath. No bra at all? Stick-on cups? That was the point, she realized, to make someone—preferably a man—wonder. Abby made a mental note to ask Pepper later about his reaction, for she knew Priscilla must have paraded herself under his nose at least a dozen times. Despite the fact that Abby and Dr. John Pepper had now lived together for over a year, Priscilla apparently still hoped he would suddenly comprehend her virtues and fall under their spell.

"Can I help you, Dr. Wilmore?" Priscilla asked formally, sitting up straight and wiggling her shoulders slightly in case Abby had missed her bounty. The waiting room stood empty; the storm had discouraged everyone. And while the lightning and thunder were waning, rain still pounded savagely on the roof.

"Sure," said Abby. "That last patient, Herman White. I want to be certain he only gets charged the minimal fee. He doesn't have insurance."

Priscilla's tiny upturned nose crimped, as if smelling something rancid, and she shot a severe look at Abby. "Dr. Wilmore, I'm sure you know I can't make that decision. FirstMed's new policy says all reduced charges must be cleared with them."

Her petite fingers flew over the keyboard, flashing with silver polish that matched her glittering eyelids. Something a twelve-year-old would wear, Abby thought.

Priscilla pointed a sparkly nail at the screen. "See? You spent quite a lot of time with him. You reviewed his meds and discussed his diabetes and his foot ulcer. You talked to him about being homeless. It's all right here. I don't see how we could even begin to justify a lower charge. If anything, he should have a higher code. I don't want to get in trouble for undercharging."

Abby told herself to be tolerant. Priscilla notoriously followed the rules if they fit her agenda. Abby knew she was tired herself, and she felt sad for Mr. White. And now she finally admitted to herself that she was worried about Pepper, his dark mood. She wanted the workday to end, even though it was only three o'clock.

"I didn't do a thing for him," Abby explained. "All I did was tell him to see a specialist in Phoenix. That's not worth a big medical bill." She braced for an irritating conflict she didn't want. "Besides, I'm not asking you to make the decision. I'm making the decision. If I could, I wouldn't charge him at all."

Priscilla's penciled eyebrows flew up as she recited the medical company's dogma. "Dr. Wilmore, FirstMed is not a charity. Maybe if I cleared it with Dr. Pepper we could—"

"Don't worry about it, Priscilla," Marcus chipped in, beaming widely at the two women. He hung up the phone and now typed quickly. "Just let me do the bill, and you can stay out of it. We can use the 99201 code for a simple new visit, then give him the 30 percent discount for a cash patient. And I can set up a payment plan for him if he can't afford it all at once. Does that help enough, Dr. Wilmore?"

Priscilla whirled on him. "Marcus Limerick, you should mind your own business! I'm having a private discussion with the doctor."

"I just thought I'd pitch in," Marcus said happily, completing the form and hitting *Print*. "I mean, I really appreciate all the help you've given me, Priscilla, orienting me to this job all week. It's time I did my share. It's so nice when we work together like this."

Priscilla fumed while Abby smothered a smile and thanked them both. As she turned away, she heard Priscilla fire back at him in a severe whisper, "If you really want my help, you should ask me about your clothes. For your information, that yellow shirt does not go with those burgundy pants. Not at all. This is a professional office, and you should dress like it."

Marcus chuckled heartily. "I know, right? My colors are always a mess—maybe I should get tested for color blindness."

"It's not funny," Priscilla hissed, as the door swung shut.

Abby gave the papers to Herman White, recommending that he wait in the lobby until the rain slackened. Then she stepped into the cramped closet they called their doctors' office, where Pepper sat with his chin in his hand, reading a medical article on the computer.

"Anything new?" she asked, scrunching in next to him.

He shook his head and smiled, reaching over to grip the back of her neck underneath her twist of hair. It was the one affectionate gesture he allowed himself at work, and she cherished it every time.

"Just more copycat drugs we don't need, at higher prices." He tilted his head to listen to the rain outside the window, which had suddenly diminished, barely dripping now. "I can hold down the fort if you want to leave early. I doubt we'll see many more patients today."

"I want to run home, but I'll be back. I meant to bring those cookies I baked last night. Everyone looks tired today—including you, by the way—and there's nothing better for morale than fresh chocolate chip cookies." She looked pointedly at him without meaning to.

"Morale?" His eyes narrowed, went frosty blue.

Abby shrugged. "Marcus and Priscilla are, um, adjusting. Sniping at each other. Although Marcus doesn't snipe—he just gets nicer and makes fun of himself, which infuriates Priscilla. And Dolores is overworked."

"And me?" he said cautiously. "I got the feeling you meant something about me."

Abby shrugged again. Quit shrugging, she told herself. "No. Not really."

"That's convincing."

This was not the place to have this conversation. "You're fine. Maybe sometimes a little distant." She smiled. "You know how you are."

Pepper shook his head, dismissive. "That's silly—everything's fine. Go get your cookies. I promise to eat a dozen and be the happiest man alive."

"Ha. You'd better watch your waistline," Abby teased. Pepper was tall and thin, and he could truthfully stand to gain some weight.

He laughed and looked like himself again, amused, a little unruly with his ruffled hair and short brown beard. "Hurry up with those cookies. Now I'm hungry."

Abby pulled on her jacket and tramped briskly through the trees. Although the rain had stopped, large cold drops plopped on her head and she tugged up her hood. The temperature dropped, and her breath puffed out in faint clouds. She wondered how much longer these storms would persist, raging along the rim every afternoon. Summer, not fall, was the usual time for thunderheads, but the weather had seemed strangely unsettled for a month: first, frantic winds ripped old trees from the ground; then, record-breaking heat parched the forest and sparked fires; and now these odd violent storms were attacking them day after day.

She made up a cheerful box of cookies, lined with a bright red napkin. So domestic, she thought—even Marcus and Priscilla couldn't resist feeling better when they saw that. Then she laughed…as if anyone could accuse her of being domestic. Most days, if she had any energy left after work, cooking was the last thing she would do. Instead she took a walk and studied the geology stacked below her, those complicated bands of stone, left behind over millions of years. Hundreds of millions. Or she might go running, something she was just starting up again.

A new thought smacked her. Could that be what bothered Pepper? Maybe she had turned too solitary, too limited, without realizing it—absorbed by her own routines. Maybe he had doubts, craved something more, something different. While they sometimes discussed their concerns about having children, neither felt ready to create that commitment. Had something changed?

Abby sat down, still in her rain jacket, the box of cookies in her lap. She reviewed their recent moments—his touch on her neck, his laugh—and she scolded herself for being silly; they just needed to talk. She grabbed a notepad and drew a little stick-figure cartoon of Pepper frowning at her cookies, a word bubble over his head saying, "Feed me cookies or else," which she propped up on the kitchen table. Then she slid a plastic bag over the box because the sky was drizzling now, a morose gray fizz, pulled up her hood, and marched back to the clinic.

Drawing near, she saw an ambulance angled into the back entry, left empty with doors flung open, a crumpled wet towel on the pavement. She broke into a jog. How long had she been gone?

Pepper, Dolores, paramedics, and rangers all crowded the treatment room where a hectic resuscitation was underway.

Pepper braced the paddles against the man's bare chest and called out "Clear!" Everyone stepped back. The body jerked, but nothing twitched on the monitor. Abby stood in the background; there was nothing she could do. The patient looked young and muscular, with thick blond hair and a spray of acne across his cheeks, still in khaki hiking shorts. He was already intubated, and someone resumed chest compressions while Pepper ordered drugs and adjusted the oxygen and Dolores filled syringes. It went on and on. Abby read Pepper's grim, unhappy face, and she knew he felt up against the wall, nothing helping, nothing happening. The energy in the room began to flag, and people exchanged glances, starting to wonder when. The mute heart in question, the center of attention, remained silent. Inert. Done.

A ranger stood beside Abby and filled her in. Over an hour ago, the patient staggered into the Kolb Studio just below the rim, wet and bedraggled, gasping. He told staff that he just finished hiking down to the river on the South Kaibab Trail, then back up the Bright Angel, a brutal trip of more than fifteen miles, forty-five hundred feet down in elevation, then forty-five hundred feet back up. A route that no one recommended for one day, even though elite runners and hikers tackled it regularly. And although he was an accomplished hiker who had done it before, today he leaned against the wall of Kolb Studio, complained of feeling awful, and collapsed. When the rangers arrived, his heart galloped furiously in ventricular tachycardia. After being shocked, it quivered into ventricular fibrillation, and after they shocked him again, it stood still in no rhythm at all.

Pepper finally stopped, told everyone to quit. They had tried for an hour. The young man's heart never thumped or bumped, not even once. The desolate process of locating his family began.

Marcus peered into the room and motioned for Abby. "There's a patient who's been waiting," he said quietly, his eyes flicking toward the form on the table. "Can you see her?"

Dolores cleaned up the body, biting her lip as she removed cardiac leads and IV lines, wiped off blood and adhesive. Pepper thanked everyone for their efforts and retired to the little office. His eyes met Abby's briefly, arctic.

"Of course," Abby said to Marcus. "What's going on?"

"She's pregnant, and her urine burns." Marcus looked somber, but as they stepped away he carried on with the plethora of information he had somehow managed to extract from the patient within seconds. "It's a boy. They were going to name him Nathan, but now the father thinks that's a sissy name and wants to name him Robert. Only she once knew a Robert that she couldn't stand, he was such a bully, so she refuses to call her baby that. Anyway, she's collecting a urine sample, and she'll be ready in a few minutes. And everything with the pregnancy has been perfect so far, and she's hardly felt sick at all, right from the start."

Abby nodded appreciatively. Typical Marcus, who rarely failed to elicit an encyclopedia of patient background. She picked up her forgotten box of cookies, which sat on the counter though she didn't remember putting it there. Then she went to the office, Pepper staring at his computer, and put the box beside him.

"I saw him last spring," Pepper said, shaking his head, "just for a rash. He was totally healthy, twenty-nine years old. No meds, no scary family history, nothing. No drug abuse. His dream was to hike in the Himalayas."

Abby stood behind him, hugged him, and kissed the top of his head, something she had never done before at work. He reached up and wrapped his long fingers around her wrist.

"Sometimes this job just sucks," he said.

She leaned against him and read the chart over his shoulder. "What do you think happened?"

"Probably something genetic. Some heart defect, maybe. Cardiomegaly, aberrant coronary arteries, who knows. A fatal arrhythmia syndrome. Something that's already there, then gets triggered by extreme exertion. We'll have to see what the autopsy shows."

Abby straightened up and nudged the box toward him. "It won't help, but have a cookie. I'm going to see that last patient."

He opened the lid, and a fragrance of brown sugar and chocolate filled the room. "Let's hope these things don't come in threes. We just lost that other guy last month, another sudden death. I mean, he was a little bit older, but he'd been healthy too. And he was only forty." Pepper bit into a cookie, chewed, and allowed himself a little smile. "This might actually help. It's really good."

The patient Abby saw was seven months' pregnant, and her urinalysis confirmed a bladder infection. Abby listened to her gravid belly and found the chirpy little heartbeat, then let the mom-to-be listen; they shared a grin. Abby sent her out with antibiotics and a careful list of precautions, since an escalating urine infection could be dangerous to a pregnancy. By the time Abby emerged, Pepper had shared the cookies with everyone and the box was empty, except for crumbs and the two cookies he set aside for her.

Hearing that tiny tapping fetal pulse was the most positive moment of Abby's afternoon.

That night, she and Pepper curled together on the back deck, watching while the clouds tore themselves apart and a half moon fought through, flooding the rim with weak milky light. Tiny stars prickled the sky, cold and distant.

They still needed to talk, but not now, not after such a day. Abby took a lighter direction and asked if he and Marcus were really going to start watching that new series Friday night.

Pepper poked her playfully in the ribs, making her squeak. "You mean you're not going to watch it with us?"

"*Vampires vs. Zombies*? I don't think so," she scoffed.

He pulled her hair aside and lightly bit her neck. "Where's your sense of adventure?"

"Stop it," she said, turning to him, trying not to smile. "I can see the sexy appeal of a handsome vampire—maybe—but zombies? Disgusting."

He drew her close, and she forgot why she had been concerned.

2

The previous summer, Abby began training for a marathon. Or maybe a half-marathon. She loved the smacking beat of her feet on the trail, filling her lungs with pine-touched air. She welcomed the moving meditation, emptying her brain of patient problems and drug interactions and everything else about work, letting it all slide past until she found that quiet core of peace. While she didn't always get there, just traveling toward it was good enough on some days.

Unfortunately, her brief summer job at Yellowstone's Old Faithful clinic turned complicated, and her running routine derailed. Now she started up again, and discovered an unexpected new acquaintance.

"Finally! I thought I would never catch you." A chunky young woman puffed up to her, grinning. "But you sure kept me going by trying."

She stopped where Abby paused for a breather and a sip of water. Abby leaned against the rough bark of a Ponderosa pine and smiled cautiously. She didn't recognize this woman with short sandy hair, wearing bright orange sneakers and a wide orange headband that covered her ears for warmth.

"Do I know you?" Abby asked. It was impossible to remember every person she might have seen at the clinic, although most people assumed she would. Someone she saw two years ago, for fifteen minutes, sometimes seemed surprised that Abby did not recall their name, or the details about their vaginal infection and difficult boyfriend.

"Nah. I've just seen you running a few times. I'm pretty new around here. And I love it! I'm Heidi Forrest—I work at Kolb Studio. What do you do?" Heidi spun in a slow circle as she talked, gloved hands stretched out. She looked up to admire the bright cold sky, late sunlight freckling her face through the branches. Kolb Studio clung to a giddy cliff where the Bright Angel Trail began, built over a century ago as a photography workshop by the two Kolb brothers. Now refashioned as a store, the studio sold art and books about the canyon.

Abby pulled off her mitten and shook her hand. "Abby Wilmore. I'm one of the docs at the clinic."

"Oh my gosh." Heidi sobered, apologetic. "I'm sorry. I didn't realize you were a doctor. I didn't mean to bother you."

"Um, I'm just standing here, resting. I don't see how that's bothering me," Abby reassured her. "It's nice to meet you. Do you like working at Kolb Studio?"

Heidi still looked serious. "Yes, I love it. It's so inspiring. I'm an artist—sort of—with watercolor. I mean, I'm not very good. It's such a challenge to paint the canyon, you know? It's so complicated, all the depths, all the light and shadow."

"I can imagine." Abby thought of Pepper's ink and pencil drawings, his careful lines and shading. A stray pencil mark could be erased, but an error with ink often meant starting over. "Watercolor is pretty unforgiving, I would think."

"Man, no kidding." Heidi appealed to the sky. "Hey. Do you mind if I tag along when I see you running? If I can keep up? I mean, I don't want to slow you down. You should just go your own speed. But it might motivate me to work harder. I'm really trying to lose weight."

"Sure, I guess." Abby shrugged, uncertain if that would work. "But you're right, I won't slow down."

"Good! I mean, I don't want to impose or anything." Heidi grinned, her cheeks stained pink with cold. She had an affable, broad face, and she swiped her drippy nose with the back of her glove. "We can make up a secret code word if you want to be left alone, all right?"

Abby laughed. Young and bubbly, Heidi's enthusiasm was infectious. "All right. If I say 'escape,' then you'll know."

"Okay then! Are you going to go again?" Heidi crouched, as if ready to launch herself from a starting line.

"Actually, no. I think I'm done." The sun sank low, long slanted rays gleaming through the woods. Pepper would be back at the house. "I'm just going to walk home now."

"Oh." Heidi looked disappointed. "Well, I'll see you soon, I hope." She straightened and started to wave goodbye, then suddenly grimaced and covered her mouth with her hand. "Hey. Did you see that guy a few weeks ago? That hiker with the heart problem, on that stormy day?"

"Yes," Abby said slowly.

"Oh my gosh, that was so scary. I was there at Kolb when he came in and passed out. He seemed so nice. He stumbled in and he looked at me with these big frightened eyes and then he said he didn't want to bother me but he didn't feel right and then he kind of reached out for me and then he collapsed and I didn't know what to do, so I called the rangers. Was that the right thing to do?"

"Absolutely."

Heidi looked down at the ground, then back up at Abby. "He looked so scared. Did he really die?"

"Yes," Abby admitted. It was public knowledge, not really confidential.

"Why? What happened?" Her face fell, tears edging her eyes.

"We're not sure." Abby felt sympathetic but careful. "I'm sorry, but I really shouldn't talk about it. It's a medical privacy thing."

"Oh. I get it. I'm sorry." Heidi looked chagrined.

"No, it's fine. We're just waiting for the autopsy."

Heidi nodded and they parted company on that somber note.

Pepper was actually cheerful that night, chatting about work and about the first silly episode of the television series that he and Marcus started watching. A good change from recent evenings where he buried himself in a book or sat at the dark window with his sketchbook, saying little, the tiny swish of his pencil shading deep clefts in a landscape. If Abby asked him whether he felt all right, he smiled briefly and said he was great. But because right now he seemed in a better mood, Abby once again put off the conversation she knew they needed.

The next day the clinic was busy—it felt as if half the population managed to injure themselves overnight.

"Gravity got mad," Abby muttered, studying the fourth X-ray of the day.

"What?" Dolores rushed to give a patient his prescription so she could room the next one, who had already waited too long.

"Gravity got mad," Abby repeated, pointing at the X-ray where the fibula looked like a twisted, cracked stick. "It made everyone fall down."

Dolores chuckled but kept moving. Abby tilted her head, hearing muffled words as Pepper talked to someone in the little office, another applicant for nursing assistant. The door opened and Pepper showed out a young woman, shaking her hand. Last week he rejected a sixty-six-year-old woman who once worked in a psychiatrist's office and had never drawn blood, and who in fact admitted she got a little queasy when she saw blood. She retired ten years ago and recently decided she was bored. Today at lunch he told Abby that he also rejected the morning's twenty-something woman who never finished high school, but claimed blood didn't bother her a bit, that she in fact rather liked blood; she found traumas fascinating.

"Our ad clearly states that you need at least a high school diploma and some medical experience," Pepper sighed. He dropped his voice to a whisper. "Besides, I'm worried she might have vampire connections. After what she said about blood."

Abby gave him a look. "Maybe you should quit watching that show."

He grinned and bit into his sandwich. "There's one more interview this afternoon. Keep your fingers crossed, because we have no more prospects."

Abby saw Mona Bell, a thirty-year-old woman with foot pain. At first glance, Abby immediately feared the patient had end-stage cancer. Disturbingly thin, her arms like skin-covered bone, her nose too large in her skeletal face. But the patient denied weight loss, unconcerned.

"I've always been like this," she assured Abby. "It runs in my family. We're small-boned. Don't worry about it."

Abby let that go for a moment. Mona was a long-distance runner and normally Abby would take a few moments to bond over that, but not this time. Her foot pain started last week. At the canyon visiting a friend, working on her distances, she ran at least two hours a day. Or maybe three hours. Abby palpated a very tender spot on her thin foot, and the X-ray showed a faint mark across the bone, the metatarsal.

"Looks like a stress fracture." Abby pointed, showing her the image. "And all your bones look pretty pale. I can't really say from an X-ray, but I worry about your bone density. That means your bones may be weaker than they ought to be."

"A stress fracture? I'm not under stress." A bit forceful. "I feel great."

"No, a stress fracture means that you've over-stressed the bone, so it gets a tiny crack. All that running. It's pretty common in athletes like you, or in soldiers, who do a lot of marching. It's more common if your nutrition is low." Abby studied her closely, her hair sparse and brittle like dried grass, her fingernails chipped and broken. "How is your calcium intake? And protein?"

Mona stared back at her. "It's fine. Normal. So…it's just a tiny crack in the bone? So I can keep running?"

"No," Abby shook her head. "Not for about a month—that's how long these fractures take to heal. You can use crutches or a splint boot if you're more comfortable that way, or you can wear a supportive shoe and just go easy on it. Lay low for a month, only walk enough to manage. That bone needs to knit back together or you risk making the fracture worse. If that happened, you'd need to wear a cast, maybe for a few months."

"I have to exercise," she said indignantly.

Abby organized her thoughts. She might only have this one chance. As if it would make a difference, this one discussion, Abby thought dismally. "Your BMI is just seventeen, which is too low. You're at risk for osteoporosis—low bone density. Which makes you more likely to get fractures. A healthy BMI is closer to twenty. At least."

Mona shook her head. "That's dumb. I'm perfectly healthy. I eat tons of vegetables."

"Do you drink milk? Eat cheese or yogurt?"

"No. Dairy products are bad for you. Besides, I'm lactose intolerant." She looked smug.

"Then you might want to take calcium tablets, maybe with vitamin D. Especially in the winter, when there's not much sun on your skin. Your bones probably need that."

"Sure. Whatever." Mona slid off the table and took a few ginger steps on her foot, her face stiff. "See? It hardly hurts."

"Do you want to try out a splint, see if that feels better? Or get some crutches? You should at least use a cane, to take some weight off it."

"No," she answered crossly, gathering her purse and jacket. "I'm not using a stupid cane."

"Well. If you're still here visiting, I'd like to check you again next week. Make sure you're getting better. How far were you running?" Abby stalled, trying to connect. "Mona. I'm worried about your weight. It's not healthy."

Mona looked annoyed. "You doctors are all alike. Always saying I'm too thin. Always saying I'm … *anorexic*."

"What do you think?"

"I think I'm just fine." Mona opened the door, ready to go. "I watch my calories so I can stay healthy, and I run to stay fit. If anything, I could probably stand to lose a few pounds on my hips. This fracture thing is really throwing me off. I might get another opinion."

"Of course. But I'm just letting you know what medical science says about your low BMI. It's likely to cause problems. It's the same as if you said you felt fine but your blood sugar was two hundred. You would still have diabetes, no matter how you felt. That's all."

Mona stared at her. "Fine. If I'm still here next week, I'll come back for another check."

"That would be great. Or go see your usual family doctor at home. They might order some tests, see if you're anemic. Check your bone density."

Mona snorted and rolled her eyes. "He's an idiot. And a quack."

Abby laughed at her comical expression. "Then maybe you need a new doctor."

"That's the best advice you've given me." Mona's lips folded, almost a smile.

Maybe she would actually return, Abby thought, but probably not. That was the delicate task, to push but not too hard. To somehow leave the door open. Abby sighed and felt inadequate.

The rest of the afternoon moved quickly: stuffy sinuses and cranky joints, a bulging buttock abscess that drained a quarter cup of pus, and back pains and neck pains and sluggish bowels and drippy bladders. Itchy vaginas and nagging coughs. Finally the patients were gone and Abby relaxed at the counter, working on her notes, as Pepper finished the last interview and let the woman out. Abby caught a glance at her back, a wide woman with a tight dark bun knotted like a fist, high on top of her scalp.

The connecting door to the waiting room caught, stuck open. Someone should fix that, Abby thought, overhearing Marcus and Priscilla.

"Your clothes don't match again," Priscilla complained. "You can't put that red and blue together. It looks like what a circus clown would wear."

Marcus chuckled. "Some days I feel like a clown. Don't you? Ever?"

"You cannot possibly be serious." Priscilla reached over and pushed the door shut.

Abby joined Pepper in their office.

He shook his head. "Well. I think I'm going to hire this last one. She's got some experience and she's a certified medical assistant."

"Your words sound convincing, but your voice doesn't."

"She'll probably be fine. She's just…a little rigid. Maybe a little overconfident."

"So you didn't hire her yet?" Abby was surprised, since there were no others.

"No, I want to sit on it for a day. We really need the help, but I don't want to regret it, either."

"That's not like you, to be so indecisive. What did she say?"

He looked uncomfortable. "I'm being judgmental."

"So what? You're just talking to me." Abby squinted, puzzled by his reticence.

"She said that this job was meant for her, an answer to her prayers."

"Well, that's not so bad, is it?" That seemed like a fairly benign statement.

"No." Pepper made a funny face, amusement and concern. "But she also implied that she was an answer to our prayers."

Abby laughed. "I didn't even know you've been praying for this."

He cuffed her on the arm. "I thought it was you."

"It was probably Dolores. She's being run off her feet."

"So I guess I'll hire her." Glum.

"If you get any more enthusiastic you're going to need sedation." She took his arm and pulled him from his chair. "Let's go home. You can sleep on it."

Pepper nodded and followed her out.

3

The autopsy report on the deceased hiker revealed nothing, no likely cause of death. His heart seemed healthy, his brain appeared normal. Frustrated, Pepper dropped the report on the desk.

"If only we'd been able to talk with him, even for a minute. How he felt, what his symptoms were. Maybe we could have found a clue," Pepper said. They were about to start their afternoon patients. Rain fell steadily past the window, and they heard cars swish past on the road.

"I might ask Heidi again," Abby said. "She was at Kolb Studio when he was still alive. Maybe she'll remember something."

The report made Abby think of her pathology class in medical school, observing autopsies. She always disliked them: the cold room, the raw smell of severed flesh and decomposing fat, a stink of waste. Skin fell away from the scalpel and the metal table gleamed dully, puddled with draining fluids. The pathologist lifted the disconnected organs onto the scale, heavy wet lungs and liver, those shiny and solid segments that once all pulled together. Now pointless. The stunned blank face of someone newly dead, like they might wake up if given another chance.

She preferred the cadaver lab with its chemically preserved and long-deceased bodies, more like rubber models. Not that she enjoyed those, either. That first day, almost dizzy from the reek of formaldehyde, she suddenly had a peculiar need to touch the body on the dissection table. As if to get it over with. Pressing her gloved fingers, a violation, making dents in the cold clay flesh.

"Heidi?" Pepper asked, distracted, picking up the autopsy page and reading it again.

"You know. The woman I've been running with now and then. You met her a few days ago, when she stopped by with me. Short, cheerful?"

Pepper nodded. "You're right, maybe we should ask her."

Marcus appeared, brandishing a clipboard and beaming. His turquoise polo shirt fought against his striped brown-and-orange slacks. While known for his mismatched colors, he seemed lately to dress more outlandishly than ever, and Abby wondered if he was trying to provoke Priscilla.

"I'm taking over the squirrel bite reports," he announced happily.

Tourists notoriously ignored warnings posted around the rim, signs sternly advising not to feed the squirrels. Signs cautioning that squirrels might carry diseases like rabies or plague. Since most of the bites were tiny nips to the finger, and because no squirrel in Arizona had actually tested positive for rabies, the physicians got involved only when necessary. Trained to assess the wounds, the front desk staff determined if an appointment was needed. But they logged in every incident for reference, no matter how minor the trauma.

Marcus's predecessor, Ginger, handled the squirrel log gravely, going above and beyond by asking each victim for detailed descriptions of the animals. She filled her pages with colorful accounts: the hue and texture of fur, the rusty reds and dusky browns. The tiny teeth, from cute square incisors to pointy little fangs. The tails, tattered or flowing. Squirrel facial expressions, determined or hopeful or angry. Marcus sighed, filled with admiration.

"This is inspiring," he said, running his finger down the list. "I can't believe Priscilla doesn't want to do this herself."

"She doesn't like vermin," Abby commented, remembering Priscilla's tirade the year before.

"Vermin?" Marcus acted personally insulted. "If squirrels are vermin, what does that make humans? I mean, just look at what we've done to our poor planet. Chewing it up, spitting it out."

"Good point. Maybe you should tell her that."

Marcus made a frightened face. "Maybe I should stick a knife in my eye."

Abby suppressed a smile. "Let me know if you have any questions. If you're not sure, just bring the patient back for a quick look. Otherwise they can leave with a handout." Abby trusted Marcus to know his limits—she had worked all summer with him at Yellowstone— and he was always kind. Patients loved him.

"I can't wait. But there aren't many squirrels right now because it's winter." He looked disappointed and trudged back to his desk.

Abby saw a new patient for lethargy, a peevish seventy-year-old man with a sulky mouth, like this was the last place in the world he wanted to be. Harry Stonewall's jumbled white hair sprang up every which way, an untidy rooster comb. His watery oak-colored eyes swam behind thick smeary wire-rimmed glasses, back and forth like goldfish in a bowl. His face caved in a little, maybe missing some teeth. He complained he just was not himself these days. A weariness had settled over him that he could not shake.

"And it ain't because I'm old." He spat the words.

"Of course not," she agreed. His clothes smelled dusty, thin layers of worn cotton, patched and re-patched. His eyeglass frame bent slightly, giving him an off-kilter glare.

"And I thought I was going to see a man doctor," he grumbled. He lifted his whiskered chin. "I've never seen a lady doctor. It don't feel quite right."

Abby was not surprised. "You're welcome to make an appointment with Dr. Pepper instead, if you're not comfortable. You can probably see him tomorrow."

"Dr. Pepper?" he hooted. "Is that a joke?"

"No, that's his real name. Dr. John Pepper." Abby had learned to keep a neutral face.

"Hee hee," he wheezed, slapping his leg, softening a little. "I guess I'll just stick with you since I'm already here. You seem nice enough, I reckon. Can't see how I need a doctor named after a soda pop."

Abby found several issues with Harry Stonewall. His blood pressure was borderline high. He admitted that he got up twice at night to urinate, sometimes needing to push and strain to get his stream going, signs of an enlarged prostate. She pointed out two likely skin cancers, on his temple and on his forearm, that should be removed soon. Because he ate poorly, mostly bargain canned chili and crackers, she worried about his nutrition. Most concerning, she heard a noisy heart murmur, a loud churning whoosh near the top of the chest, right where his aortic valve would be.

Yet he denied all signs of a poorly functioning aortic valve: no chest pain, no fainting spells, no swollen legs or shortness of breath. Abby showed him a drawing of the heart and explained the effort of the valves, those little doors that snapped opened and shut, endlessly working to move the blood through.

"Yeah." He squinted at the pictures, then waved them off. "That dang murmur thing's been there for years. Big deal."

"You really should get an echocardiogram," Abby advised. "A bad valve might be overworking your heart, making you tired. And we should check some labs to see if there's anything else."

"Leave my dang heart alone. Just do the blood tests." He removed his glasses and wiped the lenses on his sleeve, his eyes looking suddenly small and wary. Then he slid the glasses back on and they loomed again, big and blurry.

"An echocardiogram is pretty easy." Abby tried to suppress her frustration. "It's just an ultrasound, like soundwaves. Like sonar."

"This problem is not my dang heart."

"Well, you can't always tell." Did patients think she invented her recommendations? "First, let's draw your blood. And how do I reach you? There's no phone number here, no address. What do you do?"

"Nothing." His face shut. "I'll come back next week for the results."

He unexpectedly thrust out his hand, as if sealing the deal. His palm felt like sandpaper, dry and rough, his grip strong.

"All right," she agreed. "But promise you'll let me know right away if your dang heart gives you any trouble."

"Ha." His mouth started to lift into a smile when a loud knock came on the door, four sharp raps.

"Dr. Wilmore. You're getting too far behind." Candy Millhouse, the new assistant, nearly shouted through the door.

Abby glanced at Harry, who looked taken aback, and she apologized. "I'm sorry about that. She's our new MA. Medical assistant. She doesn't know she shouldn't do that."

After he left, Abby waited for a quiet moment with no one near to talk with Candy.

"It's fine to tap lightly on the door if you need something. And it's okay to remind me if someone is waiting. Just let me come to the door, and you can tell me quietly what you want."

"You were in there too long." Candy smiled grimly. She had the tiniest mouth, and when she smiled like that, her lips bunched up and nearly disappeared. Candy folded her thick dimpled arms, nodding her head once for emphasis, making the bulky bun over her head waggle back and forth. "I like my doctors to stay on schedule."

"I appreciate that," Abby said, irritated at the possessive. She wondered if everyone was trying to annoy her today, or if something was off with her. "And sometimes we do lose track of time. But try to think of our schedule as a guideline. Sometimes simple problems turn complicated and take a while, and sometimes difficult problems get handled more quickly than you'd think. It usually balances out."

Dolores exited an exam room and looked at them, sensing something. "Is everything okay?"

"Everything's good," Abby said, moving to her next patient. Dolores had enough to worry about.

Her last patient needed a Pap. Abby always enjoyed Marcy Helms, a lively fifty-three-year-old woman, a computer specialist whose menstrual periods had wandered off the monthly calendar and now followed a fitful scheme of their own.

"Make my uterus behave," Marcy demanded, though her eyes sparkled. "I thought I was done with this crap. What a pathetic system. Now I've had two periods in the last month. And I still wake up hot and sweaty every night. No wonder I'm tired and crabby. If men had to go through menopause too, we'd all be getting disability pay."

Abby sympathized. Menopause could be torturous and might last several years. They discussed how Marcy's ovaries were shutting down, no longer ovulating monthly, no longer welcoming a sperm that might come along. The human body had its own wisdom about childbearing. But the human body was also fickle and erratic and did not help a woman adjust to sudden low levels of estrogen, flashing heatwaves from head to toe, randomly leaking blood.

Abby suggested hormones. "It will reorganize your uterus, and the hot flashes will stop. Daily exercise helps, too."

Marcy made a face. "I thought hormones were dangerous."

"Yes, if you take them for a long time, or if you're at risk for cancer. If you smoke or have high blood pressure. Most women only need them for a short while."

"Sheesh." Marcy stared at her. "Well, hell. I feel horrible, so let's try it. For a few months, anyway. And I'll try to exercise more."

Abby wrote the prescriptions and gave Marcy a handout, including a summary of what she needed in the near future: a tetanus vaccine next year, a flu shot within a month. Her mammogram and colon cancer screening had been done.

She heard Pepper on the phone, sounding impatient. A few words came through, something about making choices. Hindsight. Relationships.

Who on earth was he talking with? He certainly would not use that tone with a patient. Abby dragged a stool over to the work counter instead of interrupting him. Through the partly open door she saw him grip a pen, doodling dark geometric shapes on a notepad, sharp pyramids and angular cubes, structures that somehow looked painful. Unsettled, Abby tried to ignore him and concentrate on her work. When his voice rose, she didn't want to hear it and she left her chores, escaping through the door to the front. She would ask Marcus about squirrel reports.

Candy stood before the front desk with her hands on her hips, her back to Abby, shaking her head while Marcus and Priscilla stared at her.

"...and then I told that last patient she needs to be better about her Paps," Candy declared. "Her last Pap was years ago! She thought she didn't need them every year. How dumb can you be—where did she get an idea like that? I guess I should add her to my prayers. My list is getting pretty long, let me tell you, after working here a few days."

All heads turned to Abby. Marcus's eyebrows flew up and Priscilla's eyes went wide. Candy looked smug.

"She got the idea from me, because those are the guidelines now," Abby said, quietly furious. Now she needed to call Marcy back, to apologize for Candy's wrong advice. "A middle-aged woman, with previously normal Paps and a negative HPV test, only needs a Pap every five years."

"That's news to me." Candy regarded her sullenly. "I was just trying to help."

"What else did you tell her?"

"Nothing." Candy bit the word off, then that tiny puckered smile returned and her lips disappeared. "No, wait. I noticed that she hadn't had her bone density checked yet, so I told her she needed that, too."

Abby felt her jaw clench. "That's not correct. Healthy women don't need their bone density checked until they turn sixty-five."

She made herself relax; she could not stand there arguing. Abby wanted to leave, get away from this stupid clash and get away from whatever Pepper was saying on the phone about choices and hindsight. She wanted to walk to the rim and touch stone, to survey the eons crushed beneath her, the husks of tall forests and odd extinct creatures that had nothing to do with Paps or the fleeting pursuits of humans. Especially self-righteous humans. She imagined them all reduced to a rough stripe of rock one day, millions of years from now, their cells turned to mineral dust. The vision was disturbingly satisfying.

Abby focused, saw them looking at her. She felt badly that this conflict occurred so publicly, so she tried to make things better, for everyone's sake.

"Let's do this, Candy. While you're getting used to how we manage things, you should probably just review my written instructions with the patients. Don't add anything until you're familiar with our approach. All right?"

"Sure," Candy said shortly, avoiding Abby's eyes and moving briskly past her.

Abby looked at Marcus and Priscilla, feeling compelled to say something. "Well. Are you two almost done?"

They became suddenly busy, shuffling papers. As Abby turned, her eye caught a list, a careful grid, by Priscilla's elbow, and she tipped her head to read it. The page was divided into three rows, labeled "Shirts/Slacks/Shoes," and under each heading ran a column of words in Priscilla's precise printing.

"What's that?" Abby asked.

Priscilla snatched the paper and flipped it over. She looked up at Abby, solicitous, and smiled. "That's nothing, Dr. Wilmore. I was just organizing my wardrobe during lunch."

"I should do that myself," Abby said, trying to be agreeable since she felt anything but agreeable.

She wondered if Pepper was off the phone.

4

Heidi Forrest turned out to be no burden at all. Abby quickly came to enjoy her dogged shadow when they ran together. Maybe not exactly together, since Heidi was always somewhere behind, panting and grunting a little. But when they took a break and Heidi caught up, Abby enjoyed the younger woman's contagious giggle, her delight at having someone to follow instead of plugging away by herself. She usually wore orange, a bright spot in the winter landscape.

"I always do better when I have a carrot to chase," Heidi laughed, yanking off her gloves and taking a chug of water between breaths. "Maybe that's why I like orange! But I can feel myself getting stronger. Getting faster. You make me try harder."

"That's the first time I've been called a vegetable," Abby said. A dreary day, dark low clouds, the temperature stuck near freezing. "Are you always so cheerful?"

"Yes." Heidi paused, then her smile faltered a little. "Well. Not before."

"Before what?" Abby grew suddenly alert.

"Before I quit school." Heidi looked down and kicked a pinecone. "I was supposed to be a Spanish major. They said I'm good with languages. But I just don't think I'm smart enough and I couldn't do it, couldn't make myself read all the literature and translate everything. Reading *Don Quixote* and *Cien Años de Soledad* in original Spanish… I mean, I probably couldn't read them very well in English, you know? I felt like I was drowning in words, conjugating verbs in circles, going nowhere. I got really depressed—and I mean scary depressed—until I started taking art classes. Like drawing and painting. And then I felt alive again, and anyway, I was running out of money. My parents said they wouldn't pay tuition for me to play with finger paints and anyway I needed a break from college and all the drinking and partying and so here I am. Ta-dah!" She flung her hands in the air and grinned, taking a deep bow.

"That's quite a story." Abby couldn't help but think how her own story would sound to Heidi. Her old anxiety problems, leaving Phoenix to start over. Maybe she would share it someday.

"Yep. I guess you could say that art saved me." Heidi rubbed her hands together for warmth, then bounced up and down. "So now I'm remaking myself, I guess. I'm trying to be more assertive, too, instead of a meek little mouse. Challenge things that aren't right. Stand up for myself more, take charge. That's why I decided to talk to you that day. Hey!" Her face turned serious. "I keep meaning to ask you. Should I be taking vitamins? Supplements? There's this guy who keeps trying to sell me some—he says I'll get stronger and I'll run faster if I start taking them. That I'll lose weight quicker. He's kind of pushy, but he's pretty convincing."

Abby shook her head. "No, there's no magic pills. Keep doing what you're doing. Eat healthy and watch your calories and keep exercising. Besides, you never know what's in some of those supplements, no matter what the label says. There's not much regulation. They can be full of caffeine, or worse."

They took off again, and soon Abby pulled ahead while Heidi puffed behind, her breaths growing fainter. Abby glanced up, black trees poking an ashen sky, and wished they had run along the rim instead of through the woods. Even on a dull day, the soft hues of sandstone would feel cozier than this monochrome display. That roasted bronze and rust, those ancient realms split apart. Better than this colorless gray, she thought. As if cued, lazy snowflakes began sifting through the branches, slowly dancing before her.

At supper, Abby reported to Pepper that Heidi had nothing to contribute, no more information about the young hiker's symptoms before he collapsed. Pepper nodded, preoccupied, and chewed his dinner. When he began stirring his food with his fork, not looking at her, Abby felt a seasick shift in her stomach. She set down her napkin and pushed back.

"John. We need to talk." It was past time; she had to know what was wrong.

His pale blue eyes jumped up. "About what?"

"I'm not sure. You have to tell me, because I keep worrying that it's me. And if it is, you should let me know." Better to have this out in the open, she told herself uneasily.

Pepper grimaced and stood, pulled her up.

"You're right—I should have said something. A long time ago." He moved a few steps to the closet, reached in, and tugged out their large goose-down sleeping bag. Then he scooped up their mittens and caps from the shelf, drew her to the back door. "Come on. I'll tell you a little about it, and then I'll make it up to you."

"Outside?" Abby balked. "It's freezing out there, in case you didn't notice."

"It's also snowing and it's beautiful. Come on." He pushed her knit cap down over her ears and crammed on his own, towed her through the door, and spread out the sleeping bag on the platform lounge under the porch roof. He helped tuck her into the bag, then he scooted down alongside and held open her mittens as she shoved in her hands, donning his next. The snow fell furiously, silently, a whirling white world. A few flakes drifted under the roof and eddied up and down, landing on them, tiny intricate stars.

"There," he said, gathering her against his chest. "We'll be baking in just a few minutes."

Abby shivered and ducked her head inside the sleeping bag, her voice muffled. "I don't think so. You forget that I lived in Phoenix too long. I don't do cold very well."

"If we have to, we can take off all our clothes and maximize our body heat. Like arctic survivors."

"Ah ha. So that's what you're planning here."

"Well. A man can hope." He wiggled his eyebrows. Then he sobered and pulled down the edge of the sleeping bag until her face emerged. He studied her, his eyes apologetic. "It's not you, Abby. Of course not."

29

"You haven't been yourself. I don't know what to think. You keep insisting that everything is fine, but it isn't."

"I'm really sorry. You've learned to read me too well." He shook his head. "I feel like a jerk that I let that happen, made you worry."

"You're not a jerk." She reached up and put her mitten along his cheek. "You were just sort of acting like one every now and then."

He laughed and turned his head to nuzzle her hand, kiss her mitten. "It's my sister. She's made such a mess of her life. And now she's calling me and emailing me—constantly. She's driving me crazy."

"Your older sister? The one who lives near Chicago? I thought you weren't close at all. That you'd hardly been in contact the last few years."

"All true. She and I are only two years apart, but we've always been pretty much opposites. She hung out with the popular crowd, obsessed with clothes and makeup and dating the handsome guys. You know, the football guys who wouldn't even talk to me. I was the geek who stayed after school in the science lab, feeding flies to the lizards and counting the bacterial colonies we grew in the incubator."

"My kind of man. I mean, you can't get much sexier than lizards and bacteria." Abby ran her mitten down his arm then up under his sweater, stroking his chest. It was growing warmer inside the sleeping bag, she had to admit. "So why is she calling now?"

He stirred against her touch, slipped his hand under her butt and pulled her tighter against him. "She screwed up, literally. And she keeps wanting to talk about it. And I promised her I wouldn't tell anyone." He twitched his lips. "So apparently it's made me grumpy, and here I am out in the snow, trying to make amends."

"You told her you wouldn't tell anyone, but maybe someone can guess?"

"Hm." A smile touched his face.

"She had an affair?"

He nodded. "And it's been pretty public. Mostly I feel bad for their daughter. My niece."

Abby remembered Pepper talking about his niece months ago, triggered by a photo she saw in his old wallet. He recounted fond memories of a pigtailed, curious little girl who loved asking him questions about medicine. How does the heart know it has to keep pumping? Doesn't it need sleep, need to rest? If someone has a heartache, does their heart really hurt? And how long does it take poop to get through the body, and why does it smell bad? Does poop ever smell good? Then they moved to Illinois and communications dried up. He sent her gift cards every year for birthdays and Christmas, and received the obligatory thank-you notes.

"You sort of miss her, don't you?"

"Yeah. She's the only one in my family with decent potential to be another nerd. I worry about her, stuck in that situation. The dad's not exactly inspiring, either—he's the gym coach and kind of a meathead."

Abby worked her hand out of her mitten and touched his jaw, his short beard. The snow fell so heavily that it hissed through the trees. "I don't quite get why you're tangled up in this."

"Because I've suddenly become the advisor, the doc in the family. But it feels more like I'm her confessor because I'm getting way more details than I ever want to hear. Trust me, you don't want to know. I guess I'm supposed to figure it out and tell her how to fix it."

"That's why you were upset on the phone the other day. You were talking to her."

"Yes. This has nothing to do with you, and you shouldn't have to even think about it. I mean, *I* don't want to think about it. It's all very sordid and icky. It's more complicated than what I'm telling you, too, but I won't go into everything."

"*Icky?* Is that a medical term?"

He laughed, which made her feel better. "Yes. There's lots of ickiness in medicine." He sighed. "Anyway, I think it's going to get better. I think I've talked her into some family counseling."

She moved her hand along his temple, smoothed out the troubled line between his brows. "Is there anything I can do?"

His blue eyes softened. "I can think of a few things."

He pulled off his mitten and slipped his hand under her sweatshirt, started roaming.

"Eek," she yelped. "Popsicle fingers! How come I'm warm now and you're not?"

"Maybe there's a warmer place I can put them…" His chilly hands drifted to her waistband, dipped under.

"Don't you dare." Abby grabbed his wrists. "You'll just have to—"

Bright light flashed through the air. Every snowflake stopped midflight, strobed in the glare, then the night plunged back to black. They both startled, speechless, as a loud peal of thunder cracked through the sky.

"Thundersnow!" Pepper exclaimed, delighted.

"Thundersnow?" Abby peered cautiously at the woods.

"You know, like thunder and lightning, only during a snowstorm. It's pretty rare."

The night flared again and the air broke with thunder.

"This is so special," Pepper said.

Suddenly his cold hands were everywhere, peeling off her clothes. She playfully tried to squirm away but there wasn't much room inside the sleeping bag, and he wrapped his long legs around her and held her tighter. Abby panted now, still protesting those popsicle fingers—then he silenced her by taking her mouth with his, deeply kissing until she gave in, melting, her pelvis starting to rock against him, a hard ache. The lightning blazed and thunder resounded and his hand sank along her, insistently, until she surged and burst. As she sagged, he mumbled something about not being done with her yet, still reparations to make, pulling her onto him as he quickened and she flashed again.

"Still cold?" he asked, spooning around her and huffing onto her neck. His hands were warm now.

"Not hardly," she breathed.

Their talk drifted to mundane things, work and the people there, Marcus and Priscilla with their conflicts, Dolores and Candy, clinical competency. Abby admitted how difficult she found Candy, and Pepper agreed she might not last, although she apparently challenged him less than Abby. And Pepper wandered back to feeling sorry for his niece, as if being a young teenager wasn't hard enough. He wondered who she really was now, what she cared about, her plans; he hoped she had a role model or someone for guidance since it clearly was not coming from her parents.

The snow diminished, barely falling now.

Abby watched a single snowflake wander across and settle near her on the sleeping bag, a flawless spangle of ice that gleamed once and disappeared, melted from her breath. That delicate evanescent perfection made her throat catch and flooded her mind with visions of the hopeful, hopeless dreams of everyone and no one, the universe so empty and so full of endless marvels all at once.

5

The next hiker with a heart attack fell into Abby's hands.

Pepper went to Flagstaff for the day, to visit a professor and attend lectures on epidemiology and public health policy. Abby encouraged him to go, knowing he needed to clear his mind of family problems, to think about bigger and more noble issues.

Abby found herself mired in one of those difficult days, doubting human judgment more than average. The clinic was unusually full of odd problems and unhappy patients. One woman complained of an itchy rash on her chest and arms that was no longer there, then seemed put out that Abby couldn't tell her why. She grumbled about being charged when nothing was done, even though Abby spent significant time exploring possible causes and taking a long history of food and beverage ingestions, medications and supplements, new clothing and towels and bedsheets and soaps and lotions and fragrances and jewelry and pets and chemicals used for cleaning and cooking, as well as supplies like pesticides and fertilizers that she used for her extensive indoor garden. Abby promised to work her back into the schedule, at no charge, immediately if the rash recurred.

"And what if it's gone again by the time I get here?" she asked, huffy.

"Maybe you could take a picture with your phone?" Abby suggested.

The patient remained annoyed.

Abby saw an older man who hadn't sat down for two days because of constipation and a throbbing hemorrhoid the size and color of a ripe cherry. He let her look at it but would not allow her to touch it or treat it, or do anything but give general advice about warm soaks, soothing salves, and stool softeners. He declined referral to a specialist. A teenage boy who tried Windex for his acne now had a raw, bleeding dermatitis on his cheeks. Then a twenty-year-old woman shuffled in, waddling with her legs apart because her vagina had turned scarlet, her labia swollen and bulging, after using a peeled cucumber as an internal cleansing device.

"But it was on the internet," she protested when Abby told her that produce never belonged in any orifice except the mouth.

"Just check with us first next time," Abby said, prescribing a potent ointment.

She had seen similar inflammations recently, and Abby later commented to the staff about a possible sign for the waiting room, stating that fruits and vegetables should enter a human body only in the conventional way. She was teasing, but Candy gave her a compact lipless smile and walked away. Candy stayed quiet lately, keeping a low profile—which suited Abby fine, although occasionally she saw Candy's mouth moving, as if talking to herself.

"Did you say something?" Abby asked her.

Candy looked up and squinted, her eyes slits. "Why no, Dr. Wilmore. Just thinking about my prayers."

Next Abby saw Hatch Carpenter, a patient of Pepper's with a bad virus, blowing thick yellow mucus from his nose. He looked miserable, his eyes red and crusty, hacking up wads of gray phlegm. Hatch worked near Flagstaff as a lumberman, and volunteered at the canyon with PSAR, the preventive search and rescue team. Around noon he tried to hike down the South Kaibab Trail, but a ranger saw how weak he seemed and turned him around, sent him to the clinic.

"I guess it's a sinus infection," he groaned, honking his nose into a tissue. His almond-brown hair stood up in a stiff crewcut, the sides shaved nearly bald. "How come Dr. Pepper isn't here? I always see him."

"He's in Flagstaff," Abby said as she finished her exam. Despite the cold weather, he wore a T-shirt, exposing heavily muscled arms. Popeye arms, she thought—Abby suspected he spent a great deal of time at the gym, or maybe it was his logging work. His thick forearms crawled with veins, like fat worms.

"I always get that antibiotic pack," he said shortly, interrupting Abby as she explained how antibiotics will not help a virus. He snapped his fingers in frustration, trying to remember. "I know, that Z-pack. Right? Pepper always prescribes that for me."

He peered through watery eyes, a little hostile, yet even so she saw his gaze rove across her, checking her out. She ignored that, took her time to describe again how awful a virus can make you feel, until your immune system kicks in and conquers it. How he might try taking zinc since he'd been ill for only one day, because zinc sometimes helped if taken early enough. She didn't believe him about Pepper and the antibiotics, because Pepper was even more stringent than she was about that. The medication list showed that Pepper never prescribed him antibiotics, so Hatch either forgot or made that up. Hatch was not persuaded by her explanation, so she talked about antibiotic resistance, how overusing antibiotics created legions of incorrigible bacteria that no drug could kill. Usually, her patients were convinced.

Hatch remained unimpressed.

"You're just looking for an excuse," he complained, coughing.

"Not at all. It's much easier to simply give you an antibiotic." Abby never understood why patients thought a physician would want to dupe them, but she frequently heard that lament.

In the end, Abby gave him a delayed prescription, an antibiotic to use if he wasn't better in four or five days. Most people actually never filled a delayed prescription. She recommended home treatments proven to help: a vaporizer, honey and ibuprofen for the cough and fever, pushing oral fluids, laying low.

Through the door, Abby heard Dolores review everything with him once more. When he came out, he tried to be nicer. He smiled wanly and apologized, said he just wasn't feeling well and shouldn't have been so cranky. He shook her hand and thanked her, said to say hi to Dr. Pepper. He sent her a final contrite look and glanced at her chest again.

Really, Abby thought.

"He's going to take those antibiotics right away, you know," Dolores commented when he was gone.

"Probably," Abby agreed, rubbing alcohol gel over her hands. People were never at their best when ill. Then while finishing the chart, she noticed his problem list included E.D., erectile dysfunction. Maybe that explained his manner, maybe his embarrassment at knowing she knew that. A physical exam could feel uncomfortably intimate, too, standing close enough to brush against him, pushing her stethoscope across his bare chest...a dynamic that might prompt his looks. Medical training rarely taught how to manage such nuances.

Enough of that, she thought. Just two more patients. She hoped Pepper was having a good time in Flagstaff, and didn't expect him home until late. He texted her once, commenting that health care policy was paradoxically boring and fascinating all at once. Abby smiled at her phone. She missed him, missed discussing cases with him, missed his quick mind and practical solutions. After last summer alone at Yellowstone's clinic, she knew she could function by herself, but having support was nicer.

Marcus poked his head around the corner.

"Squirrel bite!" he crowed. "You can't make this stuff up."

Abby looked at the closed exam room doors, waiting for her. "Tell me. But quickly."

"Okay, so this older woman—Helen—was worried about the squirrels, about them not having enough to eat because it was winter. She thought these two squirrels looked too skinny. She could see their ribs, she said, and their eyes looked sad. So she went into the snack bar and bought a ham sandwich. Do squirrels eat meat?"

"Mostly nuts and plants, I think. But maybe some meat, maybe if they're really hungry."

"Anyway, Helen told them to wait, and when she came back out, they were still there. So she's sure they understood her."

Abby made a hurry-up motion.

"Right. She started feeding them, tearing off little pieces of the sandwich and giving it to them. Then she suddenly noticed that the sandwich had mayonnaise, and she was afraid that would cause little squirrel heart attacks, too much cholesterol, so she tried to grab the bread away from them. And that's when she got bitten." Marcus grinned.

"Do I need to see her?"

"No, you can barely see it. I just had to tell you. Especially after that last grouch. Carpenter." Marcus wrinkled his nose.

"So it wasn't just me?"

He shook his head. "He always has attitude. Even on a good day."

Priscilla appeared. She saw the squirrel clipboard in his hand and rolled her eyes, turning to Abby. "Emergency coming in. Chest pain, any minute."

Abby turned quickly to Candy standing nearby, asked her to get the treatment room ready. Stony, Candy considered Abby. Then she stared at her watch, visibly sighed, and moved toward the room. Abby tightened her jaw and told herself this was not the time for a talk.

The young male hiker, blue and shivering with cold, kept pressing his fist against his chest as if trying to alleviate a deep discomfort. Coming up from the river, he stopped at Indian Garden, huddled breathless against a tree, unable to keep going. His pulse hammered away at one hundred twenty and his blood pressure registered so high, two hundred forty over one hundred ten, that Abby doubted the accuracy. She repeated it herself and got the same. Abby gave him nitroglycerin and watched his heart tracing, where extra beats punctured the strip like tall jagged teeth. On the EKG, places where lines should bend up were pointing down, and lines that should be level were raised up in plateaus, all signs of heart damage. But the hiker refused to buy it, belligerent and cursing.

"This is bullshit," he kept exclaiming, his face now red, his voice deep and angry. His wide pupils, like black pools, gave him an oddly alien expression. "I'm in great shape. Let me out of here—you can't make me stay." He plucked the oxygen prongs from his nose, started pulling the cardiac leads off his chest.

Abby seized one hand. The paramedic Paul grabbed the other; Abby knew him, worked with him for several years, a quiet and steady middle-aged man who had been trying to keep the patient calm.

"Easy," Abby said. Most people with heart symptoms fell quiet, fearful. His antagonism was unexpected. Her concern rose…his sky-high blood pressure and abnormal EKG made him dangerously unstable. Her thoughts ran briefly to Pepper's recent resuscitation, and she hoped to avoid a similar scene. "Your pulse is very fast and irregular. You might be having a heart attack. You have to stay quiet."

"Bullshit!" he shouted, yanking away from her grip, making Abby stagger.

"Cut it out," Paul ordered, clutching the man's hands and raising his eyebrows at Abby. He looked surprised, too. "Be nice to the doctor."

Abby ordered diazepam to sedate him, which Dolores quickly injected into his IV. Soon he lay back with his head on the pillow, his eyes half closed, softly mumbling "bullshit" over and over. With blood pressure medications and the oxygen back in place, his chest pain disappeared and his vital signs improved. His legs showed a little edema and his blood sugar came back surprisingly elevated, considering he had no history of diabetes. They found a zip baggie in his backpack filled with a jumbled rainbow of capsules and pills, many colors and shapes.

"Where did you get all this?" Abby asked, sorting through the pills, trying to find identifying marks on them. "What are these?"

"Nothing," he said slowly, his words slurred from sedation. "Just my vitamins. Keeps me going."

He didn't know exactly what the pills were, just kept saying vitamins. He didn't have the original packaging. Abby knew many athletes took concoctions of vitamins and minerals, trace elements and antioxidants, convinced it improved their performance, although this had never been proven by medical science. She made a notation in his transfer documents, asking the doctors in Flagstaff to get a drug screen, and made sure the pills went with him. When the helicopter arrived and hurried him away, Abby breathed a sigh of relief. If he made it to the ICU, he had a much better chance. But this was the second case now, maybe the third, and no one knew why. She worried about what she might have missed.

"Hi," said Heidi, smiling and waving her hand, interrupting her thoughts. Marcus had let her come back in since Abby was expecting her. "Can you still go running tonight?"

Abby shook her head, regretful. Another patient, a woman with a bad headache, still remained to be seen. And Abby was far behind in her charting.

"You're on your own, I'm afraid," Abby said. "I wish I could, though. How about tomorrow?"

"For sure," Heidi said. She rubbed her nose, holding her orange mittens and looking disappointed. "There's something I want to ask you about, too."

"Anything urgent? This last patient will take about twenty minutes. Or you can call me later." Abby still had the hiker in her mind, hoping he made it to Flagstaff.

"Nah. Same old stuff." Heidi grinned, then patted Abby's arm. "You look tired."

"Nothing new. Same old stuff." Abby smiled back.

Heidi took a few steps and looked at the framed pencil drawings along the wall, intricate lines of trees and canyons. She seemed reluctant to leave. "Hey, these are nice. Really good! Do you know who did them?"

"Pepper." Abby gazed at them fondly. "It's how he relaxes."

"Wow. I bet one of these days I'll be selling his work out of Kolb Studio. Well, I guess I'd better get going." Heidi waved and pushed out the door. "See you tomorrow, then."

Abby nodded, distracted, already absorbed in the history of the headache patient as she read what Dolores had written.

It was a moment she wished she could have gone back and changed at least a thousand times.

6

Pepper looked troubled when he returned from Flagstaff and heard about the hiker with the heart attack. Such an odd case, the patient so antagonistic and uncooperative, his dilated pupils, his extreme blood pressure. By then, Abby knew he made it safely to the hospital, now stabilized in the ICU, and seemed likely to survive.

"There's something strange going on," Pepper muttered, upset. "I just can't figure it out."

He shook it off and described his stimulating day at the university. Seeing him both energized and more relaxed, Abby made a mental note to make sure they got away more. But he was already ahead of her.

"Let's get out of here," he said that night. "Have you ever been to Jerome?"

"Who are you? What happened to the guy who wanted to kick back on his days off? Who wanted to read and draw?"

"That guy is boring. I think I can get a moonlighter to cover Saturday, so we could leave Friday night, right after work tomorrow. A romantic weekend in an old ghost town. You can't say no to that."

Abby felt thrilled to see him like this. "I love it. And no, I've never been there. It's been on my list for years."

Even though it was late, nearly midnight, he grabbed his computer and started looking up places to stay.

Then Abby remembered. "Remind me to get hold of Heidi in the morning. I promised her I would run with her tomorrow after work. I should cancel that so we can leave right away. It's at least a two-hour drive, right?" Abby felt a little bad because Heidi clearly wanted to talk with her. But Pepper came first.

Pepper nodded. "Wait till I make sure we've got a moonlighter. I think Dan Drake is between locum tenens jobs, so he would be perfect." Dan was a smart, likable family physician who Pepper helped train during his last year of residency, and Dan planned to staff the clinic at Old Faithful next summer. As a single man, he had not yet settled down, instead tackling a string of temporary jobs in rural locations, filling in for doctors on vacation. Pepper always chose him first.

Abby sent Heidi a text the next morning, once Dan Drake confirmed. Abby apologized in her note and asked if Heidi wanted to talk before they left.

Harry Stonewall returned, still worried about his fatigue, to discuss his labs. He did not feel better; if anything, he felt worse. Which seriously interfered with his prospecting, he said. His watery eyes swung behind his glasses and his furrowed face looked weary. He smelled slightly musty, making Abby think of mice, something that lived underground.

"What are you prospecting for?" Abby asked as she opened his chart.

Harry hunched his shoulders and glanced around. "Can you keep a secret?"

"Of course. That's what I do all day." She felt surprised at how quickly he had come to trust her.

"Gold," he whispered. Shadowed by bushy white brows, his eyes glinted.

"Really? I thought there wasn't supposed to be any gold around here."

"Hah." A short laugh, a high-pitched wheeze, then he lowered his voice. "Don't believe everything you hear."

"Well then, good luck." Abby smiled. "I won't tell a soul. But about your labs…"

His kidney function was off a little. He had no obvious cause for kidney problems, Abby noted, no diabetes, not taking any drugs known to damage kidneys. His mild hypertension on the first visit resolved, now normal. He took nothing over the counter, like ibuprofen or naproxen, notorious for inflaming the tiny tubules and molecular sieves that filtered blood into urine. Sometimes the kidneys just wore down with age, she explained.

"I'm not going on dialysis," he bristled. "No way."

"No, you're a long way from that," Abby assured him. "This may be something we can watch and it might never change. But you should eat healthier and cut down your salt. You eat lots of canned foods and crackers, lots of sodium. And we still need to think about getting that echocardiogram of your heart. Check out that murmur." Her eyes ran through his chart. "And you should come back soon so I can remove those skin cancers."

"Here you go again," he muttered. "Always something else."

"I hear you, but I will keep bringing these things up because I think it's important." Abby suspected he'd heard enough for one day. "It's been a week, so let's repeat your labs. If your kidney function is stable, either the same or better, we can keep checking it every few months. But if it's worse, there are some less common causes we need to consider."

"Oh, geez. Like what?"

"An inflammatory condition, like lupus. Certain drugs or metals you might be ingesting without realizing it, like lead or mercury. Cysts or stones in the kidneys. Poor circulation, so maybe less blood is getting to your kidneys. That's why you need to eat healthy and stay active, which keeps your arteries healthy."

He left in a fairly dark mood. Abby felt bad for him, because kidney disease often seemed unknowable. Kidneys were like secret organs, deep behind the abdomen, difficult to reach and exceedingly complex. She occasionally remarked to Pepper that kidneys were her least favorite organs: blood went in, urine came out, and who knew what really happened inside? And Abby worried about Harry's heart.

By midafternoon, she'd heard nothing from Heidi. Abby went to the front desk, asking Marcus and Priscilla to bring Heidi back to her right away if she came in. The two of them bent over an intricate computer spreadsheet, a grid of colored words in boxes.

"So these are what I shouldn't wear together?" Marcus said, pointing. He tugged his cherry red polo shirt down over his abdomen. Abby couldn't see his slacks, but she could imagine the clash.

"No." Priscilla sighed and shot Abby a look that suggested Marcus might be intellectually challenged. A rare moment of implied complicity. "This is what you *should* wear together. You actually have plenty of wardrobe choices that match quite well."

"Who knew?" Marcus said with mild amazement, catching Abby's eye. A tiny wicked gleam.

They had been speaking quietly, but Priscilla suddenly caught herself, realizing this exchange was not quite appropriate for the physician to witness. She straightened abruptly, glancing across the lobby where two patients waited. Abby noticed how her blond hair swooped perfectly, dramatically onto her shoulders, not a wisp out of place, a nice contrast against her clinging green sweater that seemed too small. A secret shadow dove between her breasts and welcomed a golden locket, which dangled into the depths. Her green eye shadow matched her sweater perfectly.

Abby asked them to keep an eye out for Heidi.

"Isn't Priscilla great? I can't believe she went to all this trouble for me," Marcus said to Abby. He turned earnestly to Priscilla. "You really know how to make a person feel special. Thanks so much for this."

He made a show of carefully rolling up the spreadsheet and slid a rubber band around it. Priscilla stared at him and Abby avoided eye contact as she hurried back to her work.

Her last patient, Savannah Boone, twenty-nine years old, nursed a shoulder injury from earlier that day.

"Call me Vanna," she said, shifting her left arm and wincing. "And I'm sorry if I smell like horses and manure. But Pete insisted that you check me out and you were about to close, so I rushed over from the mule barn. I wouldn't have bothered you if it was up to me."

The head wrangler, Pete Collins, was among Abby's favorites. She treated him for a rattlesnake bite her first year at the canyon; colorful and pessimistic, his dry wit always made her laugh. But Vanna didn't look like the usual wranglers—she wore sturdy work shoes and a baseball cap. Her chin-length caramel-colored hair tucked tightly behind her ears, and her face looked hard, almost angry. Her slender frame didn't quite fit with her muscular arms and hands, and small white scars pocked her forearms, scattered like stars.

"What exactly do you do over there?" Abby asked.

"I'm a farrier. A blacksmith. I put shoes on the mules."

"That's pretty cool," said Abby. "I've never met a woman farrier."

Vanna gingerly adjusted her left arm and her lips tightened. "Probably because 90 percent are men. I don't have the statistics on how many of them are bastards."

Abby frowned. "Why do you say that?"

"Forget it," Vanna said, pointing to her left shoulder. "Just fix me."

She had been bent over double, grasping a mule's front hoof between her knees and lining up the steel shoe, ready to hammer in the first nail when the mule suddenly shied and jumped against her, wrenching her arm and knocking her down, then scrambling back and forth at the end of its halter rope. Vanna got up, dusted herself off, and kept working—she said she couldn't leave the mule unbalanced with three shoes on and one off. Then she persisted, shoeing two more mules until Pete came along and saw her clumsy, uncomfortable efforts and made her stop.

Abby diagnosed a rotator cuff injury, a sprain or tear in one of the complicated shoulder tendons that attach the arm to the body.

"Please don't tell me I need surgery." Vanna looked stressed and tugged her hair tighter behind her ears. "My insurance sucks."

"No, it usually heals. But you have to be careful not to injure it again, and you have to start stretching while it heals. And really stick with it. Otherwise you might get contractures and chronic pain." Abby already guessed the answer to her next question. "Does your insurance cover physical therapy? That's the best way to go, but it's expensive."

"I doubt it. I'll just have to—"

A loud knock on the door. So help me, thought Abby irritably, if Candy thinks she can—

"Vanna? You in there?" A raspy male voice, a cowboy drawl. Pete Collins, the head wrangler.

"Come on in, Pete." Vanna sounded resigned.

The door burst open and Pete stormed in. Usually laconic and subtly humorous, Pete stomped up to Vanna and jabbed his finger in the air. He still wore his spurs and they jingled softly, but his face was furiously red and his salt-and-pepper handlebar moustache bristled.

"Which one was it, honey? Lord love me, I'm gonna kill him," he fumed.

"I'm not telling you," Vanna said mildly. "Besides, it wasn't anyone. I think it was a bird."

"It wasn't no bird, missy. That mule Peaches is smart as a whip, and she ain't about to spook at a stupid bird."

Vanna spread her hands in innocence, palms up. "Honestly. I didn't see a soul."

"Goddammit. You need to tell me so I can fire his ass."

"Pete." Her face turned cold. "I can handle this. I have to handle it my own way."

His old face hardened, but he stayed silent and Abby could see that he grasped her need. He sighed. "Are you hurt very bad?"

Vanna glanced at Abby and nodded, so Abby explained the rotator cuff injury. Pete left then, deflated, muttering threats. Abby demonstrated the exercises for Vanna and printed a handout, then asked her what really happened.

"Some of the guys don't like having a female farrier. They keep implying that I'm not very good, that the mules will suffer and go lame. But they're full of crap. I know what I'm doing and I'm good at it. So anyway. While I was shoeing Peaches, someone walked past her on the other side and I think he goosed her in the ribs."

Abby's temper flared. "You could have been seriously injured. I mean, even worse. Do you know who it was?"

"Yes. I know his boots." Vanna looked at the wall now, avoiding Abby's anger. But her face muscles twitched.

"I could report this myself," Abby said.

"Nope, this is my fight. I'll take care of it." Vanna folded the handout and stuffed it in her rear pocket. "Do you need to see me again?"

"Absolutely, in a few weeks. I need to make sure your shoulder isn't stiffening up." Abby changed the subject. "And if you don't mind me asking, what are all those scars on your arms?"

Vanna laughed. "When you hammer out a red-hot horseshoe, tiny little flakes of burning metal fly through the air. Sometimes they land on your arms."

"Ouch," said Abby. "And...Vanna?"

The other woman stopped, halfway out the door.

"Be careful, okay?"

Vanna nodded once and left.

Abby wrote up the encounter, upset and stewing, unsure if she ought to have done something more. She saw the time and realized Heidi should have been there twenty minutes ago, so she picked up her phone and called. No answer…the phone went to voicemail. Abby even stepped outside and looked up and down the road. The air felt warm for winter, the clouds low and close, pressing down and threatening rain yet again, and Abby couldn't remember when they last had a true sunny day. Such unusual winter weather—although early January, it had snowed only once, that wonderful night of the thundersnow. She stood listening, the woods silent, wrapped in gray wool. Heidi was usually reliable, communicative, rarely late. Maybe she got annoyed that Abby cancelled the day before, although that felt out of character. But what did Abby really know about her? Not much.

Abby sent another text, explaining that she would be back Sunday night. Something felt off, but if anything was urgent Heidi could always call her in Jerome.

"Come on, she's not coming. She must have forgotten. Let's get going," Pepper called to her. The car waited, packed and filled with gas, and he looked excited, anticipating the adventure. "Let's get out of here before it starts to rain."

Abby grinned and they ran to the car.

7

They hurried under the clouds as thunder scuttled through the gloomy sky.

"It should be trying to snow, not trying to rain," Pepper complained. "What is wrong with the weather this year?"

At first the storm followed them, but Pepper laughed and drove faster, hurling insults at the heavens, and eventually they left it behind. The sky began to clear and a low stern sun crept through tattered piles of burning orange cloud, residual debris. Reaching Jerome long past dark, driving slowly along the steep twisted roads, they eventually found their bed-and-breakfast and settled in, tired but happy to be away. Pepper whimsically chose to stay at The Surgeon's House, a century-old home once owned by the mining company for the local physician, overlooking a vast panorama of dusty green inclines and the distant red-and-buff cliffs of Sedona.

Jerome sprang alive in the 1880s, a bustling town that clung to the sharp hills, hills full of ore and swarming with mules, everyone chasing rampant veins of copper, silver, and gold. Over the years, the underground honeycomb of mine shafts, ninety miles of narrow passages tunneled deep beneath the terrain, yielded to the relentless tug of gravity. Destabilized, some of the land sunk, some of the slopes slipped, and some buildings began to settle and slide. After 1950, the rich ore played out and the town petered away, and a once-prosperous community of fifteen thousand shrank to just fifty people, barely a population at all. Jerome crumbled and more parts crept downhill, poised for shabby extinction.

But a few determined souls kept the vision of Jerome alive. They started preserving structures, created a historical society. Hippies joined a growing artist community, and Jerome hung on atop the empty burrows of abandoned mines, hosting an unsteady churn of galleries and cafes, biker bars and wine-tasting nooks, T-shirt stores next to custom furniture shops.

On Saturday, Abby and Pepper relaxed and took their time. They visited the historic state park, marveled at faded photos of eighteen-mule teams lugging heavy ore to the smelter. They strolled narrow switchback roads through town, lingering at galleries and craft stores. Abby kept revisiting a silver necklace with a delicate pendant of copper mountains, but far too expensive to consider. When Pepper saw her study it for the third time, he waited until she moved on, then plucked it from the case and bought it, disregarding her protests when she realized what he'd done.

"Pretend it's for Christmas," he said.

"Christmas just ended," she objected.

"Then pretend it's for your birthday."

"My birthday is in October."

He closed his eyes. "Then pretend that I like you and want to give you something special. If it helps, you can even pretend that I love you. A little bit."

This had been their tease for months, that they pretended to love each other now and then. Abby laughed and lifted her hair, let him fasten it around her neck.

"Thanks, I love it," she said, planting a kiss on his cheek. She was already imagining her next cartoon, where a stick-figure Pepper pointed grumpily at a stick-figure Abby wearing a necklace, his words in a bubble saying *Love this, dammit!* Abby insisted her little cartoons were the main glue that held them together, while Pepper claimed he considered breaking up every time she created a new one. Then he would tuck it away in his special folder where he kept them all.

That night, Abby luxuriated in a long hot bath, emptying her mind of work and medicine, of Harry Stonewall and misbehaved kidneys, Vanna Boone and glowing-hot horseshoes, Heidi who didn't show up and Priscilla with her spreadsheet and Candy with her bulky topknot and everyone and everything else but the ancient volcanic lands that made up Arizona. She envisioned the thin sea that once stirred against these hills, millions of years ago. Perhaps a few of those same water molecules now steamed her skin in the tub, now lapped against her thighs. She pictured the huge Precambrian eruption, creating the fiery ores over a billion years earlier, now crammed up into the hills around Jerome. She was sliding off to sleep with her hands floating, her toes turning pink and wrinkled with heat, when she heard Pepper on the phone in the other room.

Her mind slowly bent, sluggishly curved back to the present. She angled her head, trying to catch his words. *I don't think so,* he said. *I can't think of anyone.*

Abby abandoned her trance, finding herself firmly back in the present, wondering who he spoke with. It didn't sound like his sister; Abby had come to recognize his stiff tone with her. The conversation seemed over, all quiet now, so she closed her eyes and tried to recapture her geologic visions, but they were gone. Abby sat up and pulled the drain, reached for a large fluffy towel.

"Who were you talking to?" she asked. Wrapped in the towel, she walked into the bedroom and searched in a drawer for her nightshirt. She felt damply tropical, flushed and calm, her long hair rampant down her back, wavy with moisture.

Pepper stared at her, shifted his leg. "Are you wearing anything under that?"

Abby smiled and shook her head. "No. But I asked you first."

Pepper pulled her onto his lap. "I'm having trouble with my memory right now," he confessed, and started kissing her, first the scar on her forehead, then down across her cheek and jaw and neck, staying there.

"If you pull any of that vampire nonsense, you will be in so much trouble," warned Abby softly, breathing harder but resisting, still wondering. "Come on, tell me who was on the phone. It sounded serious."

"Sh. Don't distract me." He loosened the corner of towel tucked between her breasts. "I'll tell you in a minute, after I'm done here. You know us men, we can't multitask very well."

"In a *minute*? It will only take a minute?"

"Will you hush and let me concentrate? That's only a figure of speech...I think you know me better than that." He reached and turned off the light, and he proceeded to show her just how long and delicious a figure-of-speech minute could be.

The room was dark, the house silent as they recuperated. The small towns glimmered below them and a bright clutter of stars spanned the wide black sky. A faint eastern glow heralded the rising moon.

Limp against him, Abby let her hand glide across his chest.

"So what was that phone call?"

Pepper sighed heavily and raised up on his elbow, considered her. "I was hoping you'd forget about that. Can't we just leave it until morning?"

Abby scrutinized him. "Are you hiding something?"

"Is that so bad? Maybe I just don't want to talk about work. We're supposed to be on vacation."

"Except I can tell you're thinking about it anyway. You have those little squinty lines at the corners of your eyes." She smoothed them with her fingertips. "I'll just keep worrying, so you might as well tell me."

"Fine." He sat up, ran his fingers through his hair. "That was my friend Ed—the doc in the Flagstaff ICU."

"Oh no," Abby startled, suddenly fearful. "Is it Heidi? Was she in an accident?"

Pepper looked puzzled, his thoughts interrupted, then realized what she meant. "No, it's nothing about her. It's about that latest hiker with the heart attack. The guy from a few days ago, the one you saw."

Her eyebrows rose.

"They ran his drug screen, and his amphetamine and caffeine levels were through the roof. And probably some barbiturate, too. They think he's jacked up with anabolic steroids as well. He's got edema, and acne, and breast tissue. And his thyroid level is super high. They're still waiting on the steroid results. And they've sent his pills for analysis—they might find more garbage."

"That could explain a few things." Abby recalled his belligerence, the dilated pupils, the alarming hypertension. "Did he ever say where he got those pills?"

"Yeah, but it's crazy. He bought them from a ranger months ago, early last fall. Someone he met along the trail, below the rim. He said the ranger offered them as kind of a secret, because he had more than he needed. This ranger supposedly told him that all the rangers took them for strength and endurance, and told him not to tell anyone."

"Are you serious? Who on earth did that?" Astonished and upset, Abby could hardly imagine.

"That's the thing. He described someone with dark red hair. Curly red hair, green eyes."

Abby frowned. "I don't know them all, of course, but I can't think of anyone who looks like that."

"Right? And they checked with park headquarters—there's no such person. Never was."

What a peculiar, disturbing story. Now Abby wished she had listened to Pepper's wisdom and left it till morning. Amphetamines, caffeine, anabolic steroids, thyroid. Probably other drugs, too. Maybe barbiturates. Her face twitched, remembering her unfortunate near-fatal brush with barbiturates in August, and she unexpectedly shivered.

Pepper watched her closely. "You're thinking about last summer, aren't you?"

Abby nodded, pressing her hands against her temples, as if she could touch her brain. "It still shows up every now and then."

He wrapped his arms around her. "I wish I could make it go away."

"It's better." She lifted her chin. "I've gotten pretty good at turning it off—I just change the channel, you know? Like right now." A faint smile. "So, this guy, the hiker. He was taking some sort of performance-enhancing drugs?"

"Looks like." Pepper settled back in bed, pulled her against him. "It makes me think...maybe the others with heart attacks were taking them, too—the ones that died. They were never tested, so we don't know."

The gibbous moon suddenly peeked over the hills, glazing the basin with silver light. The same moon that everyone had watched since people were people, Abby thought, depending on when you defined humans. A few hundred thousand years ago, or a few million years ago…not that it mattered. The same moon that shone on the thick hides of dinosaurs, the same moon whose light filtered through the soupy seas of enormous Devonian fishes. Everything always changing, and some things never changing. She almost said so to Pepper, but it took too much effort to explain, and he would smile at her and accuse her of escaping into distant epochs. Damn right I am, she thought, feeling bristly about a conversation that had not happened.

"What are you thinking?" he asked, feeling something.

"Nothing. Silly stuff. Getting myself caught in time warps."

"Your specialty," he said fondly. He listed his head. "Do you ever regret it? Going into medicine instead of astronomy?"

"No." She looked rueful. "Too much math. Besides, I might have lost myself in all that time, all that distance. Disconnected. I'm not sure who I would have been."

The next morning, they dawdled over breakfast, sharing a sunny sitting room with friendly strangers and soufflé, French toast, and quesadillas. Then they procrastinated more, taking a long walk and visiting more galleries. Eventually they packed up and headed home beneath a mess of fretful clouds that raced and collided and pulled apart, curls and knots of vapor twisting across the powder-blue sky. They agreed the weekend had been a wonderful escape, and now they drove sedately, putting off their return.

Nearly dark when they arrived home, Abby studied the canyon sky, again unsettled and threatening rain. A few stars sputtered between bulky gray cumulus, and flips of lightning glowed here and there, but no thunder sounded. Pepper unpacked the car while she went to open the door, surprised to find a formal-looking notice attached to the frame. It was from park service enforcement, her name carefully printed on the official envelope: *Dr. A. Wilmore, immediate attention requested.*

What the heck, Abby thought, tearing open the letter and reading in the dim light of the porch. Her stomach lurched and she looked up in alarm.

"What's that?" Pepper asked. "Is something wrong?"

Dismayed, Abby read it out loud. The notice asked her to call them right away, that they wanted to talk to her about Heidi Forrest, who had been missing since Friday morning.

Abby may have been the last person who saw her.

8

Investigations apparently took a break on Sunday night. Abby found no one to talk with about Heidi until the next day.

Monday heralded one frustration after another, and Abby could do nothing except slog through each obstacle as it came. She slept badly, imagining a dozen fates that might have befallen Heidi. A hike down the trail and a stumble near an edge, that was all it took. Taking a shortcut and twisting an ankle, stuck, with no one coming by. Abby tossed while little rushes of rain came and went on the roof, sometimes pounding, sometimes tapping, like the worries rapping on her brain.

Pepper stirred. "Awake again?" he murmured, sliding his arm around her. Abby feigned sleep and he drifted off.

She dressed early, made coffee, and was out the door before Pepper showered.

"Don't forget to turn off the pot," she called. Since she was awake anyway, she figured she might as well take care of paperwork before her patients arrived.

Within minutes, Abby saw the prospector Harry Stonewall's lab report, showing further deterioration in his kidney function. She had no phone number, no way to reach him, just a post office box. He needed closer monitoring, more tests, and consultation with a nephrologist. Which meant going to Flagstaff, which she doubted he would embrace. She had no idea whether he had a car. Abby nearly groaned at all the barriers. While she supposed he would show up eventually, it might take days. She made a mental note to ask if any rangers knew where to find him. Then, not trusting her memory with little sleep, she wrote herself a message and stuck it to the wall.

"Your first patient is waiting, Dr. Wilmore," said Candy shortly as she moved past the office doorway.

Abby dragged herself up as Pepper came in the back door. He gave her a concerned look, so she summoned a smile and waved him off. Worry about Heidi nagged her constantly, a prickle in her mind, but she left a voicemail with the inquiring officer, so now it was up to him. The morning clinic bustled, everything from broken wrists to broken toenails, broken hearts causing ulcers and depression, broken glucose monitors leading to badly managed diabetes. One man overslept and missed his mule ride into the canyon, then broke three toes when he kicked a hotel chair in frustration, then was irate about being billed for the broken chair. The whole world seemed broken.

The officer showed up just before lunch. Abby hurried through her last patient, Angela Barnes, a young woman with low-grade pelvic pain who had endured two miscarriages and desperately wanted to be pregnant again. Angela already conferred with two different obstetricians, who found no abnormalities after countless tests.

"I just know something's wrong," Angela said, chewing on her fingernail. Her eyes huge, imploring.

"Reproduction can be tricky," Abby commiserated, and launched into an exhaustive history of symptoms, trying to discover something new or hidden, without success. "We don't understand everything. I'm sure you've heard the stories of couples who give up after years of trying. They decide to adopt, and suddenly within a year they're pregnant."

"What should I do? Are you saying I'll have to adopt a child in order to conceive my own?" Her eyes even more huge.

"Absolutely not." Abby never meant that, felt appalled that Angela said that. "All I meant was that stress can affect your ability to get pregnant. There are probably stress hormones that we don't recognize, something that affects the egg or sperm."

"So I should just give up?" Her voice caught.

Abby realized now what Angela sought: a definite path. Encouragement to keep trying, or permission to stop. Angela already admitted they could not afford more medications or fertilizations.

"I don't know," Abby admitted. "No one knows. It's something you and your husband need to decide. Have you considered counseling?"

"No." Her voice quavered, then her face changed and bitterness crept in. "He wouldn't do that. He just looks at me like I'm defective. His sperm are perfect, of course. Probably the most perfect sperm anyone has ever seen."

Abby did recommend counseling and suggested focusing on a healthy lifestyle: daily exercise, good eating, ample sleep. None of which Angela achieved these days. Abby tried to be present for her, to listen closely and answer thoughtfully, but she kept thinking of the waiting detective, who Dolores already warned her seemed impatient, pacing in the lobby.

Officer Derek Shipley introduced himself, shaking her hand briskly and running his small calculating eyes over her, making Abby feel like a specimen at best and a suspect at worst. He explained how Heidi did not show up for work on Friday and failed to respond to multiple phone calls. Everyone liked her and everyone worried. Her car remained parked at her place, just outside the park. When she didn't appear the next day either, concerns rose and the investigation began. Her parents from Reno arrived quickly, and they discovered her connection with Abby from her calendar.

Abby answered his questions the best she could, but she simply did not know much about Heidi. Abby knew of no boyfriends or even close female friends, didn't know if she drank alcohol or used street drugs. It had never come up; they talked mostly about running and her job, her watercolors.

Abby did not appreciate Shipley's judgmental attitude.

"Her parents say she had quite a history of depression," he commented, looking sharply at Abby, his pen poised. His stubby fingers had short clipped nails. "Did you treat her for that?"

"She isn't my patient," Abby countered, increasingly irritated. "I've never treated her for anything."

"Maybe your partner, then? Pepper?"

"No, she's never been seen here at the clinic. Not as a patient."

"But you used to exercise together, right? You must have talked about your lives. Was she happy, or did she seem upset?" He paused, as if awkward to say it. "You know, girl talk."

Abby shook her head, feeling worse. "We talked about our running, and we talked about art and painting. To tell you the truth, we didn't talk that much. It's not that easy when you're breathing hard. I mostly encouraged her. She really wanted to improve herself." It bothered Abby that he kept referring to Heidi in past tense, leading her to do likewise, so she tried to take control. "She's always upbeat. Cheerful. She loves it here, and she's trying to be healthy and lose weight. She doesn't seem depressed."

"Hm." He frowned at his notebook, the page mostly empty.

"Sir? Do you have any clues at all? I mean, Heidi is usually reliable. This is really upsetting." Abby caught herself biting her lip, made herself stop.

"We've got almost nothing. Who knows? Maybe a friend picked her up and they took a trip. Maybe she went for a hike in the canyon and fell. Maybe she hurt herself or got sick and got trapped somewhere. And of course, maybe it's suicide. We've starting searching, but no one really knows where to go." He squinted tightly. "What happened that last time you saw her? What was the last thing she said?"

Abby told how she cancelled running with Heidi that Thursday evening because of the cardiac case. How they switched their plans to Friday, before she and Pepper decided to go to Jerome. How Abby tried to reach her all day Friday without success.

"So you just left anyway?" Almost accusing.

"I figured she'd forgotten. I left her messages. I mean, we've really only been running together for a short time, not even a month. Maybe six or seven times. We don't even know where the other lives. All she said was…" her voice trailed off. Shipley stared, waiting, and Abby swallowed. "All she said was that she wanted to talk with me about something. But she said it could wait. And I told her to call me sooner, if she needed me."

Shipley pursed his lips. Then he seemed to shift, now mostly disappointed. "Well. I was hoping you'd have some clues."

"What will you do next?" Abby asked, distressed.

"I don't know. Without any more leads, we're at a dead end." He grimaced, as if realizing he should not have said *dead*. "Sorry. But right now, suicide is tops on the list. What with her history of depression, you know. Her parents say she was suicidal in college. We've checked all the usual places, though, and haven't found anything."

Which meant they looked at the bottom reaches of cliffs and drops. Places like The Abyss along the western curve of the rim, a sheer three-thousand-foot fall to the rock below. But a suicidal person could step off into nothingness in so many places, at so many overlooks, along so many trails—just about anywhere. The opportunities were endless.

Abby had little time for lunch after that, and it ruined her appetite anyway. Tense and distracted, she chewed a few crackers and called it a meal, then launched herself into the afternoon.

Priscilla waited for her after her last patient. She wore a shapely red woolen dress with long flared sleeves and a short skirt that barely covered her, set off by shimmery gold tights and black stiletto-heeled boots. Her red lips and nails matched the dress, her eyes masked in coal liner. She looked like a Christmas elf gone awry.

"Dr. Wilmore," Priscilla said formally, awkwardly, clutching a clipboard. "Can I go over a squirrel bite report with you?"

"Of course," Abby replied. "But I thought Marcus was doing those now."

Priscilla pressed her glossy lips together. "He is. But he asked me to do this one." She entreated the ceiling with mascara-fringed eyes. "He thinks it would be good for me."

"Good for you?" Abby kept her face straight. What was he up to?

"He thinks—" She avoided Abby's eyes and stared at the clipboard, tapping her pen. Her fingernails gleamed like fresh blood but she acted uncharacteristically tentative. "He thinks I'm too...he thinks I should...he says he worries about me because I don't appreciate nature. That I would be happier if I did."

"What do you think?" Abby was amazed that Marcus could throw her so far off balance.

"I think I'm perfectly happy," Priscilla said, haughty, straightening her shoulders and raising her chest. It was almost a relief to see her back in form. "Why wouldn't I be? I have a good job and I like the people I work with." She glanced over as Pepper appeared from another room and her shiny lips curved into a coy smile, staring at him a little longer than necessary.

She caught herself—her eyes jumped back to Abby and she consulted her papers, all business but also a little hopeful. "I can ask Dr. Pepper if you're busy, now that he's available."

"No, I'm fine. Go ahead."

"Okay." Priscilla looked disappointed. "So, this little boy's parents made him pose for a photo with a squirrel while he was trying to feed it a potato chip. From his hand. So of course he got bitten. Those parents should be charged with child abuse."

"Does the bite look bad?"

"No. It's a teeny tiny scratch."

"Did it bleed?"

"No, not even a drop."

"Do I need to see it?"

"I don't think so. Marcus just wanted me to run it past you." She glanced again at Pepper.

Abby waited, knowing there must be more, but Priscilla stayed silent. Finally Abby said, "Didn't Marcus have you ask anything else? Anything about how the squirrel looked or why it bit the boy?"

Priscilla rolled her eyes. "Yes. He told me to do that, but I don't see why. It's just silly. The squirrel was brownish red and it had blackish ears so it looked like it was wearing a little black hat, so the boy laughed at it and I think the squirrel got mad because it didn't like being laughed at, so it bit him. Serves him right."

"It sounds like kind of a cute squirrel."

"I thought so, too," Priscilla admitted. "He shouldn't have laughed at it, poor little thing."

She nodded firmly and went back to the front desk, leaving Abby to stare after her. Never before had she heard Priscilla refer to squirrels as anything but disgusting vermin, nor ever heard her utter much empathy or kindness.

"What's up?" Pepper asked, seeing Abby's puzzled expression.

"I'll tell you later." She smiled. Then Shipley and Heidi came rushing back into her head. She suddenly wanted out of the office, away from the antiseptic smells and gleaming surfaces, away from everything clinical and artificial and human-made. She needed ancient rock.

Pepper could tell. He pulled her into the little office and shut the door. "Nothing new about Heidi, huh?"

Abby shook her head. "They're thinking suicide. That doesn't feel right, but you never know for sure. I mean, what if she really did need to talk to me that night? What if that's what she wanted to tell me? And I just put her off, told her to go away." She heard her own voice rise, as if it belonged to someone else.

"Stop." Pepper sat her down. "Give yourself a little credit. If she'd been distressed that way, I think you would have picked up on it."

Abby was not so certain. Upset about the combative hiker, engrossed with his blood pressure and skipping heart, she might easily have overlooked the degree of Heidi's torment. How seriously had she ever taken Heidi? Abby put her hand on his, gave it a little squeeze.

"I'm going to take a walk out on the rim," she decided. "I need some fresh air."

"Hang on. Let me finish this and I'll go with—"

"No, please. Don't be offended, but I want to go alone." Abby kissed his hand and gave it back. "I just need some empty time and space."

"Are you sure?" Worried.

"I'm sure. It's just my way of dealing with things. You know me." Abby smiled to prove her stability.

"Okay…" He fixed her with a cool look, but said nothing more and watched her leave.

She pulled her jacket on quickly before he tried again, saying she would be home soon. As she exited the back door, Marcus walked past with a box of paper and she stopped him.

"You may be dangerous," she said, poking her finger into his arm.

"Ouch." He rubbed the spot as if it really hurt, his round face wide and innocent. He looked good, Abby realized, wearing black slacks and a pale blue shirt. Marcus went on. "I don't know what you're talking about."

"Right. Because Priscilla really wanted to do that squirrel bite report herself."

He smiled primly and turned to move on.

"Have you lost some weight, Marcus? You look nice."

He shrugged. "Maybe a little. I'm getting in shape for golf season. I mean, it's early in the year, but it's been warm enough that they're opening the driving ranges. So I'm starting to practice."

"Good for you." Abby was pleased. Marcus had previously abandoned a promising golf career because of performance anxiety. "Let me know how it goes."

She walked quickly through the winter woods and out to the rim, where the planet suddenly broke open and fell into itself, collapsing into a nearly unbearable display of broken gingerbread and cinnamon cliffs, golden splintered towers. The sun sat on the horizon, a low butterscotch globe about to abandon the sky, inching down and igniting the edges of small huddled clouds. Deep down, out of sight, the formidable river rubbed and purred against the oldest stone, mumbling its mysteries and carrying prehistoric silt across the continent. Night then day, then night again then day again, on and on, over and over. All the same spectacle whether or not fragile humans—facing joy or tragedy—watched it and wondered.

Abby couldn't stop herself from searching—as if her weak naked eyes might find what the rangers had not after their detailed probe of the vertical terrain with their high-powered binoculars. But she felt her gaze scanning the drops and talus, looking for a crumpled form, an orange hat or scarf. You're an idiot, she thought suddenly—she hadn't told Shipley to look for orange, that Heidi always wore orange. But they would have noticed that without being alerted, if it was there.

Her breath caught. Heidi could not possibly have been that depressed. Could she? Abby imagined going dizzily off the edge, falling through time, a blur of eons flashing past, all those compact worlds of ferns and fishes and shells and cells and molecules jumbled together. Landing among them. Becoming them.

Her steps slowed as the sun slunk below the horizon and the sky charred. Venus emerged, a bright eye staring back, more than one hundred million miles away. Too close, Abby thought, and she turned her back on Venus to study the dark eastern sky. Still hours until Jupiter rose, that huge gaseous hulk, more than three hundred million miles away but still locked in orbit like Earth, still subject to the sun's insistent gravity. Distant Jupiter with that massive red storm, raging blindly across its surface for hundreds of years. Abby nodded to the east, as if acknowledging Jupiter's dominance and its mindless tempest. Maybe she would get up tonight to see it rise and share some moments with that furious world.

Her phone chimed, a text from Pepper: *I'm lonely.*

Abby surveyed the canyon once more, now dripping with black shadow. She checked on Venus, thought again about Jupiter and its vast, venomous atmosphere, and headed home.

9

Abby jumped when someone tapped her shoulder.

Typing instructions for her patient, she sought just the right words to expose the flaw in his plan, to reduce his five nightly cocktails "as soon as his stress improved." He warily agreed he might cut back a little, and he certainly doubted whether he needed to see her again. She knew he wasn't ready.

It was all about keeping the door open. And advising him not to drive when he drank.

Abby turned at the shoulder tap and Hatch Carpenter stood there, grinning sheepishly, his baseball cap in his hands. He was on the way out, having just seen Pepper. He looked considerably healthier than when Abby last saw him, snuffling and miserable with a virus. Now his almond hair stood up stiff and shiny with gel, a pale arc of bare skin above each ear, freshly shaved.

"Hey, Doc," he said, sticking out his meaty hand. "Thanks for helping me a few weeks ago. Sorry if I was a pain."

Abby shook his hand, her fingers crushed in his grip. She smiled cautiously and refrained from asking if he had taken the antibiotics. "No problem. I'm glad you're better."

"I hate those sinus infections. The miracles of modern medicine, right?" That answered her unspoken question, but he already moved on. "Anyway. I was just talking with Doc Pepper about these hikers and heart attacks. He says no one knows what's going on—maybe something with supplements? What the hell. But I want to be on the lookout when I'm down in the canyon, doing my little volunteer rescue thing. What should I be watching for? What should I be asking?"

Abby glanced back at her laptop and her interrupted task. But she appreciated his effort. "Nothing you wouldn't already know. Ask them about chest pain, shortness of breath, palpitations. Maybe carry some aspirin with you—if you give patients aspirin early in a heart attack, they do better. Make sure they're hydrated. Get help right away."

He grunted. "Like that's easy. Getting help way down there."

"It's challenging, isn't it? Kind of hard to drive an ambulance down the trail. And helicopters can't just land everywhere. But you've got a radio, right?"

He nodded. "I hope Doc Pepper figures it out. This is bad stuff."

"He's very determined," Abby said, "and I'm putting it mildly. If anyone can get to the bottom of this, it will be him."

Hatch waved and moved on. "I see you're busy. But thanks, that's really helpful. I'm going to pick up some aspirin right now, and I'd better hurry. Have you been outside? Looks like a nasty storm coming."

Abby returned to her work, relieved to see that he wasn't completely annoying; he seemed to mean well. People were complicated, and rarely was anyone all bad. Or all good, for that matter. Then she remembered and called after him.

"Hatch?"

He turned.

"Have you heard about a ranger selling vitamins—someone with red hair? Did Pepper ask you about that?"

He shrugged. "Yeah, but I don't think it's real. It sounds sort of made up."

"Thanks. You might be right." Abby suspected the same, that the patient created a false trail. Hiding something illegal.

No signs of Heidi surfaced. Abby never had the young woman completely out of her head, always hoping that she would suddenly show up, embarrassed at what silly thing she'd done, some wild stunt like running off, having a fling. The search was losing steam, no clues, no leads. Abby tried to run one afternoon but eventually quit because she kept imagining footsteps behind her, kept turning to look. She felt haunted and slept roughly. Over and over she recalled

Heidi's look of disappointment that last afternoon and questioned what signs she might have missed.

A roar of thunder startled her, a gust of wind shaking the clinic windows, a rattle of rain. The overhead lights seemed to intensify as the sky darkened. Abby stepped back to the glass door at the rear entrance to look, leaves and debris flying by, tree branches lashing wildly. Then a blinding flash lit the world, and a deafening, overwhelming crack of thunder shattered the air. The lights stuttered and went out, and Abby found herself crouched with her hands over her ears.

"Everything okay?" Pepper called out, hurrying down the hall. He started toward Abby but she straightened and put her thumb up, still too stunned to speak. Pepper quickly opened the doors to two exam rooms where patients waited, rooms now utterly dark with the power out. Marcus and Priscilla appeared in the doorway, and Dolores popped out of the bathroom, eyes wide. Abby realized she was holding her breath and blew it out.

"Everyone okay?" Pepper repeated, and they nodded mutely.

A burst of hail hammered the building, and they gathered to watch as it bounced exuberantly off the pavement, leaping up and down in an icy dance, rapidly whitening the ground. Marcus laughed and everyone started to relax as their ears recovered, although the clamor of hail made talking difficult. Then Dolores remembered the generator for emergency power, and weak light washed through the clinic.

Abby and Pepper wrote their patient instructions by hand since the generator only covered a few outlets, none close to the large printer. They offered the patients to stay and wait it out, but both worried about their families and left.

"Guess I won't go running now," Abby commented as the rain pounded down. She had planned to try again, see if she could handle it this time.

Pepper gazed at her. "That's too bad. You probably needed that."

"Um hm." She didn't trust herself to say more, felt surprisingly close to tears. Maybe it was the rain, the dark melancholy day. Maybe it was—

"Hurry," called Dolores, hastening past. "Ambulance."

The back door banged open with a rush of cold wind and rain, paramedics and rangers pushing a man on a gurney. Water and mud slithered off everyone, puddling quickly on the floor, a slippery mess. Dolores ran to assist and slid instead, her feet flying out and she sat down hard with a squishy plop. Abby scurried to help her up as they wheeled the cart into the treatment room. She had no idea where Candy was.

"Lightning strike," called the paramedic, panting, swiping rain from his face and leaving a streak of mud on his cheek. "We tried to call you but everything's out. This lightning is nuts."

Pepper bent over the patient being transferred from the cart to the table; Abby saw blood trickling from his ear. The drenched middle-aged man stared around, water dripping off, blinking and dazed. His shirt was in shreds, his chest nearly bare, and a raw superficial burn mark zigged from his right shoulder to his left hip and disappeared under his wet plastered jeans. His left shoe barely clung to his foot in black tatters, an odor of burned rubber. Dolores reached to unfasten his jeans to remove them, and the paramedic handed her scissors.

"That zipper's melted shut," he explained.

Abby helped pull off what was left of his shirt and saw feathery marks fanning across his shoulder, a spidery fern of red tracings like the branching of a tree. Like an odd echo of the lightning itself that caused it.

"A Lichtenberg figure?" Abby pointed, amazed at the strange pattern, recalling an old lesson in emergency medicine. "Have you ever seen it before?"

"No, just in photos," Pepper said. "Wow. It's pretty rare."

"What? What happened?" The man gaped at everyone around him. "Who are you all?"

"Do you remember anything?" Abby asked, knowing that amnesia was common. Pepper was studying his electrocardiogram.

"Ouch. My ear really hurts." He raised his hand to touch it, then saw blood on his fingers and gasped. "Whoa. I'm bleeding."

"It's okay. Your eardrum might be ruptured. From the lightning. Do you remember the lightning?"

"Lightning?"

They pieced the story together from bystanders. He had been standing near the rim, watching the storm approach. "It was spectacular," added a ranger, still in awe, "and terrifying. The worst scary dark clouds I've ever seen."

The soaring black mass flicked and flashed with bent lightning, when a wide bolt flung itself to earth about forty feet from where the man stood. Only he was no longer standing, now a victim of ground current that raced through the soil and blasted him from below. A nearby schoolteacher who more or less knew CPR started thumping on his chest, and his pulse came banging back.

The patient turned out remarkably stable. His cardiogram was normal and his ear stopped bleeding. The burns were superficial and only mildly painful, but he shivered with cold and Dolores piled on another blanket. Though still bewildered, his thought process slowly improved, and he kept asking if he had really been hit by lightning. And why he was still alive.

"Most lightning strikes are actually not fatal," Pepper explained. "Many people survive—especially when there's not a direct hit, like with you. The electricity traveled through the ground and you happened to be standing there in the wrong place."

"Just my luck." Warmer now, he sat up and stared at his blackened sneaker. "I just bought these shoes. How hot does it have to get to burn up a tennis shoe?"

"Um." Pepper hesitated, clearly unsure whether to answer and maybe upset the patient. But the man looked at him earnestly, so he went on. "Lightning is at least fifty thousand degrees—hotter than the sun's surface. Of course, it wasn't that hot by the time the current reached you."

"Whoa." The man laid back down and closed his eyes.

Marcus appeared. "There's no way you're getting a helicopter in this weather."

Abby was not surprised. Thunder still boomed and rain drummed hard on the roof. "That's okay…he's doing really well. He can go to the hospital by ground ambulance." She looked up toward the ceiling, listening to the clatter. "If they drive slowly."

By the time the ambulance left and Abby and Pepper closed up the clinic, the storm had diminished into a dull silver overcast, the world dripping and cold. No sunset, no stars, no planets, just a gradual darkness that took over and swallowed the day as they sloshed through puddles and hurried along the road home. Once inside, Abby sat down wearily on the couch, strangely exhausted.

"I'm thinking I might not go to Marcus's place tonight," Pepper ventured.

"Isn't this your night for *Vampires vs. Zombies*?"

"Yeah, but I'm tired."

Abby knew that wasn't what he meant. What he meant was that she looked tired. They had talked about how she wasn't sleeping well, wasn't eating very well. Abby assured him he needn't worry, that she was fine and her disquiet would pass. It just took time.

"You should go," she insisted, plucking his jacket from the chair and tossing it to him. "I'm just going to read a while and go to bed. I'm sure you don't want to miss the next breathtaking plot turn of your great film classic."

"That was very sarcastic," he scolded. "Besides, the plot is already shifting. The zombies are becoming more self-aware. More clever. They've captured a vampire and they're holding him hostage, instead of mindlessly devouring him like they should. The implications are quite disturbing." He made a hideous grin and licked his lips.

Abby crammed a pillow over her face, her voice muffled. "Don't you ever do that again. Go. Get out of here. You're giving me the creeps."

Pepper pulled the pillow away from her, his words now soft, his eyes probing. "Call me if you get lonely, okay?"

Abby smiled and nodded. When he was gone, she sat staring at her book, feeling hollow, listening to the house make its little night noises, humming and ticking. Water dripped unsteadily from the eaves, an undecipherable code.

Hopefully time would work its magic soon.

10

Pepper's sister started calling again.

The family counseling did not go well. Her husband went twice, then refused to continue, claiming his wife blamed everything on him and took no responsibility for herself. The niece, Ashley, stared at the counselor and said nothing, refusing to look at her parents.

"It doesn't get fixed overnight." Pepper sat in the small office, on the phone. He leaned back in his chair and caught Abby's eye as she passed the door. "It takes a lot of work. And patience. And trying to be kind to each other. If you don't think that counselor is a good fit, then please try someone else."

Abby moved on as he explained to his sister that he must get back to work.

Abby hoped he might become more resigned during this new round of talks. But his sister could feed dry kindling to his flame in an instant, a needling ability to ramp him into aggravation with only a few words. Doubtless, this sprung from deep in their childhood interactions.

The farrier Savannah Boone limped in, returning for her shoulder checkup but also presenting a fresh wound for Abby's inspection. A touchy young mule, annoyed at balancing on three legs, yanked his hoof from her grasp and stomped on her foot, crushing Vanna's outside toes. Though she always wore sturdy work boots, the big bay mule Kamikaze weighed nine hundred pounds, and he knew how to lean in. Vanna commented that he triggered some of the best profanity she had ever produced.

Abby ordered the x-ray and examined her puffy black toes, blood still oozing from the nailbeds.

"So it was really an accident? Nothing suspicious?"

"Just a normal accident, I think. Occupational hazard. I mean, it never seemed like anything else."

"That's not very convincing."

Vanna shrugged, a quick gleam in her eye. "I think things are getting better. Most of the guys are treating me okay now."

"Most of them."

"Yeah, well, some take a little longer than others. But Pete's helping me." Vanna grinned and asked Abby if she had time for a story.

A few days ago, some of the wranglers hung around after their trail rides, knocking off the dust, watching her work. Some chewing and spitting, joshing one another, cowboy humor. Then one started in on her. Roy sidled up behind Vanna, bent over, and watched her hammer home a nail, three strong whacks.

"Looks a little crooked," he remarked, angling his head to gape at the others.

Vanna described Roy as a scrawny thirty-something, a man who smiled a little too much, always glanced around to see who was listening, who might think him funny. Stubble dotted his pointed chin, and greasy hair hung from under his hat, but he was oddly vain about his cowboy boots, a black-and-tan eagle pattern, and he kept a rag in his hip pocket for swiping off the dust when he thought no one was watching.

Vanna smacked in the last nail and gently set the hoof down, waiting a second for the mule to find his equilibrium. Then she straightened her back and looked at him.

"If that nail is crooked—which it isn't—it would be because somebody's standing in my light."

The others chuckled and nodded.

"Oh yeah?" he retorted. A long pause. "Well, we sure do miss Johnny Winston, our last farrier. He was so good that he went to competitions. You know, that national horseshoeing contest? He was so good he came in fifth last year—almost made fourth, missed it by just a few points. Damn, I miss that guy."

"That so?" The head wrangler Pete Collins appeared around the corner of the barn. Abby imagined him ambling over with his bandy gait, his spurs chiming. Touching the brim of his hat at Vanna, always polite. "Guess it's too bad old Winston never got a chance to meet our Vanna here, ain't it?"

"Why's that, Pete?" Roy chortled, anticipating a joke.

"No, wait, I forgot. I recollect he must've met her after all. Back last year, when Vanna came in third at that shoeing contest. That same one where Winston got fifth place. Ain't that right, missy?" Pete looked at her, rubbing the mule's withers.

Vanna told Abby how she kept a poker face. She scratched her head like she couldn't quite remember, picked up her nail clincher and her hoof rasp and bent to the mule again.

"Geez, Pete. I think so. It was so easy and it happened so fast that I can barely recall who all was there."

Loud guffaws, Roy awkwardly joining in.

Abby showed her the X-ray. The fourth and fifth toes were fractured, both short phalangeal bones cracked through, but fortunately the alignment was only slightly off.

"Yikes," said Vanna, raising her foot and studying her purple swollen toes. "I liked it better when I didn't know what the bones were doing in there."

"They should heal without any intervention, but you need to go easy on your foot," Abby said. "We can tape the toes together for support, and you should wear your most protective shoes or boots. Can you take some time off? The pain will improve in about two weeks, when the bones start mending together. Full recovery in about six weeks."

"No." Vanna shook her head, her caramel-blond hair swinging. She tucked it behind her ears, her lips a thin line. "I can't take time off just for this. It's not like I get sick pay. I'm finished around here for a few weeks, but I'll be shoeing in Flagstaff and Williams. I've got a lot of clients, and the horses can't wait. Their hooves will get too long and they'll get sore."

It felt like a long day, even though Abby arranged a short afternoon for herself. She saw drippy penises and wheezy lungs, burning feet and itchy armpits, crusty eyes and aching muscles. She saw three diabetic patients; one who gained weight, one who lost weight, and one who stayed the same. Abby thought of Goldilocks. Each case needed thoughtful management and education. Do this more, do that less. Eat fewer carbs, get more sleep. This is contagious, this is not. Quit smoking. Please quit smoking. Here's how to quit smoking if you're ready. Are you ready? How close to ready are you?

The few times she spoke to him, Pepper seemed distracted.

She diagnosed a new case of depression and spent considerable time explaining the pros and cons of medication, the value of counseling; unconvinced, the patient wanted neither drugs nor discussions and instead demanded unorthodox blood tests, including a peculiar thyroid panel Abby never heard of—it wasn't listed in the laboratory catalog. The patient grew angry, as if Abby was trying to dupe her, so Abby left the lab book with her and went on to the next patient, who had been waiting far too long. Dolores later told Abby that the patient sat there twenty more minutes, searching the pages, before leaving without a word.

At last Abby sat at the counter, working on her notes, when Candy appeared. Her face curdled.

"I told that smelly old man that we're done for the day, that you can't see him," she complained. "He insisted you had an arrangement. As if. I also told him he ought to have the courtesy to bathe before he came to the doctor."

"Who are you talking about?"

"Stonewall. That grubby old prospector, or so he says he is. Old coot." Candy's nose wrinkled up, a piggish look.

"Candy." Abby narrowed her eyes. "You didn't really say that to him about bathing, did you?"

"I certainly did, Dr. Wilmore. Can you imagine if you had to sit next to him in the waiting room?" Indignant, she balled her fists on her hips and the heavy knot of hair bobbled over her head. "I'll go tell him to come back tomorrow when you've got an opening."

She turned to leave.

"No," Abby said forcefully. "I'll see him right now. He has a kidney problem and we don't know why. Please get his vital signs and put him in a room."

"Dr. Wilmore." Candy scowled. "You're done. You already saw your last patient. I have a lot of cleaning up to do."

Abby flushed. "It's only four o'clock, and you're scheduled to be here until six. I kept my schedule light today on purpose because I worked extra last weekend. We'll all get finished sooner if you bring him back right away. Thank you."

Abby returned to her laptop and didn't look up. She wanted to get done because she planned to finally go running that day.

Candy stood a moment, then whirled and stalked to the front office. Abby breathed deeply, made herself calm down. This was ridiculous—she would talk to Pepper tonight about letting Candy go. Abby closed her eyes and slowed her pulse, counted backward, made herself quit stressing. For the moment. She had to concentrate on her work.

Harry Stonewall shuffled in, dejected, admitting to more symptoms. His patched clothes were rumpled and a little crooked, but Abby sat close to him and could not discern even a whiff of bad odor. Just his usual faint dustiness, not unpleasant. His stomach cramped and his feet tingled; his appetite faltered and he lost three pounds. He was very unhappy about his worsening kidney tests, and especially unhappy about Abby's recommendation to see a nephrologist in Flagstaff.

"I'm not going." He lowered his shrubby brows and stared at her through smeary glasses. "I got no truck with a dang specialist. They just get rich off you."

"I wouldn't send you to someone like that." Abby used her best persuasive voice. "How about this. You also need to see a cardiologist about that heart murmur. Maybe you could go and get it all done in one trip." She longed for a social worker to help make arrangements.

Harry didn't buy it. He guessed he would just muddle along.

Abby did convince him to get the tests for unusual causes of kidney damage. A few days before, a ranger told her that Harry had been escorted from the Orphan Mine site twice in the last month, but she knew better than to ask him directly. He might worry about his territory, his elusive gold.

"Have you been working around any mines? Any exposures to uranium or asbestos, anything like that?"

His eyes swam cautiously. "What have you heard?"

"I haven't heard anything. I just know there's some uranium contamination not far from here. Uranium and other heavy metals can harm your kidneys."

Few tourists realized that an abandoned uranium mine sat on the canyon's edge, just a few miles west of the village. Established in the late 1800s, the Orphan Mine cranked up its uranium production in the twentieth century when the arms race accelerated and governments craved the shimmery gray metal like candy. Eventually the hunger for uranium waned and the mine was abandoned, leaving an unsightly work camp, a hazardous deep shaft dropping a thousand feet into the canyon, and radioactive terrain. Exactly how radioactive seemed uncertain. When Abby searched online, official statements about planned environmental cleanup had petered out a few years earlier. While the area was fenced off, some people considered the barricades more a suggestion than a law.

Harry seemed to be weighing his options.

"I might've poked around that mine a few times," he said finally. "Is there a test for uranium?" Then he added quickly, "And just so you know, there ain't nothing like gold there, neither. So don't tell anyone that there is."

Abby listened to his heart with its swishing murmur, and confirmed numbness in his feet by prodding his toes with a nylon filament. And once again she recommended he return for his skin cancer removal.

"One of these days." He pushed himself up to leave. "When I feel better."

Abby sighed.

If she wanted to exercise, Abby knew she needed to go right now. She had postponed it so many times, for weather or fatigue or anxiety. Too many excuses. Abby changed into her running outfit—she could finish her charts when she returned to pick up her clothes.

She felt wonderful out on the trail, the slap of her feet, the chilled forest air in her lungs. She knew she shouldn't overdo; she hadn't run in weeks. But soon she found herself cruising along the rim, savoring the vision of crusty tiers cascading below her, the wide gulp of air and sky. She thought of the great shadowed river in its private cleft, sinking into rock. This was exactly what she needed, and she could hardly believe she had gone so long without it.

Eventually, Abby slowed a little, feeling tired, aware she had gone too far, and she began to loop back through the woods. She reached for her water bottle at her waist and chastised herself at finding it nearly empty—she meant to fill it, but was upset about Candy and forgot. Now she fixed on how she needed to talk to Pepper about Candy. About how to help Harry Stonewall. About how to support Pepper with his family problems. Distracted, she tripped on a root, stumbled a few steps, and flew sprawling into the dirt.

What a klutz. Abby stood and brushed off her legs.

She saw it behind a stand of trees about twenty feet away. Something that didn't belong, something orange on the ground. Orange.

Her breath stopped and she froze. No, surely not.

Go on, just go see what it is, she told herself, while another part of her brain stared with dread. Her pulse pounded as she took a small step, then another. Abby halted and looked around, checked to see if anyone was near. Maybe she should wait, go get someone. But what if it was nothing? Another step. You can handle this, no matter what, she told herself sternly—you're a doctor, for god's sake. You've seen everything. She thought of Heidi's pink cheeks, her cheery grin. Abby's teeth caught her lip painfully. She leaned around the tree.

A large orange traffic cone, dented and flat, lay in the dirt.

Abby closed her eyes and huffed, half a laugh, half a sob. What on earth was that stupid cone doing out here, not even close to the road? Battling a strange mix of relief and dismay, Abby bolted away, running faster and faster to escape the images, real and imagined, that flooded her mind. Heidi on the last day, unhappy, planning to return the next afternoon. Heidi talking about her watercolors, working on her craft. Heidi admiring Pepper's drawings. Heidi splayed at the bottom of a canyon cliff, broken and ruined. Heidi decomposing in the forest, decayed and rotting flesh.

Abby ran harder, unevenly, recklessly off the trail, dodging stones and branches. She ran on and on until her calves began to cramp and cry at her to slow down. Her thoughts finally began to clear. She blew heavily and dropped into a jog as the visions faded. The light through the woods shone low, a dull scorch. She glanced at her watch, nearly six o'clock…uncertain how far she had gone, at what pace, she felt a little shaky and knew she needed to sit down. Her heart flew too fast and her lungs heaved, her skin suddenly sticky with sweat. She quit jogging and walked into the clinic, pushing through the back door.

Dolores looked up. "Dr. Pepper's been looking for you."

"Sorry," Abby said, still puffing, "I went longer than I meant to."

She felt funny, off balance, and the lights seemed unusually bright. Her ears roared and for some reason the floor was tilting.

"Dr. Wilmore? Are you all right?" Dolores moved hastily, reached for her. "Abby?"

The lights faltered, then winked out.

11

When Abby came to on the floor, shortly after fainting, the first thing she saw was Candy's round puckered face floating over her like a pink balloon. Then Dolores appeared, anxious, having just propped up Abby's feet on a chair. Dolores jostled Candy aside and knelt next to Abby, snagging her wrist to check her pulse, and frowned.

"Don't just stand there—go get Dr. Pepper," Dolores snapped at Candy. "Hurry. I think he's up front talking to Marcus."

Abby blinked and stared vacantly around. "Mm?"

"I think you're okay," Dolores said, brushing hair from Abby's face. "But you just passed out, honey."

A door slammed and a rush of footsteps, and Pepper crouched beside her, his face filled with alarm. Almost terror. Abby dimly realized his dread, his fear that she might be the next cardiac case, so she smiled feebly to prove she was fine. Her muscles seemed watery, loose, barely attached. Marcus, Priscilla, and Candy stood a little way off, watching quietly, anxious. She suddenly felt self-conscious lying there on the floor, her hair loose and tangled underfoot.

"I'm okay," she mumbled. "Dolores said so." She started to sit up.

"Wait, wait." He held her down. "Don't get up too fast."

"Her pulse is one hundred thirty," Dolores told Pepper, her brows pulled together.

"What?" He tugged the stethoscope from around his neck and slid the disc under her sweatshirt, placed it against her heart. He listened intently a moment, his expression grave. "I think it's slowing down."

His uneasy eyes connected with Abby's. "And it's steady. No arrhythmia. Have you had any chest pain?"

"No, of course not. I'm okay," she repeated, feeling stronger now, trying to rise. Her muscles were coming back. "Let me up."

"Not yet," he insisted, pushing her back. He nodded at Dolores to put her feet down, then he sat on the floor with her and crossed his legs while Dolores slid a cuff around her arm and checked her blood pressure.

"Normal," she said, sounding relieved.

"Nice work, Dolores." He picked up Abby's water bottle where it had fallen and shook it. "It's empty. Did you drink all of this?"

She closed her eyes, trying to recall. "No. I think I forgot to fill it. Ouch—you're sitting on my hair."

He smiled briefly and shifted his weight, pulled her hair out from under him. His face tightened. "How much fluid did you drink this afternoon, before you exercised? What did you have for lunch? Dolores said you went for a long run, that you were gone at least an hour. When did you last pee?"

"Um. That's a lot of questions. Kind of personal." She looked over at the staff.

Abby could not remember the last beverage since her morning coffee. She couldn't recall breakfast, and wasn't completely sure about lunch. She took the time to listen to Vanna's story instead, and then she worked on her charts to get finished early. But probably she ate something, a quick snack. To be honest, she hadn't been very hungry for days, for weeks. And she had no idea when she last urinated, but it had been a while.

"Abby." He shook his head, somehow that one word bearing an intricate mix of caring and frustration. His fingers found her pulse. "That's better now."

He helped her sit, and when that went well, pulled her up off the floor and gripped her shoulders as she moved into the office. Abby dropped in her chair and rubbed her face, feeling closer to normal. Pepper thrust a water bottle in her hand and said *Drink all of it, every last drop* in his best authoritative voice, then he talked with Dolores in the hall. Abby breathed deeply and took long swigs, suddenly thirsty. She drained the water while she logged into her laptop and brought up her last few charts, still incomplete. Harry Stonewall's note was mostly blank.

Dolores slipped in next to her, a rubber tourniquet and glass tubes in her hand, an alcohol swab.

"Doctor's orders," she explained at Abby's questioning look. "Just a few tests."

Abby submitted grudgingly, knowing Pepper would have a fit if she refused. She thought crossly that she would talk to him later about how he might improve his communications with her.

Dolores had finished, holding gauze against her skin, when they heard loud voices from the front office. Pepper, harsh and upset. Abby was shocked—he never raised his voice at work. Or anywhere. Someone retorted sharply. Was that Candy?

"Oh dear," Dolores breathed, glancing over her shoulder. She reached behind and shut the door, sealing them off.

"What's going on?" Abby asked, craning her neck. "I can't hear what they're saying."

"Wait a minute." Dolores calmly taped the gauze over Abby's vein. "I think maybe Dr. Pepper just told Candy to leave."

Feet scuffed in the hallway outside their door. A drawer opened and closed, a cabinet door banged. Something dropped and they heard Candy swear, a few very unholy words. Then her footsteps rapidly receded and the back door swished shut.

Their office door sprang wide and Pepper stood there glaring.

"Well, that's over," he announced brusquely, his face flushed and severe. But he softened as he studied Abby. "How are you?"

"I'm good now. Pretty much normal. What just happened?"

He stepped away and came back with another water bottle, handed it to her. "Drink this one, too. I think you were just plain dehydrated. And what was the last protein you ate?"

"John, for heaven's sake. Tell me what just happened."

Dolores ducked out of the room with her equipment and disappeared discreetly into the lab.

He still fumed. "I just fired Candy. You don't have to put up with her anymore."

"Why? Did she say something? What did she do?" Abby tried to imagine. But she felt struck by her own relief, as if he just lifted a boulder off her back.

"It's not important. I should have done it a long time ago." He pointed at the water. "Drink that while I go get the car—you can't walk home." She started to protest but his eyes turned frosty and she backed down as he went on, now pointing at her. "Just stay put, right there in that chair, till I get back. Okay?"

Abby nodded. "Yessir."

Pepper glowered and stomped away. Abby suspected that the trip through the forest would do him good.

As soon as he left, she walked up to the front desk where Marcus sat, finishing up. Priscilla had already gone and Dolores puttered in the lab.

"Are you all right now?" Marcus asked. His brow wrinkled and she could tell he debated whether to step around the counter, ready to support her just in case. "Shouldn't you be sitting down? You scared us to death."

"It wasn't my best moment. But seriously, I'm fine now. See?" She raised the water in her hand and took a long drink. The second bottle was half empty and she began to appreciate how truly dehydrated she must have been.

"All right…" He seemed dubious. Although he wore a bright apple-green polo top, his tan slacks made the picture professional. His clothes hadn't clashed much since Priscilla produced her spreadsheet.

"Marcus. You have to tell me what happened with Pepper and Candy. He won't say anything."

"Um." Marcus looked apologetic and glanced toward the door as if planning an escape. "Dr. Pepper said you didn't need to know."

Abby scowled. "Of course I need to know. Imagine if everyone here knew something about you, except you." Marcus's eyes widened, looking trapped. But Abby spent last summer with him at the

Yellowstone clinic, and she knew he wouldn't fail her. He never had. "Come on, Marcus. We go too far back. I won't tell him."

"I'm going to be in so much trouble." He leaned forward, his voice dropped into a whisper. "The door stuck open—you know how it catches like that sometimes?—and Candy had her back to it, so she didn't see Pepper come up. She does that, comes out and unloads on us. And she was carrying on about you. I always tell her she's full of horse-pucky and to cut it out, and she backs off for a while, then she starts in again." Abby's eyebrows climbed at that bit of information, not to mention that Marcus never used strong language, so horse-pucky was pretty rank, coming from him. He gulped and forged on. "She was saying that you don't have the sense that god gave a mouse, and that Pepper ought to watch you closer because you don't have a clue what you're doing."

Abby went speechless.

They both turned as Pepper entered through the front door. He coldly appraised them in a long arctic-blue stare and flicked a glance at her empty water bottle.

"Damn it, you two. Sometimes I don't know why I even waste my breath around here." He took Abby's arm and pulled her toward the door.

"Wait," she said, resisting. "I still have to finish my charts. I left the computer on."

"You can log on from home, or you can finish tomorrow. And Marcus will go shut down your computer. Won't you, Marcus?"

"Of course," he said quietly, not looking at either of them.

"Don't blame Marcus. I made him tell me," she said as he towed her out the door.

They rode silently on the short drive home. Abby leaned back and watched the early evening sky slip along, ashy piles of cloud under the blackening dome, and wished she could float away with them. Pepper simmered the whole way and she felt bad, knowing his stress with his sister, and she just exacerbated everything by adding herself and Candy and Marcus to his list of aggravations. And now Marcus was upset because she made him betray Pepper, who tried to protect her from Candy's mean gibes. How could she have been so rash, to run without keeping hydrated? So clueless? To be rattled by that ridiculous traffic cone. To ignore her own symptoms. She felt so foolish.

Pepper settled her on the couch and made her tea, then fixed her a sandwich. Tuna with pickles and almonds, one of her favorites. She started to talk, to explain what a wreck she was, but he said *Eat first* and waited until she was done. Now he looked subdued, kind and sad, and Abby felt worse. She started to clear her plate, but he stopped her and did it himself, then sat next to her and took her hands.

"I'm sorry—"

"I'm sorry—"

They both spoke at once and stopped. Abby leaped in.

"I made such a mess today," she said in a rush, putting her fingers against his lips before he could stop her. "I started out just fine and I was really enjoying my run until I saw this dumb orange traffic cone, only I couldn't tell what it was at first, because it was behind this clump of trees, and so I started thinking about Heidi because of, you know, how she always wears orange. Then I started imagining her dead body lying there and I sort of freaked out and I kept running faster and faster to get away from it all and I don't even know how long I went but I was just an idiot because I thought it was going to be her decomposing body in the woods. I just lost it. And then I made a fool of myself and fainted and scared everyone including you and I made you fire Candy even though she needed to be fired anyway because she's a terrible person, but I know how you hate this kind of stupid gossipy drama, and then I made Marcus feel bad because I made him tell me what you told him not to tell me even though he told me you asked him not to tell me. I mean, I made him say horse-pucky, and for him that's pretty vile. And then—"

"Stop," said Pepper. "Hit your brakes for a second and let me say something. Please."

Abby sat silent, staring at her hands in her lap. He tipped up her chin with his long fingers and gently kissed her.

"None of this is your fault," he said. "It's all on me. You're having a really hard time, thinking you could have helped Heidi. I disagree, but I get that. I would probably react the same way. But right now you seem kind of stuck, and I wish I knew how to help you.

"But I got too wrapped up in my family train wreck, again, and feeling sorry for myself, when I should have been paying more attention to you. I had no idea how nasty Candy was. Who knows why, some sort of power struggle, I guess. When I heard her say those things today…" He stopped. He wrapped his arms around her and pulled her against him, holding her so tightly it hurt.

"Can't breathe," Abby squeaked, her face squashed against his chest.

Pepper laughed then, loosening his grip. "So I owe Marcus an apology—I'll call him tonight. It wasn't fair for me to ask him that, to put him in the middle, and it wasn't fair to hide it from you. You have a right to know this crap." His face darkened. "When I saw you lying there, I almost fell apart. I mean it, Abby. I think I aged ten years in about two seconds."

"Good thing you're pretty healthy, so maybe I won't notice how old you are now." Abby smiled. Then she squirmed. "And I hate to ruin the moment, but I really, really have to pee now. Finally."

"Hang on." He dug in his pocket, pulled out a small packet and put it in her hand.

"Really?" She held up the pregnancy test kit. "You know I'm on the pill."

"No contraceptive is foolproof. And you understand that pregnancy is part of the differential for passing out." His look was impenetrable. "Just do it, okay? I didn't want to give it to you at the clinic where there's no privacy. Because I'm sure by now that everyone knows you're mildly anemic."

"What? Everyone but me! Is that what Dolores said my blood showed?"

"Yes. Probably because you've been eating poorly. You can start taking iron tomorrow."

"Iron tastes terrible."

"Tomorrow." His face stony.

Abby went to the bathroom, emotions jumbled, her thoughts chaotic. What if she actually was pregnant? But she couldn't be—she didn't feel pregnant. Right, she told herself sternly, and you didn't feel like you were going to faint, either.

She did not want to be pregnant, not right now. Could she handle that, adjust her internal timetable, even though she wasn't certain what that timetable was? She was not completely sure she should have a child at all. Whether she could manage the demands, control her anxiety. Whether she would transmit that anxiety to an innocent child.

Pepper would stand by her, whatever she decided.

She blew out a breath and performed the test. Waited with her eyes shut and kept her brain empty. Then she clenched her teeth and opened her eyes, peered at the stick.

Negative.

She brought it back to him and watched his reaction. As usual, his face stayed inscrutable.

"Well," he said, gazing up at her, neutral. "That's a relief. Isn't it?"

Abby sat on his lap. "Yes. For now. I just don't think I'm ready yet for a little Pabby."

"What the hell is that? Pabby?"

"You know. A cross between Pepper and Abby."

He burst out laughing. Then he quickly sobered and searched her face, stroked a strand of her hair into place, rearranged her hair. "Thanks, I needed that. But I want to know what I can do. For you. To help you through this."

"I've already decided. I need to talk to my people. Lucy and Karen." Both women had helped Abby with her anxiety problems over the last few years. Lucy, a retired gynecologist in Phoenix, was her friend and support system and substitute mom; Dr. Karen Goh had been her telephone psychologist. She should have called them both, weeks ago.

Pepper nodded, and he went to phone Marcus. For now, Abby gave up trying to sort out her complicated emotions and drew him a cartoon instead, Pepper handing her a water bottle and demanding that she drink every last drop.

12

Pepper seemed up to something. Every now and then Abby caught him watching her with a mysterious smile. If she asked, he turned dour and said she imagined things. Once, she found him speaking quietly with Marcus, bent over a computer, pointing at the screen. *That one*, she thought he said. Seeing her, he straightened abruptly, stumbled over a few words, then asked her about a patient. By the time Abby moved to where she could see the screen, Marcus wore a deadpan face and the computer showed two tawny puppies wearing little cowboy hats. Abby shook her head. She didn't like pets dressed in human clothes; it seemed somehow demeaning to the animal.

"Really?" she remarked, looking back and forth between the two men. "You two were admiring puppies?"

"We love puppies," Pepper said somberly, while Marcus nodded enthusiastically.

Abby wondered if Pepper planned to get her a dog, but the puppy screen felt like a decoy. Then she realized she might actually like having a dog, some warm friendly mutt, and now worried she would be disappointed if he wasn't planning that. Her thoughts felt convoluted.

"Are you getting me a dog?" she ventured.

"No." Then he saw her expression, which seemed to surprise him. "I mean, do you want a dog?"

Abby shrugged. "It might be nice."

"You've never mentioned this before." He squinted, trying to calculate her.

"You've never looked at puppies before," she pointed out.

She resumed her tasks. Without Candy, Dolores reverted to her frantic solo routine. As difficult as she was, Candy had performed many duties, so Abby tried to help where she could. Sometimes she roomed a patient herself, or gave a vaccination, without bothering Dolores.

Abby thought she was coping a little better. She dove deeply into discussions with both Lucy and Karen, opening up her fears like a patient on an operating table and letting them cut away at her guilt, a sensation so sharp it physically hurt. It felt like undergoing surgery without anesthesia, but it helped untangle her emotional entrails. While her sleep remained restless, her torment decreased. Somewhat.

"You might want to see this," Pepper said, sticking his head in the office at lunch, where she was just biting into her sandwich. Abby diligently ate regular meals now. But he looked ominous and withdrew quickly. "Another chest pain."

A fit woman, thirty-three, tall and muscled, the patient looked built like an Amazon wearing ultralight hiking gear. She hiked down to Phantom Ranch early that morning on the South Kaibab Trail, then returned the same way. Only at the rim trailhead, she buckled to the ground, breathless, dull pains crawling down her left arm. After Pepper administered nitroglycerin and got her blood pressure controlled, the angina subsided.

Abby studied the initial EKG, taken when the patient's chest still hurt. The lines curved and wiggled into patterns of heart muscle strain.

Abby talked with her while Pepper phoned for transport and alerted the emergency doctor in Flagstaff. Impatient and agitated, the woman sat on the edge of the table and repeatedly tapping her toe against the wall, throwing dark looks between Abby and Pepper. Since he started the case and didn't need help, Abby faded into the background and watched.

"So I'm fine now," the woman said, irritated. Her voice deep, a little coarse, almost a man's voice. "So it turned out to be nothing."

Pepper disagreed. "I wish that was true. But unfortunately, you just had a pretty severe attack of angina. Your heart muscle wasn't getting enough blood. If that continued, you would have had a heart attack. The nitroglycerin you took—that pill under your tongue—helped open up your arteries so the blood could get through. And lowering your blood pressure took the strain off. Your blood pressure was really high. Dangerously high."

The woman made an exasperated face. Abby noticed her pupils were a little dilated and saw the acne clustered on her chin, scattered down her chest.

"I know you told me you don't take any prescription medications," Pepper went on, ignoring her aggravation, "but what about supplements? Do you take anything for bodybuilding or weight loss? Anything for stronger muscles?"

She glared. "Of course. Everyone does. Because it helps."

"Can you tell me what, exactly?" He appealed earnestly. "We think some supplements around here are contaminated with bad chemicals." He gave her a cold gaze. "People have died."

That rattled her. She looked suddenly unsure, crossing and uncrossing her arms. With a little more persuasion, she fished in her backpack and pulled out a plastic bag that looked all too familiar, containing multicolored pills and capsules. She handed it to Pepper for inspection, her words defiant but her voice faltering.

"Those supplements really work. I've cut tons of time off my hikes."

Pepper looked grim and asked where she got them. When she hesitated, he explained that her life might depend on it. She gave in, then, describing an odd man at the river she met a few months ago, with a dark braid over one shoulder and loose cotton clothes. He tied a red bandana over his head like a skullcap, and a black patch covered his right eye.

"He looked like a pirate," she admitted. "I know it sounds dumb, but he did. He even had an anchor tattoo on his arm. I mean, it was probably from being in the navy, you know? But he actually seemed really smart, and he knew a whole lot about nutrition and performance and competition. A lot," she emphasized.

"And you bought pills from this guy?" Pepper was incredulous.

"Really—he was completely convincing." She spread her hands, defensive now. "He said how he was an alternate for the Olympics a few years ago, only I can't remember what sport. And he said how all the athletes used this stuff. But he had a surplus and was selling some of it off. It wasn't cheap, either." She looked nervous, her annoyance gone. "Can you tell me what's the problem? What do you think is in them?"

Pepper explained the other cases, the heart attacks and cardiac arrests. He told her about the corrupt mixture of drugs, a wicked blend of amphetamines, steroids, testosterone, caffeine. Thyroid hormone and traces of barbiturates. She looked appalled.

Abby slipped out, hurrying back to her lunch. Pepper convinced the woman to be checked in at Flagstaff. And for her supplements to be tested.

Abby swallowed her second bite of sandwich when she heard Priscilla yelp loudly up front, almost a shout. Before Abby could find her feet, Priscilla stormed back, furiously waving a sheet of paper, her face red. Abby had a fleeting thought that Marcus would have calmed her down, whatever was wrong, but Marcus took the afternoon off to go golfing. It was unnerving to see Priscilla so overwrought—her usual haughty disdain rarely went missing.

Priscilla shoved the paper under Abby's nose and dropped it, snatching back her hand as if scalded.

"I touched this!" she screeched. She shook her hand vigorously, as if trying to shed something clinging to her skin. When Abby looked puzzled, Priscilla pointed to the diagnosis, stabbing the air with a long lavender fingernail. Her pearly purple lipstick had smeared in one corner. "Look at that! I touched that after the patient touched it! Lice!"

Abby set down her food and picked up the sheet, saw where Pepper had entered *pediculosis*. Head lice.

"It's okay," Abby said soothingly. "It's not contagious like that. You need really close body contact, like head against head." Abby reached out to reassure her, but Priscilla jerked away. "And this responds well to treatment, so the patient will be fine. Besides, we haven't seen any cases of 'super lice' around here."

"Super lice?" Priscilla went pale. "Oh my lord, what are super lice?" Her eyes flew desperately around the room, searching for monsters.

"It's okay," Abby repeated. "Super lice are just lice that have become resistant to the usual treatments. They still respond to prescription medication. It's been a small problem in some parts of the state."

Priscilla sat down in Pepper's chair, her chest rising and falling.

"Don't hyperventilate," Abby said. She coached Priscilla to hold her breath and count to ten. Priscilla nodded weakly and did it and her panic improved.

Pepper came in and looked back and forth between them.

"She's okay," Abby said, pointing at the paper and trying to be generous. "She was afraid we might all get lice."

Priscilla grasped Pepper's sleeve. "Oh, Dr. Pepper. Will I be all right? My heart is racing so fast."

Pepper expressed proper sympathy and listened carefully to her worries. Then he escorted her to Dolores, asking Dolores to check her vital signs and keep her under observation for a short time. Priscilla thanked him profusely and finally released his sleeve, her fingers trailing down his arm. Pepper returned to the office and briefly closed his eyes, then sent Abby a suffering look that said everything.

The ambulance picked up the hiker with angina and took her to Flagstaff for monitoring and a cardiology consultation.

After that, the afternoon remained blissfully uneventful. At the end, since it was Friday, Abby pulled up her computer schedule to check Monday and see what patients to expect. But something was off—all her appointments were empty. Startled, wondering about an error, she clicked on Tuesday and found the same mistake. The rest of the week, blocked and empty. Pepper came in and stood behind her, watching her search through the week again.

"Anything wrong?" he asked mildly.

"Look at this." Abby pointed, upset. "This is completely messed up."

"Hm." He looked at her instead of the schedule. "I wonder how that happened."

Abby narrowed her eyes. "What's going on?"

A smile tweaked his mouth, but he warily raised his hands, just in case. "Don't be mad at me, but we're taking a vacation. I think we both need a break, don't you?"

"What? Where?" Rarely had he thrown her off this far, and she wasn't certain she approved. Abby knew she lacked flexibility at times, but she liked to be included in plans and didn't care for surprises.

"Do you know where your swimsuit is?"

"John. So help me—"

He sat down and took her hands. His eyes shone, and he looked so impish and pleased that she tried to shed her vexation.

"You know how much you like volcanoes and hotspots and all that geology stuff? How after last summer you said you have a personal relationship with Old Faithful?"

"We're going to Yellowstone?" Abby nearly jumped with anticipation. She pictured the bubbling, steaming terrain, the reek of sulfur. The scalded aqua pools, brimming and slurping with heat. She nearly laughed out loud. "But what about the clinic? What about—"

"I've got a moonlighter all arranged. But it's not Yellowstone. We're going just a little bit farther."

"Rainier? Mount St. Helens?"

"No," he scoffed playfully, shaking his head. "Even I know those are stratovolcanoes, not hotspots. I thought you liked volcano hotspots."

"You don't mean…?" She couldn't finish the sentence, too astonished to believe he would plan such a trip on his own.

"Yep." Pepper grinned. "We're going to Hawaii. The Big Island. Kilauea."

Abby grinned back.

13

Abby had never flown over the Pacific.

Although nothing but ocean and sky filled the window, she could not tear herself from the glass, lost in that endless mint blue above and below, searching for where sea met air in a thin pale blur. While of course Abby knew in her head that seas covered nearly three-quarters of Earth, now she held it in her heart and deeply experienced how she lived on a watery planet spinning through space. Solid land was practically an anomaly, a stony stroke of luck for her species.

They emerged from the plane onto a surreal landscape with clinging tropical humidity and broken, blackened terrain, with charred chunks of lava as small as pebbles and as large as boulders. Waiting for their luggage, they reveled in the exotic air, heavy and warm, the steady breeze fragrant with blossoms and salt. They marveled at the open baggage area, offering a wide view of the bright turquoise ocean.

Pepper's intrigues were not done.

Abby reached for her suitcase as it trundled by on the conveyor, but another man's hand grabbed and hoisted it first. She looked up in surprise and saw a familiar face, cinnamon hair, warm brown eyes.

"Hi there, Abby," he said.

She felt a dazed moment, unable to comprehend how her friend William Bridges from Montana could be standing there, smiling, holding her suitcase. Then a short slender woman with shaggy sable hair emerged from behind him and shrieked with delight. She wore a long flowered skirt, and a rattlesnake tattoo curled down her left arm.

"Abby!" Her eyes danced with mischief.

"Gem? William?" Abby stared with her mouth open, struck nearly dumb, as Pepper embraced her.

"Don't be mad," he said, turning her to face him. "I almost told you a million times."

"I'm not mad," Abby laughed. "Are you kidding?"

Gem hugged her and William shook Pepper's hand and everyone talked at once. Abby could hardly believe that Pepper pulled this off. Last summer at Yellowstone, Gem and William had become her fast friends. Gem worked as the clinic nurse and William as a seasonal ranger, a shy and devoted geologist, and the two found each other there. Competent and feisty, Gem didn't put up with much of anything; cautious and gentle, William would soon become a professor at the end of this semester. They complemented each other like salt and pepper.

While Abby suspected that coming to Hawaii would seem like paradise, she never dreamed it would feel like heaven.

The change in time zones prompted early rising, and the next morning they walked the beach early. Soon Pepper and William forged ahead with their long-legged strides, discussing something about careers, but too far away to hear.

The women strolled more slowly, enjoying the sand between their toes, the sharp calls of shorebirds, the foamy hiss as the sea rushed up to touch them, then ran away.

First Abby updated Gem on Marcus, recounting Priscilla's wardrobe spreadsheet and the squirrel reports. It was wonderful to laugh so much, their peals of joy mingling with the sounds of birds and waves. Abby felt liberated, a different person, and she cringed a little inside to think just how somber and haunted she had been.

But Gem was rarely one to delay; she tackled problems with vigor. She stopped and faced Abby. The men were far down the beach, chatting and gesturing, faintly audible in the breeze.

"So how are you doing now?" Gem's light brown eyes searched Abby's face. "Pepper told me about your friend who disappeared. But it's been weeks since I talked with him about it."

"I figured he had." Abby wasn't upset; she knew how worried he was back then. "Did he ask you to come here to fix me?"

"No, not at all. He asked us to come because it would be fun. Because we all need that. He didn't even tell me what happened until after we decided to join you."

Abby smiled, for that was exactly how she expected Pepper to behave. He never assumed, and he rarely pushed his own agenda on others, almost to a fault. Even now he avoided mentioning his sister's calls, reluctant to bother Abby, although she encouraged him to vent.

"I'm better," Abby said simply. "Both Lucy and Karen have been helping. They've been dissecting my reactions to Heidi's disappearance. Her possible suicide. They've pointed out that I may not be 100 percent perfect. Who could have guessed?"

"And can you embrace that?" Gem asked, a small frown. "Because how many times have I told you that? But you've never believed it. I mean, you know how you are—you always expect yourself to know everything. To never make a mistake. And then you're really hard on yourself if you think you don't measure up."

"Well. I'm trying to get there. And I really appreciate that you're asking. That you care." Abby grasped her hand affectionately. She squinted against the glare off the water, the sun climbing and starting to blast them with heat.

"You know I do. You'll never escape me." Gem threw a bear hug around her, then sobered. "Is there anything new? Any more information at all?"

"Nothing. It's like she vanished into thin air." Abby shook her head. "I think it would be easier to deal with something concrete instead of nothing. Even suicide—at least we would have some closure. As it is, there's still the chance she could turn up, maybe alive, maybe dead. It's just unsettling. Waiting for the other shoe to drop."

Gem nodded sympathetically. "Maybe this vacation will help. Give you some distance."

"I actually think it will." Abby was ready to change the subject. Sometimes she wearied of the theme herself, so she could only imagine how everyone else must feel. And she knew it would never fully resolve, not unless Heidi reappeared, which seemed increasingly unlikely. She realized she would always doubt herself about this, at least a little, and must learn to live with that.

"And what about you and William?" Abby nodded toward him and Pepper, standing on the smooth sand, taking turns throwing something into the sea, some sort of contest. Men, she thought. "Are you moving in together yet?"

"Maybe." Gem turned shy, stared out across the open water, shading her eyes with her hand, as if she might actually see Asia if she tried. "I mean, yes. We just did."

Now Abby gave her a bear hug. "You mean—"

William suddenly shouted and scampered into the dazzling water, dove under a wave. He emerged sleek and shining, shaking his hair, scattering diamond drops.

"Hey, wait for me!" Gem cried, running after him, plunging in.

They played in the water for hours. They built a complicated sandcastle, designed fancy turrets and moats, and then cheered their destruction by the incoming tide.

The next day they booked a snorkel trip to Kealakekua Bay and floated over the mystic corals, some shapes spiny and some smooth, some twisted and blunt, others knuckled and gnarled. They peered in dismay at bleached remnants and stubs, the dead and dying corals, killed off by overly warm waters and poisoned by chemicals in sunscreen. Abby lost herself among the fishes, sunny yellow tangs and iridescent parrotfish, black triggerfish with neon blue stripes, and the ludicrously long thin trumpetfish. The fish nibbled, swayed with the waves, darted and flashed together in dense, mesmerizing clouds, dappled by sunlight. Abby lolled and drifted in the brine and let the rolling waters rinse away her stress. Some of it, at least.

Not every moment was peaceful. Pepper's sister renewed her calls, several times every day. Urgent, strident—Abby heard her voice even when he pressed his phone to his ear. He cast his eyes and walked away as he talked, as if to spare Abby.

Best of all, though, was the island itself, the jumbled terrain, the rough lava blocks strewn across the landscape. Abby loved it, seeing the island build itself as they stood there, seeing the mantle of her planet burp up its fiery guts. She walked reverently on the recent lava, which had oozed up from hundreds of dark miles below and, in awe, she stroked the ropy black whorls of cooled pahoehoe. When they visited Hawai'i Volcanoes National Park, Pepper was almost as eager as Abby.

"I didn't know you were so interested," she said.

"I'm excited to watch you be excited," he explained.

"That's kind of complicated."

The evening crater of Kilauea glowed, an eerie light cast up from the restless lava lake, an unnerving steamy orange cloud that climbed to the sky. Abby could have sat there all night, fathoming the earth's crust, sensing the deep shifting magma and the violent heat of the core, still outrageously hot after four billion years. She felt comfortably meaningless, an ephemeral speck.

Except for the phone calls, Pepper seemed as happy as she'd ever seen. Sometimes he dismissed the calls quickly, back to himself in seconds. Other times a disquiet shadowed him for a long while.

They bought fresh pineapple and cups of poi at a farm stand set deep in the trees, a dark green oasis in the midday sun. Pepper showed them how to properly eat the sticky taro paste, scooping it up with two fingers. Then, while Gem and William were busy looking at carved wooden bowls for sale, Abby took his hand and gently sucked the traces of poi from between his fingers, licking the bland gluey film from his palm, a trickle on his wrist.

"Abby," he said thickly, shifting his hips. He looked around at the trees, the deep inviting grove.

"No. No way," she said firmly. "You have to wait."

Gem and William seemed mildly surprised when Pepper abruptly announced they should leave. He drove a bit fast back to their beach resort where he professed fatigue and begged off until dinner, hurrying Abby along to their room. There, he spent the rest of the afternoon inventing quite a few other ways one person could consume poi off another.

Later, while he napped, Abby found a hotel notepad and drew a cartoon for him, where he pointed longingly at a palm grove while

Abby said *No!* She was in the bathroom, getting ready for dinner, when she heard him laugh.

It was their last night. They lingered hours over dinner, fresh fish and crème brûlée baked inside a pineapple. Abby debated whether to mention it, then finally commented that Gem's snake tattoo looked a little pale and blurry. Gem admitted softly that she started laser treatments, that with William in her life now she no longer needed her snake's protection. He took her hand and gently kissed the fierce fanged head, such a tender moment that Abby felt tears sting her eyes.

Much later that evening, the phone call lasted long and shrill. Pepper's expression turned stormy, so Abby took her book and moved out to the lanai, slid shut the door to give him privacy. She watched the sky, splattered with huge radiant stars that drifted downward and fell slowly into the ocean.

The door yanked open and Pepper's face appeared, unhappy. He came out and slipped behind her in the lounge chair, pulling her against his chest between his knees.

"She's lost her mind," he grumbled.

"Now what?" Abby leaned back against him, tried to track the motion of the stars.

"It's ridiculous. But at least now she says I can tell you everything. Mostly because she wants something."

"What are you talking about?"

Pepper played with the tips of her hair, twisted a strand around his finger. "I can't remember if I told you what she does? That she's a high school counselor?"

"No, you didn't. That's sort of ironic, huh."

He nodded. "Right. So she had an affair with the principal, and everyone found out, and it's gone all over social media. Then somehow everyone also found out that a year ago she had an affair with the music director. So out of character."

"What's out of character? To have two affairs?"

He laughed. "No, it's out of character for her to sleep with someone who's got any culture."

"Ouch."

"Exactly. And her husband is the coach at the same school. He teaches some bland class like health studies, where probably all they talk about is abstinence. I really don't care what they've done to themselves, but my niece—Ashley—is caught in the middle, and everyone knows. She gets teased all the time, and she's regressing. Withdrawing. I can't even imagine."

"Sounds awful," Abby agreed. "What a tangled web. How old is she?"

"Just fourteen, I think. They had her skip a grade even though I advised against it. So she's a freshman, halfway through her freshman year, but she's young." He shook his head. "They plan to move her to another school next year, but right now they just want to pull her out, get her away. I suggested maybe the parents should leave the school, but that didn't go over well."

"She's just going to stay at home? Alone? That doesn't seem wise."

"Exactly." He fluffed her hair. "They actually had the audacity to ask if she could come stay with us for the rest of the semester. You know, while they try to patch up their marriage. I told them no, that it wouldn't be fair to you."

Abby sat very still while her thoughts took off, racing in tight circles, an odd surge of…something. Undefinable. "You mean that if you were single, alone, you'd do it?"

"No," he scoffed. "How would that look?"

She studied the sky, wondered which star that was, about to drop into the watery horizon. She thought about the trillions of miles the light from that star had traveled to meet her eye, all the thousands of years that beam had been running toward her. She thought about the child's photo in Pepper's wallet, the way he talked about her curiosity. How she had once charmed him with her wonder. Abby considered what a good man he was, and she reached up and took his hand.

"Do you want to do it?"

A long pause. "It's not fair to you. It could be messy, let's face it. I suspect she has some pretty significant issues. Who wouldn't?"

Abby shrugged, a bit amazed herself that she might be okay with this. Maybe it had something to do with Heidi—another lost soul, her chance to help. Maybe she just knew Pepper wanted it. He had been so considerate with her, so generous, and she understood without a doubt that he would do this for her if the situation was reversed.

"Well," she said slowly, feeling her way. "It's just a few months. Three, maybe four. We have an extra bedroom. I mean, it's tiny, but it's there." Abby scrunched her face, already imagining, planning. "She would have to go to school, so that would be hard on her, to face everything new for such a short time. She would need to be pretty independent. And at the same time, she'd have to agree to follow our rules."

Pepper pulled her around, looked in her eyes. His gaze was cool, puzzled, as he searched her. Abby smiled—he was not the only one who could behave unexpectedly.

"Are you serious?" he asked.

"You would do it for me."

"I don't want you to feel obligated. You shouldn't do it just because you think you should."

"It's not that." Abby could not define the feeling, but it was not obligation. "I think it's something that I need to do. Want to do. Let's not overthink it."

Pepper laughed. "This might be one of the few times you actually need to overthink something."

Abby agreed to sleep on it. But she knew she had already decided. The long flight home provided plenty of opportunity for overthinking, and her decision stayed the same.

14

All vacations end. Everyone falls back into their routine, Abby thought, although these days nothing felt routine.

While a trace of uranium showed up in Harry Stonewall's metal screen, the surprise was his highly elevated lead level. Any reading over ten micrograms was serious, and Harry's lead level hit fifty micrograms. To make things worse, Abby could not find him; he had not appeared for several weeks. The rangers knew of Harry—everyone saw him poking around at one time or another—but no one had put eyes on him lately. Abby fretted and they all promised to send him her way if he materialized.

In another unexpected but more positive development, Marcus found a new medical assistant to replace Candy. Golfing in Williams, an hour away, he struck up a conversation at a diner with an older woman behind the counter. According to Marcus, who never failed to uncover copious personal information immediately from everyone he met, Bessie Corn came from Missouri and grabbed the diner job for something to do while settling her mother's estate, battling through Arizona's complex probate laws. But she found she abhorred serving food and watching people eat, said it nauseated her, and she was hoping to work in the medical field where she had years of experience. Rangy and thin as a rail with a long mournful face, she dyed her severely short hair an unlikely coppery orange. Seventy-year-old Bessie said little, worked hard, and seemed ruffled by nothing. Dolores began smiling more and clinic efficiency picked up considerably.

Phone calls flew between the canyon and Illinois, arranging for Ashley to come in two weeks. Pepper handled everything. He registered her at the local high school. He talked with her privately several times, welcomed her, and reviewed the rules he and Abby drew up about homework and chores, hours and curfews, about no smoking or alcohol or drugs. Ashley agreed immediately to everything, no problem. Pepper commented to Abby how Ashley was so eager that she probably would have signed a contract in blood with a vampire.

"Maybe you should quit watching that show," Abby said for the twentieth time.

Pepper and Abby finalized a new project at work, sending out an email newsletter to their patients, full of advice about recent medical developments and reinforcing healthy habits. At the last minute, Pepper added a brief warning:

Caution: Avoid buying or taking supplements/vitamins from any individual in this area. These supplements may be contaminated with dangerous drugs such as steroids and amphetamines (speed). A seller has been described dressed as a park ranger or a man with an eyepatch.

Please report any such activity to medical or park staff.

"Good idea," approved Abby. She made a copy of the announcement and pinned it in the waiting room.

Next she saw Tammy Arnold, a sixteen-year-old patient with nausea for two weeks. Bessie handed Abby the vital signs outside the exam-room door, making a long face.

"What?" Abby asked, beginning to discover how Bessie was a keen observer.

"Hot mess." Bessie moved on to her next task.

Tammy and her nervous mother sat on opposite sides of the exam room, the air crackling with tension. Tammy's bright blond hair waved around her face, cheeks pink with blusher, her scarlet lips crimped in a pout.

"It's nothing, Mom," Tammy said, exasperated. "I told you I'm fine. You always overreact."

"She's not fine," Mrs. Arnold pleaded with Abby. "She's lost weight. I've heard her throw up in the bathroom at least three times. Something's wrong."

The vomiting made Abby think of Mona from months ago, the runner with anorexia. But Tammy did not fit that profile: she was not underweight and she liked her figure. She said she avoided exercise because she detested getting sweaty and because it ruined her makeup. When Abby explained to Mrs. Arnold that she always liked to chat alone with a teenager about their symptoms, the woman left the room so fast she nearly tipped over her chair. Abby called after her to wait in the lobby until Bessie fetched her.

After piercing Abby with a hostile glare, Tammy stared at the wall and answered questions in an edgy drone. She denied stomach pains, diarrhea, and constipation. Abby tried to be friendly, tried to connect, shifting to get into her line of vision. Tammy denied fever, a change in her diet, or any sick friends. Abby tried a smile, and Tammy slid her eyes away to another spot on the wall.

"I know all this seems boring, but there's quite a few things that can upset your stomach," Abby said. "That's why I have to go through this long list. But we're almost done. Have you used any drugs or needles? Smoked anything, been drinking alcohol?"

A brief pause, a dark glance. "No."

"Do you have regular periods?"

A longer pause. Her face twitched. "I don't know."

Abby knew there was no way to soften it. "Do you think you could be pregnant?"

Tammy's eyes caught Abby, defiant. Then her face crumpled and her voice caught, fell to a whisper.

"Maybe."

Abby examined her abdomen, which was soft and benign. No enlarged or tender liver, no kidney or bladder discomfort. No soreness over her upper abdomen, which could indicate an ulcer or gallstones.

"Let's get some lab tests," Abby suggested. Tammy swallowed hard and nodded.

The pregnancy test was positive. Abby talked with her about options, but Tammy had frozen, unable to express what she wanted or how she felt.

"Are you going to tell my mom?" she finally asked, rubbing her eyes. Her mascara smeared now.

"She'll have to know. I can tell her, or you can tell her. I can be here with you, or I can step out. Whatever you want."

Tammy blew out a long breath, steeled her face. "I probably should do it."

Abby called Mrs. Arnold into the room and left, quietly closing the door. She sat at the counter typing her note, hearing the muffled rhythm of their conversation, fits and pauses of talk, occasionally sharp but mostly subdued. Bessie walked by and gave her a look; Abby saw what her assistant had suspected from the beginning.

When everything seemed quiet, Abby tapped on the door. She hoped to find them sitting close, maybe even embracing over the enormity of the situation. But they had retreated again to their corners, like boxers facing opponents, both faces striped with tears.

"Now what?" Mrs. Arnold asked hopelessly.

"Well. It depends on what you decide. On what Tammy decides. Did you talk about it?"

They shook their heads, miserable. Abby gave them names and numbers, the nearest obstetricians and the nearest Planned Parenthood. She offered information and timelines based on the last menstrual period, gave them space to talk, made suggestions for counseling, and finally proposed they visit with her again, because both remained shell-shocked and had no questions. When Abby guided them toward another appointment in a few days, though, Mrs. Arnold said maybe, then silently walked out ahead of her daughter.

Give a hug, Abby wanted to shout at them. She wanted to physically push them together, make them wrap their arms around each other, make them say they still loved each other. It was one of the emptiest, most hollow moments she could imagine, and she felt like pulling them back into the room and demanding they start over, communicate better, actually say what they were feeling, for better or worse. Show somehow, at some level, that they cared about each other. Show anger or sorrow or determination or regret or resolve.

Something. Anything.

But the other rooms were filled, patients waiting, each with his or her own needs and worries and questions that craved her attention. They had chronic tennis elbow and acute knee strains, nagging allergies and coughs that wouldn't quit. All the ups, all the downs: high cholesterols and low thyroids, high blood pressures and low white cells, high sugars and low libidos. Throughout the afternoon doubt nagged at Abby, how she should have done better, found some subtle key to unlock them. She decided to call each one tomorrow, first Tammy then her mom, and see if anything had shifted. But it still felt terrible.

Then she imagined the teenager about to join her and wondered what on earth she had been thinking. Wondered what unrealistic fantasy she had invented. Abby the savior. As if.

Pepper seemed tense, too. He started taking long evening walks, an old habit from his single days. Sometimes Abby joined him, if she hadn't already gone running. Sometimes he went long after she fell asleep, hiking to the rim and occasionally a little way down the Bright Angel Trail.

"Are you worried about these plans?" Abby asked. "Should we back out?"

"Sure, I'm worried." His mouth turned, part of a smile. "Who wouldn't be? But no, we can't back out. That would be wrong—she's really counting on this. And I can't blame her. It's going to take all my willpower not to mention how worthless her parents have been."

"Do you think they'll end up divorced?"

"Who knows?" he shrugged. "At this point, I almost wonder if that would be best."

Abby talked again with Derek Shipley about Heidi, how the investigation was going. Missing-person flyers were posted in Arizona and nearby states, and they continued to look for her body. Kinder now, Shipley mentioned that Heidi's mother had been going through her daughter's papers, looking for other contacts and clues. Unknown to Abby, Heidi kept long, detailed journals and diaries, exploring her feelings, musing on other people, making plans and weaving her dreams.

"I wonder if something happened suddenly, maybe that night, after she left you," Shipley said. "Something upsetting, maybe an unexpected rejection. Something that devastated her, you know. Enough to do something impulsive."

Abby had to think he might be right. Maybe it would turn up in her journals.

She tossed restlessly that night until Pepper joined her, her head crammed with too many people. Tammy Arnold and her mother never returned her phone calls. Abby knew she must let it go, but couldn't quite shed them from her thoughts. Ashley loomed in the near future, an unsettling unknown. Pepper had been reading in the other room, sleepless as well.

"We're a pair," he commented, sliding into bed and finding her awake.

Abby nestled against him. "A pair of what?"

He smiled and stroked her hair, and Abby finally dropped into sleep. She slept deeply, hungrily, as if she couldn't get enough. Until she fell far into a dream, down a dark tunnel with echoes and cries, looking for something lost. Something critical, but she couldn't remember what and—

Abby woke with a jolt, damp with sweat despite the night's chill. Pepper was no longer there, just the rumpled sheets. You're fine, she told herself, it was just a stupid dream. He had probably gone out to read again, probably slept there on the couch. Wide awake now, she padded out to find him, but the lights were off except for the tiny nightlight in the kitchen, his chair abandoned. In the dim gray, she saw his book splayed open on the table, next to a half-drunk mug of tea. She opened the back door, thinking maybe he took the sleeping bag out to the deck. But the lounge was deserted, a rime of frost glinting in the starlight.

What time was it? Abby felt confused, couldn't recall the day of the week. Did he go to Marcus's place to watch that stupid show? No, of course not, he would have returned long ago. She found her phone, shocked to find it was two o'clock—he had never been gone at such an hour. She quickly called him.

His phone rang in the bedroom. He left without it.

Relax, Abby commanded herself. He obviously couldn't sleep and went walking to settle himself. He would be back soon. She turned on the lights and washed the dishes in the sink, wiped off the counters, put things away. She turned the TV on and off again. Thirty minutes went by, forty-five. After an hour she found herself pacing. Finally she pulled on her clothes and a jacket and left the house to find him.

Abby walked rapidly; it was a fairly long way to the rim. Where would he be? He was a thoughtful, measured man—surely he hadn't hiked far. No one was about, the night silent except for her own breathing and low rumbles from the hotel, the machinery of humans. She peered down the long stretch of trail, too dark to see much, not sure what she expected to find, while far away on the horizon a small storm blinked now and then. The canyon shone weakly in starlight, no moon, the endless towers and cliffs more felt than visible. Tiny rustling sounds moved along the ground, maybe a mouse. Abby stared and stared and began to wonder what she was doing, why she had come there. Any chance of intersecting his path was minimal. The massive space plunged before her, grave and indifferent, keeping its dark secrets to itself for a few more hours until daylight gathered again. She felt those millions of years clinging together, this opened burial ground of obsolete landscapes and creatures, billions of long-extinct beings.

The growing beat of rotors, not too far away, broke the spell. Abby turned and scanned the sky, saw a helicopter nearing what must be the clinic area. She broke into a jog and went to grab her phone, then realized she had not brought it with her since Pepper didn't have his.

Emergency vehicles parked at the helipad strobed red lights through the night, the woods throbbing with flash. By the time she arrived, the medic helicopter was already loaded and about to leave, revving higher as Abby hurried up to where Paul, one of her favorite paramedics, stood watching. A few rangers waited nearby.

"What's going on?" Abby shouted over the noise, bracing against the battering air, touching his shoulder to get his attention. She snatched her hair as it flew up. "You haven't seen Pepper, have you?"

"Abby!" he cried, shocked to see her. "Dr. Wilmore! I've been trying to call you!"

"Sorry, didn't have my phone." She opened her empty hands. "Is there someone I need to examine? Is everything under control?"

"Oh my god, Abby." He grabbed her arm. "It's Pepper. He must have stumbled off the Bright Angel Trail in the dark and broke his leg. I think it's an open tib-fib fracture, but we got it stabilized and splinted pretty well. We don't know how he didn't fall all the way. Somehow he dragged himself back up."

"*What?*" Abby stared at him, uncomprehending. The accelerating whine and roar of the helicopter was deafening, befuddling. Then all at once she grasped it, aghast.

Frantic, she whirled and ducked low to escape the rotors, running toward the helicopter. But she only made it a few steps when Paul tackled her heavily, took her to the ground with him.

"Are you crazy—you can't run under those blades! You'll be killed!" he yelled.

Abby thrashed, trying to escape from him before Pepper left. She nearly broke away when another pair of hands seized her arm, one of the rangers. She didn't know him—he looked upset and his grip was so tight that she yelped, but it partly cleared her head.

"It's a small chopper, one of the little ones," Paul kept saying loudly in her ear as the helicopter rose and the hands released her. "There's no room for anyone else."

Abby gazed wildly up at the disappearing helicopter, trying to make her mind work. The sudden drop of sound and wind was disorienting, like a vacuum.

"Tell me again," she insisted violently, clutching Paul's arm. "Tell me again what you said. What happened? Is he okay? Does he know I'm here?"

"He was in a lot of pain," Paul said, quieter now as the noise receded. "We gave him some morphine, so I don't think he knows much of anything right now."

"I must go," Abby said abruptly, pulling away. Everything she had to do started clicking into place. He might have other injuries. He would need orthopedic surgery on his leg. He would be in the emergency room for a while, and he needed her to be there. "I have to drive to Flagstaff. Right now."

Paul flung his arm around her, looked sternly in her eyes. "Listen to me. Are you listening to me?"

Abby shook her head, squirmed in his clasp. She was unaware of tears streaming down her face, unaware of how her hands shook. "No. I have to leave. Damn it, Paul. Let go of me."

"Look at you—you're a wreck," he exclaimed. Then more kindly he said, "Anyone would be. But you're in no shape to drive seventy miles, and you probably haven't had much sleep. I would go with you myself, but I'm still on duty. Who can drive you? Who can we call?"

Abby's breath caught, trying to think. There was only one answer.

"Marcus," she said urgently. "Call Marcus Limerick. Do you know him? Do you have his number?"

"Of course," Paul assured her, taking up his phone. "Everyone knows Marcus."

15

Pepper came home from the hospital four days later. Because First-Med scrambled quickly and found a moonlighter, the clinic closed for only one day after the accident. Abby refused to leave Pepper in Flagstaff alone.

Fortunately, he had a closed fracture, not open—no bone pierced through the skin, even though the scrapes and bleeding made it look like it. But the fall shattered both bones of his right lower leg, the tibia and fibula, and it took extensive surgery to pin them back together. Pepper was abraded and torn from sliding against rock and the spiky, scrubby undergrowth—until a tiny bush on a tiny ledge snagged him and stopped his descent. Once Abby and Marcus arrived in Flagstaff that night and found him in the emergency room, they had stared in dismay at the x-rays, the ghostly images of splintered bone.

No one could fathom how Pepper dragged himself back to the trail, traversing eight feet of steep inclined stone, leveraging himself upward by finding miniscule rifts for his fingers and his one able foot. One slip, one miss, and he would have fallen eighty feet. Then fortune came his way in the shape of an insomniac hiker, a man who left Phantom Ranch hours earlier for a starlit trek out of the canyon. The startled hiker came upon Pepper struggling up over the edge, not very far from the top. He helped pull him up and ran for aid.

Once he was home, Abby busily rearranged furniture to make way for crutches. Pepper propped scowling on the couch, his leg swathed from foot to thigh in a blue fiberglass cast.

"I can't do this," he muttered, his eyes stormy, his face drawn. He shifted the cast, seeking a more comfortable position. "I want to bend my leg. I want to take a walk. I'm no good at being an invalid."

"I don't think you have much choice," Abby pointed out, adjusting a pillow behind him and putting another one under his cast. The drive from Flagstaff had been rough, unable to elevate his leg very well.

She sat beside him and took his hands, seeing his pinched mouth, the deep line between his brows. His left cheek was scuffed, still raw, his right forehead bruised. Small cuts laced both hands. For the thousandth time Abby felt a hollow catch in her chest, that she had almost lost him.

"You look like you're in pain. Can I get your meds?" she asked.

"No, I'm fine." He laid back his head and closed his eyes, then went on without opening them. "You must have a ton of things to do. Don't worry about me."

Abby sighed. She did have much to do, and she had to resume work tomorrow. Marcus already reported how they were counting the minutes until she returned. No one liked the moonlighter, a terse old physician from Las Vegas trained in internal medicine, who knew little about treating children and less about traumas. Marcus guessed he hadn't sewn up a laceration in decades: his hands tremored and Dolores had to keep showing him which equipment to use. Clumsy at typing, he took forever to finish his documentation and wouldn't move on to the next patient until he was done. Bessie summed him up on his first day with a variation of her favorite phrase, murmuring "old mess" as she walked away.

"And he *smokes*," Marcus whispered to Abby over the phone. "So he's always stepping out for a cigarette."

That took Abby aback, for very few physicians used tobacco. Doctors had the lowest smoking rate of most professions, for good reason. Then she caught herself, realizing this man probably regretted his decision to fill in at the canyon, no doubt accustomed to an adult urban practice and not realizing what he was getting into. Instead of judging him, she felt annoyed at FirstMed for hiring someone so ill-suited for the job.

But work wasn't until tomorrow. Today Abby needed to stock the kitchen with groceries, tidy and clean the messy house, manage a mass of emails, and keep an eye on Pepper. Make sure he ate something and drank enough fluids, help him wash and navigate. He seemed both exhausted and restless. Abby could tell something else bothered him, too. Something furtive, but he denied it when she asked. Much had been left unsaid…she wanted to question him about how on earth it happened. But he would likely feel bad if she pressed it, so she tried to let it go.

"You'll do better when you can start putting some weight on your leg," Abby said, wanting to encourage him.

"That's not for a week," he replied dismally.

"Well." Abby needed to tell him what she had arranged. She had put it off too long, and he would surely be mad at her. But yesterday her worries and isolation drove her to call Gem for support. Gem offered more than support, for she immediately dropped everything and insisted on coming, to help him out for a week. After that, Ashley would arrive.

And that was another dilemma.

Two days after Pepper's surgery, Abby called Ashley and her mother. Pepper had fallen into fitful sleep, and Abby walked outside the hospital with her phone to deliver the news and discuss delaying Ashley's trip for at least a few weeks, maybe indefinitely. Pepper himself agreed her arrival would be problematic, to say the least. Abby admitted to herself that she felt a little panicked, trying to juggle so many roles: working the clinic alone, caretaking Pepper, and parenting a teen.

First Abby spoke with Pepper's sister, who quickly disregarded it all and passionately pled for not changing plans. She asserted how much Ashley needed to escape the toxic school atmosphere and how badly the parents needed to work out their differences—alone. Abby listened patiently and tried not to condemn this wheedling woman who had barely asked about her brother's condition. Pacing the sidewalk under the trees, sunlight flashing through pine needles and cotton-wool clouds dotting the sky, Abby longed for her normal life of a few days ago, and felt guiltily happy to be out of the hospital.

Then she heard muffled arguing through the phone and Ashley's voice, young and sharp.

"Go on, Mom," Ashley said. "Please leave the room. Let me talk to her alone."

"Hello?" Abby said into the ensuing silence.

"Yeah. It's me." A hard exhale. Her voice no longer shrill, but low and sad. "Is Uncle John okay? I've been worried sick."

"Thanks for asking. He's doing all right. Mostly recovering from surgery right now."

"Listen, Mrs. Wilmore. I mean, Dr. Wilmore. Tell Uncle John to let me come. Please. I can't stay here. It's just horrid, and my parents are making me crazy."

"Ashley. I appreciate that, I really do. But we'll be spread really thin. Your uncle may need nursing help and—"

"I can do that! Last summer I was a volunteer at the hospice here in town and I was really good with people. I did all sorts of things. I even worked with catheters and IVs and everything. They asked me to come back. I can get you references from them. I can—"

Abby hoped Ashley couldn't sense her smile. "Well, he's not dying, you know."

A small snort. "I know, I know. But I could help you out, a lot. I mean, help him. I promise, I won't be any trouble at all."

Maybe she was correct, Abby thought. It would be good to have someone at home while he recovered. But there was so much more to the equation. "I'm sure you're right. But you must understand that we have to keep an eye on you. And that's going to be hard with John laid up and unable—"

"Exactly! If he's home all the time, he'll be with me more. You won't have to worry about me because he'll be there, right? He'll make sure I do my homework and eat my veggies, right? He can be like a stay-at-home mom."

Abby paused. She hadn't considered that.

"*Please?* I'm already packed—I've been packed for days. I've checked my plane ticket so many times that it's tearing in half and I had to tape it together. I mean, it's like I'm Charlie Bucket and that's my golden ticket. Tell Uncle John that he's like my Willy Wonka. Promise me you'll tell him that."

It was hard not to laugh. Pepper broke into a grin when Abby told him he was Willy Wonka, the most pleased he'd looked in days. In the end, they cautiously agreed to let her come, although Abby wondered how soon they would regret it.

But Ashley was a week away. Gem would arrive in a few hours.

"That's a lot of food," Pepper commented as Abby unloaded groceries, making another trip to the car. He managed to nap that afternoon and looked more rested, a little less gloomy. "Are you trying to fatten me up?"

Abby put the last food in the refrigerator and sat down.

"I'm glad you slept and you're feeling a bit better." She looked closely at him. "I have a confession to make."

"Oh no." Pepper put his face in his hands. "You're trading me in for a better model?"

Abby laughed. "I should, but no. We're having company, though."

"Really?" He frowned, no longer amused. "Pretty bad timing."

"This is going to be a rough week," Abby said. "So I've arranged for someone who can fix your meals, take you places, help you out. While I'm at work."

"That's ridiculous. Whoever it is, call them and cancel. I'm not that impaired." His eyes flashed at her, annoyed.

"John. You actually are impaired. You can barely get to the bathroom, can hardly get down that narrow hall with your crutches. You still have a lot of pain, and you're weak, and I'm worried you could fall. When you banged your leg on the door today, you turned gray and you looked like you might pass out." He shook his head but she forged on. "I'll be gone all day and you might need assistance. Maybe you won't, but it will be good to have someone just in case." She put her fingers on his lips before he could protest again. "It's okay. It's Gem. She insisted on coming. I don't think I could have stopped her if I wanted to."

Abby braced for a reaction, but it never came. He was surprisingly okay with having Gem there.

And Gem was wonderful. She immediately took over, sending Abby to her tasks while she and Pepper strategized what he needed. She arranged the furniture again, to her own liking. She watched him use the crutches and made suggestions, testing his strength and forbidding him to navigate alone. When she saw the uneaten lunch Abby had fixed him earlier, she reheated it and commanded him to consume it all. Which he did.

"You'll never get stronger without good nutrition," Gem insisted sternly.

Abby narrowed her eyes as he meekly obeyed.

"What the heck," Abby said, picking up the empty plate.

Pepper admitted he was a little afraid of Gem. Gem overheard and muttered *damn right*. But she smiled.

That night, Abby and Gem invited Marcus over and cooked a hearty dinner of pasta, fresh bread, and salad. It was just like last summer at Yellowstone, Abby with Gem and Marcus, relishing each other's company, teasing Pepper about the lengths he went to, just to get out of work. Abby sighed with relief, seeing him relax, joining in.

Work the next day was crazy, of course. Even Priscilla seemed glad to have Abby back, and she made Abby assure her several times that Pepper would be okay.

Abby threw herself into work, answering a backlog of messages and questions on both her own and Pepper's patients, between examining puffy joints and searing heartburn, wheezy asthma and a raw blistered rash, puncture wounds and cat bites and hearing loss. A frail elderly woman brought in her frail elderly husband, worried about his derailing memory and escalating paranoia, but Abby only had enough time for a quick assessment, which confirmed his dementia was worse than suspected. She asked them to return for a longer appointment so she could test him better and make the right recommendations. Abby felt bad about that, because the woman looked so anxious and depressed, but Abby was almost an hour behind. She had Dolores come in and arrange the dementia evaluation in a few days, and she appreciated that Dolores spent extra time talking with the wife.

Abby was tired by the end of the day, but at least she hadn't worried much about Pepper. She talked with either him or Gem several times; he complained that Gem was too much like a drill sergeant and made him do his exercises more than necessary, while she complained that he was a difficult patient who only wanted to lie in bed and eat chocolates. Abby smiled at their banter, valuing Gem endlessly and feeling deeply indebted.

Abby checked up front with Marcus and Priscilla, making sure there were no more questions before she left. Priscilla was straightening the waiting room, restacking magazines precisely, putting the tissue box where it belonged, when Abby noticed that the flyer she put on the wall last week, warning about the supplements, was no longer there.

"What happened to that?" she asked.

Marcus and Priscilla both looked surprised. They hadn't realized it was gone.

"That's strange," Abby muttered, looking around as if she might find it. "I wonder why anyone would take that."

She made another flyer and stuck it up again. Then she walked home to find dinner on the table and more stories about Pepper's rehab under Gem's supervision. Hungry, Abby enjoyed her meal and mused aloud that she might have to arrange for Pepper to get injured more often.

The week flew. Pepper grew stronger and his pain improved somewhat. He slept better and started putting a little weight on his leg, letting his foot touch the ground as he walked with the crutches. No one wanted Gem to leave, but it was time.

Abby embraced her tightly. "I can never repay this. You made this week so much easier, for both of us."

Gem smiled. "You can repay me. Come visit William and me this summer."

"Done," Abby and Pepper promised together.

That night they ate leftovers from Gem and still had more in the refrigerator. They moved to the back deck, Pepper hobbling out the door with more dexterity, swinging better on the crutches. They snuggled together on the lounge, enjoying their last private night before Ashley arrived the next day. Dusk came later now, the air warmer with spring on the way, and Venus shone like a nightlight in the sooty sky. Abby worried to herself how much she would miss her solitude once Ashley joined them.

"We probably should make the most of this," Pepper said, pulling Abby against him and kissing her forehead, stroking her ear and down her neck.

"Are you sure you're up to it?" she asked gently, tilting her face and kissing him at length.

"What do you think?" He took her hand and put it on him there.

"I guess," she smiled, feeling him rise, starting to unfasten his jeans. "But I don't want to hurt you."

"We just have to go gradually, and you'll have to do most of the work. Don't worry, I'll tell you if you need to stop."

"If you want to go gradually, then you'd better slow down those hands," Abby warned, her breaths erratic.

Afterward, they agreed that sometimes the best things are those you anticipate the longest.

They talked far into the night, the tensions of the week sliding away. Abby admitted she felt bad for the maligned moonlighter, so out of his depth. She noted that Harry Stonewall remained missing, and how the flyer about supplements disappeared.

Pepper fell silent and she felt him tense up.

"What's wrong?" she asked.

His nose flared and his eyes gleamed at her, then away. "We haven't talked about it. I know you haven't asked because you didn't want to sound critical. Because you didn't want to seem like you were blaming me. But it's the elephant in the room, isn't it?"

"What are you talking about?" She was nearly certain and wished he had not approached it. Not now.

"I'm talking about why I fell. How I could do something so stupid, so careless." His words rough.

Abby shook her head. "Don't be so hard on yourself. You probably stumbled. Maybe you didn't see a rock in the dark, or maybe your ankle turned. Maybe you accidently got too close to the edge, or your foot skidded in the dirt. It could happen to anyone."

"I don't think so."

"Well, maybe you—"

"Abby. Stop. I've been trying and trying to talk myself out of this, but I can't. For a while I thought I shouldn't tell you, but that's not right, either." He faced her and gripped her arms, and his eyes speared into hers, wintry. "I don't think I fell. I think I was pushed."

16

Originally, Pepper planned to drive to Phoenix and pick up his niece at the airport. Because that was now impossible with his fracture, he instead arranged for her to travel by shuttle to Flagstaff, then take another shuttle to the canyon. While he worried that she had to navigate alone, she assured him it was nothing.

"I take the train by myself into the Loop all the time, to go to the museums," she told him. "My parents are allergic to museums, so I have to either go by myself or I don't go at all. Have you ever ridden the El through Chicago? Trust me, this is nothing."

Pepper didn't argue. Arizonans were mostly friendly and safe, despite their penchant for firearms.

With Ashley scheduled to arrive late afternoon, Abby tackled a full day of work. FirstMed contemplated hiring a temp while Pepper was disabled, but their communications were poor and nothing happened. Worried they might again hire someone inappropriate, Abby let it drop and shouldered it all.

The frail old woman with her frailer older husband returned for his memory test. Eighty-two-year-old Winnie Swanson led in eighty-seven-year-old Jerry Swanson, pushing his battered aluminum walker down the hall. One leg of the walker bent inward, making it list to one side, pulling Jerry crookedly to the wall.

"What happened to your walker?" Abby asked, watching him drift.

Jerry looked blank, so Winnie told how last year he slammed the car's trunk shut on it while the legs were still sticking out. She admitted she should not have yelled at him quite so loudly, but he scared the dickens out of her. When Abby suggested a new walker,

Winnie rubbed her finger and thumb together in the universal sign for money.

Abby patiently performed the dementia exam. Winnie sat by him and kept tapping her hand against her mouth, as if to stop herself from blurting the answers. Once, she accidentally prompted him and Abby reminded her to let him try; Winnie nodded tightly. She wore a brown sweater bearing a large golden brooch, a smug-faced swan with green glass eyes. Every now and then she reached over to brush lint off his shoulder, or adjust his uneven tweed lapels, or fuss with his hair. Abby saw her dismay mount as Jerry declared the current year to be three decades earlier, and when Abby held up a pen and asked him to name it, he mumbled a string of odd syllables until he finally called it a panda.

For the last part, Abby drew a circle on paper, then gave him the pencil and asked him to fill in the numbers like on a clock. He seemed frozen, so Abby started him off with the twelve and encouraged him to keep going. In a shaky hand, he slowly put the number one in its place, then painstakingly followed with the rest of the numbers right next to it, on top of each other, running them off the page. He looked wretchedly up at Abby.

Winnie's lips quivered and a tear worked down her cheek.

"It's worse than I thought," she said, patting his arm, using her other hand to wipe her face. "He used to read me Shakespeare, you know. He loved doing all the voices. Once we stayed up all night while he acted out Macbeth. I know it's a tragedy, but we laughed so hard. Especially when he did the witches."

They discussed what to do. He might have an occult head injury called a subdural hematoma, a puddle of blood at the edge of his brain—something that could be treated and he might improve. He needed a head scan to look for that. He might have a vitamin deficiency, a low B12 that caused poor brain function, or his thyroid might be haywire. But by far, Abby explained, the majority of cases like his came from Alzheimer's.

"So what now?" Winnie asked softly.

"Let's make sure there's nothing complicating this," Abby said, turning to Jerry, who twisted the pencil in his hands. "We'll check your thyroid and B12, and you can get a brain scan in Flagstaff. If you want, you can consult with a geriatrician, and you might want to arrange for help at home. If you need it." Winnie nodded grimly. "You can also get involved in Alzheimer's research down in Phoenix if you're interested, but that's a long way."

"Aren't there medications?" Winnie raised her hand, her fingers out, as if literally grasping at a straw.

"There are meds, and they might help temporarily. But they don't make much difference in the long run. And they have lots of side effects."

Deflated, Winnie said they had a son in Prescott who might help; they contemplated moving there, although she would have no friends. Abby felt badly but she had to keep going, other patients waiting, so she promised to call Winnie with the lab results. While Winnie seemed grateful, Abby knew her solutions were woefully inadequate. They needed so much.

She wondered if Ashley had arrived. How Ashley and Pepper were getting along. Abby yawned, for she'd slept poorly after Pepper's declaration that he had not simply fallen from the trail.

She didn't know what to think. Abby had to believe him—he was hardly prone to wild imagination. But where was the sense of it? He described the trail that night, so deep in black shadow. Anyone in dark clothing could have crouched invisibly in a rocky niche. He'd heard a noise, something out of place, and he paused to listen, standing near the edge and gazing into the great dim space before him. He recalled a tiny bobbing light far down the trail, likely the hiker who helped him, wearing a headlamp. Then when Pepper turned to walk on something struck his leg, a flash of pain, and he went skidding down the stone.

No logic explained it. Pepper had no enemies they could imagine—at least, no one who wasn't in prison, like the man Pepper testified against in a domestic violence case. They even checked to make sure that man remained incarcerated. And who would be out there in the middle of the night, waiting for him? Pepper's activity was unpredictable—his last midnight walk had been days ago. Though reluctant to doubt him, Abby wondered if the trauma and morphine jumbled his perception. No one thought he suffered a concussion. But in the spirit of support, she encouraged him to talk with the rangers, maybe contact Shipley. Pepper agreed, although even he seemed hesitant to claim it officially.

Hatch Carpenter came in with an infected finger. A few days ago, he cleared a broken limb from the trail and a jagged twig pierced his work glove, spearing into his fourth finger. Because he knew it was a deep puncture, he came to the clinic immediately, where he saw the older physician from Las Vegas. That doctor glanced at it, according to Hatch, pronounced it to be nothing, and sent him out with instructions for warm soaks twice a day. Now the finger looked like a swollen red sausage, hot and throbbing. A few drops of pus seeped from a tear along the knuckle. Hatch was not the kind of man to let mere pain bother him, but he flinched and grunted when Abby touched the finger and tried to bend it.

"That looks bad," Abby agreed. The chart note was scant: *Minimal trauma, superficial scratch, warm soaks.* No precautions, no instructions about what to watch for, no mention of a tetanus vaccine. Abby was incensed. Hatch couldn't remember his last tetanus shot, so she ordered one right away.

"Was your exam really normal? Just a scratch?" she asked. "It says here there was almost nothing."

"Hell, no," he growled, indignant as if accused of lying. "It was still bleeding some. He said it looked *like a scratch?*"

Abby worried that the infection could turn serious if it traveled down his finger and into the tendon sheath, which would infect his whole hand. That development would become an emergency hospitalization, and she emphasized the importance of taking antibiotics immediately.

"If it looks worse at all by morning, even a little bit, you must let me know." She instructed him to elevate the limb and watch for red streaks up his arm.

"Thanks. At least you know what you're doing." He made a face and stretched his thick neck. His arms seemed more beefy than ever, ropy blue veins running under the skin, his hair stiffly gelled. "And hey! How's Doc Pepper doing? I heard he got hurt really bad."

Abby nodded. "He fell on the trail and broke his leg. He'll be okay, but he won't be working for a while."

"Well, dang. Tell him I miss him." Hatch's broad brow wrinkled up and he looked genuinely concerned, which warmed Abby's heart.

"Of course." She appreciated that he had dropped his macho façade and no longer looked at her breasts like last time.

"And what about those vitamins, and those hikers with the heart attacks? I've been asking around, just like Pepper said I should, but I got nothing so far." He pursed his lips. "I'd sure love to catch those bums. Do you think they're still around?"

Abby shrugged. "We don't know. Pepper thinks it might be just one guy, someone using different disguises. Knowing Pepper, he'll figure it out while he's lying in bed. He's downright dangerous when he's got too much time to think."

Hatch laughed. "Have him call me. I'm serious. He can be the brains, and I can be the brawn. We'd make a great team—he'll figure it out, and then I'll go get the bad guys. I'd love that."

What an unlikely accomplice, she thought. Internally she still fumed over the negligence of the physician who failed to ask Hatch about tetanus, whose record-taking was abysmally inadequate. She wondered if she should notify FirstMed, caution them to never hire him again. Abby made a mental note to check the medical board website, to see if there were complaints against him.

Everyone on staff, Marcus and Priscilla, Dolores and Bessie, admitted to Abby that they told every single patient he saw to come back and see her, because they didn't trust him.

Abby finished her notes and put her stethoscope away when she noticed Swanson's dented walker parked beside the nursing station.

"How did they forget that?" she asked. "He's had a hip fracture and hasn't walked right since then."

Dolores told her to ask Marcus.

Marcus looked mildly surprised at first, as if he couldn't imagine they left it, but he finally admitted that he gave them the clinic's walker instead, a more sturdy and expensive model.

"I appreciate the sentiment," Abby told him, "but FirstMed will have a cow when we ask them for a replacement. They'll say it's not in the budget, and they'll want to know what happened to the first one."

"Not to worry," he beamed. "I've already ordered a new one, and I paid for it myself."

Priscilla lowered her perfectly drawn brows and stared at him.

"By the way," he went on, looking back and forth between the two women. "I'm taking tomorrow afternoon off. I'm meeting a new friend for a round of golf. I didn't think it would be a problem."

"Why don't you just wait and play on the weekend?" Priscilla asked, miffed.

"It'll be fine," Abby said, to placate her. The last thing she needed was for them to start sniping again. "Priscilla, you can save most of the billing forms for Marcus, for the next day. Who's your friend, Marcus? Is he a good golfer?"

A prim look from Marcus. "The courses are less busy during the week, Priscilla, so that's a better time to go. And my friend is a she, and yes—she's a very good golfer."

Now both Abby and Priscilla stared at him, as he turned and walked out the door.

Abby's phone buzzed with a text from Pepper. *She's here, all safe and sound. Hurry home.*

Abby couldn't tell if that was a normal "hurry home," or a pleading "hurry home." She pulled on her jacket and walked through the woods, slower than usual, enjoying the long amber shafts of sunlight through the trees. Storms were forecast for later, which made her treasure the quiet sunlit forest.

She felt like she missed her peace already.

17

Ashley greeted Abby nervously, standing quickly and wiping her palm on her jeans before shaking hands.

"How was your trip?" Abby asked, knowing how exhausting it must have been. First the long flight, then two shuttles. Three hours of that climbing, curving highway from the desert to the mountains, watching the saguaros dwindle and the pines gradually rise, from hardy pinyon to stately Ponderosa. Then another hour across the high plateau to the canyon.

"Thanks so much for letting me come," Ashley said in a rush, as if she had to get it out immediately, not even hearing the question. She chewed her lip and looked closely at Abby. "You probably saved my life. I mean it."

"Well. I hope it wasn't quite that serious." Abby glanced at Pepper who sat on the couch, looking slightly anxious, but he remained silent and let them sort the moment out. Abby pointed at Pepper. "And it was your uncle's idea to have you come."

"It was that serious," Ashley said solemnly. "And he said it was your idea."

Ashley looked fondly at her uncle, then her eyes leaped back to Abby, grabbed her. A few freckles sprinkled her cheeks, and her raven hair fell below her shoulders except for her bangs, which dropped bluntly past her eyebrows. Abby fought an impulse, because the girl unmistakably had Pepper's eyes, to brush those bangs aside and stare that pale cool blue. It felt almost disorienting.

Abby motioned her to relax back on the couch and sat down herself. "We really are happy to have you, Ashley. And I'm sorry about your bedroom being so tiny—it's almost a closet. But if you—"

"I love it. Please don't worry." Ashley made a little face. "And… if you don't mind, I don't really go by Ashley. It's the worst name ever."

"Really?" Abby could relate to disliking your name. What were her own parents thinking, calling their newborn daughter Abigail? "I always thought Ashley was kind of a classic name. You know, like in *Gone with the Wind*."

"Um, that Ashley was actually a man."

Abby felt a little foolish. "You're right, of course. Ashley Wilkes— Scarlett thought she loved him. I wasn't thinking."

"You know that my last name is Ember, right?" Ashley waited until Abby nodded, then pushed on. "So that's me, Ashley Ember. It sounds like a porn star. Or maybe like a woman in a trashy romance novel."

"No, it doesn't sound like that," Abby objected, knowing that it did. "No one would think that."

"Oh yeah? Ask pretty much everyone in my high school," Ashley said acidly. Then she lightened. "So please just call me Madd. As in m-a-d-d. It sort of sums up the way I feel about my life right now. Or you can call me Maddie, too."

"Maddie?"

"I kind of like it." Pepper finally weighed in. "Now that I'm getting used to it."

Abby blew out a breath. This young woman seemed intriguing, to say the least. "All right, then. Maddie, let's think about making some supper. Are you hungry?"

"I'm way ahead of you," she crowed, gesturing toward the kitchen. "I already threw together a casserole, noodles and spinach and tuna. Uncle John said you liked tuna, and he said we had to include veggies. He tried to help, but I was afraid he'd fall over and hurt himself or something so I only let him sit there and tell me where everything was."

"She's kind of pushy," he complained. "She and Gem should start a club."

Abby touched her on the shoulder. "I bet you'd get along with Gem. But I like it when a woman knows what she wants."

Maddie beamed. "Sometimes I do. And they gave me some good training at that hospice, so I know how to work with patients. Difficult patients." She looked at Pepper.

"Hey," Pepper protested. "Remember, I'm not dying. Don't forget to resuscitate me if something happens."

Supper conversation was lively. For someone who reportedly clammed up and refused to say anything during family counseling sessions, Abby found Maddie animated and clever. She had imagined someone more surly, more edgy. Maybe Ashley—Maddie—was just trying really hard, wanting to make a good impression. Nothing wrong with that.

Pepper explained how Maddie planned to be a writer and was working on her first novel, and Maddie eagerly dove into the details of her middle school fantasy, a web of children abandoned by obnoxious parents, struggling through their school with toxic teachers while tackling a shadowy fourth-dimensional world of demons and guardians.

"That actually sounds pretty interesting," Abby admitted, caught up in the plot. "I hope we can read it someday."

"I would really like that, but it's only half done." Her face darkened. "My parents won't read it. They say that my writing should be my own private space. But that's just their excuse for not bothering." She stared back and forth between Abby and Pepper, and Abby felt unbalanced again at seeing Pepper's frosty gaze in her eyes.

"We'd love to," Abby assured her. "Do your parents call you Maddie?"

"They do if they want me to answer them."

Abby shared her battle with her own name. Being named after her great-aunt Abigail made her feel old and stuffy, like a grandmother.

"Sort of the opposite of your problem. And what made it worse was that I was kind of like that—a little fussy about things. I still am." Abby laughed, for she never told Pepper that story and he looked surprised. "I made them promise at my high school graduation that they had to announce me as Abby or I wouldn't walk across the stage."

Maddie grinned. "I love it, Dr. Wilmore. And now I know what to do at my own graduation."

"Don't you dare tell your mom you heard that here," Pepper warned.

"Wait," Abby said, stuck at being called Dr. Wilmore. "You can't call me that. It's too formal. Just call me Abby."

"Can't do it. My parents would kill me. They're really big on respect for your elders." A twitch of mischief crossed her face. "How about if I call you Aunt Abigail?"

"Absolutely not." Abby tried not to smile. Impertinent little scamp.

"Okay. How about Auntie Ab?"

"No way," Abby scowled. "That sounds too much like Auntie Em, from *The Wizard of Oz*."

Maddie sobered and flashed a blue glare from under her bangs. "Well, that fits. I just came from Oz."

Then she yawned hugely, unable to stifle it. Drained from traveling, she went to bed early, before they resolved the question of how she would address Abby.

Abby picked up in the kitchen and Pepper propped himself at the sink, washing dishes on one leg until Abby made him sit down. They made plans for the weekend, what to show Maddie, how to help organize her. Abby liked her, liked how her charm came gleaming through the angst. Maybe they truly could help her.

Pepper crutched out to the living room on his way to bed, but in a moment he reappeared in the kitchen where Abby wiped down the stove.

"This was lying on the side table," he said, handing a notebook to Abby, the cover flipped open. She saw a page with a haiku at the top, then a gap, then notes about the shuttle ride. Scribbled descriptions of saguaro, something cryptic about a dry arroyo waiting for rain. "She must have been working on this when I showered. I didn't mean to read it."

Abby took the notebook, the pages bent and ratty at the corners. Her heart stung as she read the haiku, and she wondered how long ago it was written.

Your words are hot coals
That fall on my skin and burn
With the fire of hate

Pepper closed the notebook and put it back on the table where he found it.

18

Marcus found the prospector Harry Stonewall.

Driving back from golf, Marcus passed a campground in Tusayan, just outside the national park. A sudden hunch struck him and he made a U-turn. Marcus cruised slowly through the campground until he discovered Harry's red rusted-out VW Beetle at the farthest, most secluded site, deep in the trees. The VW was familiar to Marcus because they often talked about its sputtering, unreliable performance while Harry waited for his appointments. He found Harry resting wearily on a cot inside a large old army tent, the canvas worn and mended. Although Harry refused to let Marcus bring him to the clinic right then, he promised he would appear in the morning.

Abby listened with concern to Marcus's description of Harry's place, although it didn't surprise her. Stacks of canned food lined the walls of the tent, and cardboard boxes crammed with lumpy rocks sat everywhere—tucked under the cot, piled in corners, flanking the doorway. An old ice cooler, a rickety lawn chair, and a tiny propane heater were the only other items. Harry's cookstove and a large water jug sat on a picnic table outside, and more jumbled rocks sprawled in heaps behind the tent.

"He's been living there this winter? With all these storms?" Abby could hardly imagine; it sounded miserable.

"A tent site at that campground only costs ten dollars a day, so he can stay there for three hundred dollars a month," Marcus pointed out.

"Did you tell him about his high lead level?"

Marcus shook his head. "I just told him he really needed to see you. That you might know what's wrong."

"Probably wise." Abby noticed how much leaner Marcus looked. His polo shirt no longer stretched far out in front, his belly now just a small bump. His plump face seemed less round and showed a hint of cheekbones. "Were you golfing in Flagstaff? With your friend?"

Marcus glanced down at his hands, then back up. "Yes, she can be fun. A little temperamental. But you know how golf is."

"That's nice." She didn't, of course, know how golf was, but that was not the point. "She isn't like a girlfriend, is she?"

"Oh, no," he said quickly. "No, that wouldn't work at all. She's nothing like me."

"You know what they say," Abby teased, "about how opposites attract."

"No." He shook his head firmly, a little frown. "She's kind of a hot-head. I just try to keep her calm so she can focus on her game. I try to get her to laugh. That's all."

Abby dropped it, not completely convinced. But Harry Stonewall had just arrived, and she hurried to make space for him in her crowded schedule. It would still be weeks before Pepper worked again, which kept Abby functioning just below panic level.

Instead of complaining about Harry like Candy had, though, Bessie took him under her wing. She coaxed him to be patient, that he might have to wait a while, then asked about his last meal and brought him juice and graham crackers. Abby heard them behind the closed door, Bessie chatting and Harry's wheezy chuckle.

Bessie came out and Abby smiled at her.

"Did you actually get Harry Stonewall to laugh?" Abby asked. He and Candy used to glare daggers at each other.

Bessie's long, seamed face pulled even longer, her eyes almost misty. "He reminds me of my pa. He was so cranky that you couldn't help but love him. Harry's just like an old piece of pie, all hard crust on the outside and all sweet goo on the inside."

"You're the best," Abby said.

Harry apparently recovered from Bessie's charms by the time Abby saw three more patients and finally entered his room, where he slouched crossly on the table, his scruffy gray eyebrows drawn low. When Abby explained about his lead levels, his brows dropped even lower and his eyes nearly disappeared.

"Lead?" he grumbled. "Where the hell would I get lead? I don't believe it."

Abby showed him the lab report as proof, but he shook his head.

"Poppycock. I could trust that, maybe, if it said uranium, but lead is stupid. Makes no sense at all."

"Well, you do have a small trace of uranium, but your lead is dangerously high. It's sure to be causing most of your symptoms, including your kidney condition. Your stomach problems, your numb feet—all from lead poisoning." His face darkened and she switched tactics, tried to be collaborative. "Let's see if we can figure it out, okay?"

Abby opened the CDC website on her laptop and they ran through the possibilities. Harry denied using any old paints, or owning anything with flaky, lead-based paint, which could contaminate his tent. He took his drinking water from the campground spigot, so Abby made a note to contact the health department and have it tested. Because he primarily ate canned foods, she asked that he check the cans for lead seams—products from other countries might be sealed with lead solder. He didn't use leaded gasoline, or handle car batteries or eat game meat killed with lead shots or bullets. At every question, he looked distrustful and muttered *no, no, no,* increasingly irritated, until she asked about his dishes. Whether he ate off plates made of glazed pottery, anything from central America.

His oak-colored eyes woke up, big and startled, behind his thick glasses.

"Huh."

"Lots of those colorful glazes are made with lead, and it leaches into your food," Abby explained, trying not to show her excitement that she may have found a cause. It was hard to imagine that his dishes could raise his lead so high, but who knew? She had only one more question. "And how about medications from Mexico, anything for upset stomach? Especially if it's colored yellow or orange. Some of those folk remedies are full of lead."

Harry raised his hand to his mouth, shaken. "Dang. I take that elixir every day. Two or three times a day if I'm feeling poorly. Which is most of the time. My crazy old cousin lives in Baja and she sends me a bottle every month."

Without meaning to, Abby jumped up and gave him a little hug, overjoyed to have figured it out. Startled, he bristled and pulled away.

"Sorry," Abby said, gathering herself, "but I'm just excited that we're getting to the bottom of this. Can you bring me that orange medicine? We can find out what's in it and make sure it gets disposed of properly."

"All right, all right, young lady. I mean Doctor Lady. I mean lady Dr. Wilmore…" Ruffled, he fussed with his shirt, straightened his eyeglasses. "I don't mean no disrespect. But let's just all calm down. 'Cause maybe that's not what it is, you know?"

"Of course," Abby said formally, still smiling.

She wanted Harry to see a toxicologist, to see if they recommended chelation therapy to lower his lead levels faster. But Harry would have nothing to do with specialists. Instead he vowed to throw out the glazed dishes and to quit taking the elixir, and he agreed to return in a week to recheck his labs.

At lunch, Abby congratulated Marcus on his initiative, first finding Harry and then convincing him to return. She suspected Harry had given up on medical help, and it scared her to think how he might have scraped along, barely managing, progressively deteriorating as he dumped canned food into his leaded plates, as he swallowed more and more lead-laced tonic.

Maddie's first few days at the canyon coincided with spring break, creating some good bonding time for her and Pepper. Now she went to school, and in the mornings she walked directly to class, but afterward she walked or jogged in large loops through the woods, trying to improve her fitness. Surrounded by so many hikers and runners, so many people focused on their fitness, her skeptical outlook shifted. Back in Illinois she disdained exercise, too conventional, but now she admitted that the exertion helped her relax, and how the forest felt spiritual. She began to range farther, east and west through the village and along the rim, and she talked about hiking to the river someday.

"I need to see how Mother Nature made this crazy place," she said.

Abby agreed they might do that—obviously, Pepper couldn't make the hike with his leg—if she could secure a campground spot at the river. Those campsites were booked out for months, but she did know a few people after all. Maybe they could snag a cancellation.

Though better, Pepper still had pain. Every few hours, he needed to lie down and elevate his leg to stop the throbbing ache of his fractures. It grew worse if he spent too much time up on his crutches, which he was stubbornly prone to do, putting more and more weight on his injured leg. But if he did too much around the house or yard, the pain troubled his sleep, although he rarely took his pain meds. At least twice that Abby knew of, Maddie came home from school to find him hurting, and she took his crutches so he had to stay put. He could only win them back with good behavior.

Maddie impressed Abby with how few demands she made, how well she adapted to the rhythm of their lives. Because she spent hours alone with her notebooks and little laptop, briskly typing stories, Pepper made a point to check on her screen activity. She willingly agreed and he found with relief that she avoided social media sites. When he remarked on that, trying to support her, her response was quick and hot.

"If you'd been attacked on Facebook a thousand times about how slutty your mother is, and what a creep your father is, you'd stay off it, too." Maddie glared up through her bangs, waiting for a reaction.

"I'm sorry," Abby said. "That sounds awful."

Maddie stared at her a moment longer, then resumed typing.

Once Abby asked if her parents had communicated with her much since she arrived. They certainly had not called Pepper.

"Now and then," Maddie remarked shortly. "Once because they couldn't remember the computer password when they had to reboot it."

Most of the time, though, Maddie seemed content to live a quiet life without drama. She adored her uncle, was endlessly curious, and many supper conversations centered on the medical cases Abby saw that day, the trickiest diagnoses and stickiest personalities, the obvious and the mysterious symptoms, and the subsequent management. Abby carefully masked identities to maintain patient confidentiality, but the one time when she slipped and accidentally used a name, Maddie called it out and reminded her to be careful.

"Have you made some friends?" Abby changed the subject.

Maddie shrugged. "I don't really have friends. Not back home, and not here. I get along better with my teachers. But that's what happens when you skip grades and start high school too soon. Apparently I'm too young and immature for all these sophisticated high school kids."

"Well. Maybe you'll connect with someone here. I hope you might," Abby said neutrally. "How are your classes?"

"Pretty boring." Maddie sighed. "And this time I'm not being sarcastic or mean. I've just already had most of this material. I was in the advanced math curriculum, and here it's plain old normal algebra. And I've already read *Fahrenheit 451* and *Catcher in the Rye* on my own, a few years ago. So it's hard to be motivated."

Pepper fixed her with his gaze, suddenly alert. "What are you saying?"

"I'm saying that it's kind of slow and dull. It's hard to get excited about studying stuff you've already done. Sometimes I sit there and work on my own book instead."

"So." The gravity of that one word, dropping heavily from Pepper's lips, made her look up quickly. "You're saying that you know the material, so we can expect that you'll be getting straight As in all your subjects. On all your tests. Correct?"

Abby felt tart electricity zip between their eyes, blue to blue, then Maddie looked down.

"Um. Sure, Uncle John. No problem."

"That's what I thought," he agreed pleasantly.

The next night, Pepper fell asleep early. Abby and Maddie sat quietly in the living room, sipping hot chocolate; Abby studied a medical journal while Maddie scratched away in her notebook, writing in fits and starts. The storms had paused for a few weeks, but now rain pattered steadily on the roof and thunder grumbled, the windows flashing now and again with lightning.

"What are you writing?" Abby wondered out loud, seeing the girl's fierce concentration.

Maddie raised her cool eyes and pursed her lips, calculating. "A haiku for my parents. You want to see?"

"Sure." Abby reached over and took the offered notebook. Several marked-up versions of the poem had been crossed out, a clean copy near the end of the page.

The more you complain
That I'm quiet, the louder
My silence will grow.

"Pretty dark," Abby commented, handing it back.

"Yeah." She stared at her words. "I guess that's how I handle all this crap. Turn it into something else."

"Didn't you have a counselor? Did you ever show her the stuff you write?"

"No, Auntie Ab." Defensive, a little challenging. "I never talked to her. She said she wanted me to open up. But trust me—she didn't."

Abby let the *Auntie Ab* go. "You could still send her your writing without talking to her. Just share it. You never know…maybe that would help. I mean, she does know all the sides of your family's story."

"Right." Maddie rolled her eyes.

"Just a thought." Abby shrugged one shoulder.

They sat silently, neither one reading or writing, listening to rain drip off the porch, the muttering thunder.

Maddie glanced at Abby. "My mom says you and Uncle John aren't married. Is that really true?"

Abby nodded. She hoped the next question was not going to be why.

"Auntie Ab?" A hopeful smile pulled at her pale lips. "Remember what we talked about? Can we please hike down to the river? *Please?*"

"I'll see what I can do. So keep exercising. I'm not strong enough to carry you out."

19

Prevention is a tricky task, Abby thought for the millionth time.

Marietta Appleby lived with her son Wilbur, a friendly interpretive ranger with a long neck, prominent teeth, and a sparse moustache. Combined with his polite smile and black-framed glasses, he reminded Abby of an affable ferret, and he knew just about everything there was to know about Grand Canyon critters: all the birds and lizards, all the rodents and scavengers, the bugs and slugs and things with wings. He loved sharing the complicated geology and the river's cubic-feet-per-second flow, and he could quote the annual rainfall for the last twenty years.

Eighty-six-year-old Marietta understood her body the way her son appreciated the canyon. She knew the volume of her lungs and the cadence of her pulse, the rhythm of her bowels and just when her gallbladder contracted. As she was healthier than most people twenty years her junior, Abby often did not quite understand what prompted Marietta to appear in the clinic every few months. Her concerns felt a bit contrived, but they required intense attention to satisfy Marietta.

Abby always spent much of her passion on prevention, talking to her patients about eating and exercise, reducing alcohol and eliminating tobacco, promoting the best tests for cancers and denouncing the worst schemes from charlatans. So it felt curious when Marietta announced firmly that she was done with prevention.

"I've had it with you doctors and your experiments," she proclaimed sternly, her face severe, her knobby hands gripping the large black purse in her lap. Her white hair wound tightly in a braid, bound against her skull by a maze of bobby pins and clips; just looking at it gave Abby a headache. Marietta wore a simple cotton dress peppered with tiny flowers, and chunky brown shoes with Velcro straps. "I'm old and I'm going to die soon, so I don't see any reason to let you keep poking and prodding at me, looking for something that's not bothering me."

Her son Wilbur had greeted Abby warmly and now sat quietly in the corner of the exam room, reading something on his phone, not looking up. Abby suspected he was used to staying out of such discussions.

Abby scrolled through her chart, checking the last few visits, finding no such recommendations she had made.

"What are you referring to?" Abby asked, clicking through screens, still searching. "I hope you don't plan to quit getting your flu shot. Older people are more likely to have influenza complications."

"Oh, posh. I'm not talking about a flu shot—of course I'll get that. I'm not crazy. I'm talking about sticking scopes up my colon and squashing my breasts with that mammogram machine. About shoving that cold metal funnel up inside my lady parts." Abby saw Wilbur cringe at that one, while Marietta nearly spat with disgust. "When you get to be my age, you earn a little respect. And you earn the right to make decisions about all this nonsense."

"But I haven't recommended any of those for you lately."

"Excuse me? We talked about this just a few months ago."

Abby shook her head. "Maybe a year ago. There actually isn't very good research about whether to look for early colon and breast cancers after the age of eighty-five. Maybe do it, maybe don't, depending on your health. Since your last mammogram was two years ago, it's time to talk about that." Marietta looked sour and Abby forged on. "You haven't had a Pap test in years because we quit doing those at age sixty-five. And you had a good score on your bone density scan a few years ago, so we don't need to look at your bones for at least another six years, probably never again according to some studies."

Abby stopped. She realized she got carried away, overdoing it, giving too much information too fast.

"I'm sorry, that's a lot to take in," Abby apologized. "I can write it down for you. Do you have any questions about all that?"

Marietta tightened her clutch on the purse and leaned forward. Wilbur sent a brief apologetic glance toward Abby and seemed to hunch smaller in the corner.

"What are you saying?" Marietta demanded. "Do you mean that you've given up on me? That I'm not worth it?"

Her abrupt about-face caught Abby off guard.

"No, I'm saying we should discuss it. The pros and cons." Abby felt certain they had talked about this before.

"Well. I never." Marietta leaned over to poke at Wilbur with a bony finger. "Are you listening to this?"

Wilbur sighed and put down his phone, looked up mildly. "Yes, Mom. It all makes sense. I think you confused Dr. Wilmore, because at first you said you didn't want any more testing, and now you're acting upset if you don't get it."

"Well," she huffed. "I don't like it when people write me off. Maybe I'm old, but I'm not dead yet."

Abby tried to take control. "Actually, you're the sort of older patient who might benefit from a little more screening. Because you're so healthy. If you had other serious medical conditions, like heart disease or emphysema, the screening wouldn't matter as much. But ultimately, it's up to you, what you want."

Marietta stared through her tiny eyeglasses at both Wilbur and Abby. She decided she needed more time to think, so Abby sent her home with handouts and recommendations. And Abby thanked her stars that they didn't need to go through the muddy and ever-changing advice about prostate cancer screening.

Pepper began appearing at the clinic, off and on, much to Abby's concern. Too boring at home, he claimed, and he had to get out. Once Maddie left for school, he carefully drove the short distance, his left foot on the pedals and his casted right leg thrust into the passenger footwell. He liked visiting and reading medical articles on the computer, even though he could, of course, read them at home. Once when Abby found herself especially busy, he saw one of his patients while braced on his crutches, and he talked about scheduling a few more. Abby disagreed, knowing how he still tired easily, how he ached at night after spending time at work.

He always tried to be home when Maddie arrived after class, although she walked and jogged farther now to build up her stamina. She made big circles through the village, trekked a mile down and up the Bright Angel Trail with her book-laden backpack.

"I think I could be a geologist," she said a few nights ago. "Have you ever put your hand on that Kaibab limestone and thought *I'm touching stone that's over two hundred million years old*? I mean, there's little crumbs of fossils, you know, like mollusks and trilobites that lived back then. Way before the dinosaurs…it blows your mind."

"I think about it all the time." Abby loved her sense of wonder. "Back before the end-Permian extinction. You should talk to William."

Then the next night Maddie said, "I think maybe I could be a water expert. What's that called—a hydrologist? I can't believe that the water we use here comes piped up all the way from the Colorado River. From across the river! Is that crazy? All this controversy about water conservation and water rights is fascinating. Would I need to be a lawyer for that?"

"I think so. You really should talk to William," Pepper said. "Maybe you could go with us to visit them this summer."

Everyone paused and looked at one another. While Abby and Pepper had promised to visit Gem and William, Maddie should be back with her parents by then.

"Are you serious? I could really go with you?" Maddie asked quietly, biting her lip. She ducked her head and her hair screened her eyes.

"Well." Pepper realized he had overstepped, carried away by her enthusiasm, and Abby saw his face spasm with regret. Very out of character for him not to check first with Abby, and not to consider Maddie's parents. "I'm getting ahead of myself, aren't I? We'll have to see how things are."

"Sure, Uncle John." Maddie tried to hide her disappointment.

Pepper began teaching Maddie to drive. Late afternoons, before Abby got home, Maddie cautiously navigated the winding roads around their house with Pepper instructing from the passenger seat. When Abby protested to him that Maddie was too young, not quite fifteen and legally unable to have a learner's permit, Pepper concurred but continued the lessons. He claimed it was a safety issue, in case something happened and Maddie needed to drive him somewhere to get help.

"Because everyone's phone might suddenly break at once?" Abby asked.

"Exactly," he agreed.

Abby let it go. A mishap seemed unlikely with Pepper right there, and they stayed on quiet streets. Or she was pretty sure that they did. The driving lessons did keep Maddie busy, though, gave her focus and responsibility, and promoted their connection.

Abby pulled herself back to the present. Marietta Appleby's visit that morning had been the first in a series of unsettling encounters, people full of misgivings, and Abby felt relieved when the last patient left. She heard Priscilla lock up the front lobby, heard Marcus talking with her. Then Priscilla pushed the connecting door open and stuck her head through.

"That sign is gone again," Priscilla announced, crinkling up her tiny nose. Her eyelashes sparkled with pink glitter, her lips a matching bubblegum tint. "You know, that supplement warning sign."

"What on earth?" Abby was baffled, and it added one more wrinkle to the odd day. She would make up another sign tomorrow—today she just wanted to leave.

The walk home soothed her, the springtime woods warm and musky, a clean blue sky with feathered tails of cirrus, until she came around the turn and saw a park enforcement vehicle at their house. Her first thought was a car wreck, Maddie driving. Nervous, pulse pounding, Abby rushed inside.

Thank goodness—Pepper and Maddie sat safely together on the couch, Officer Derek Shipley perched across from them in a chair. No one looked happy, though, and she knew from Pepper's dark gaze that something serious was wrong. Maddie looked blank, sitting stiffly cross-legged, immobile.

Shipley stood and shook Abby's hand, grimacing. "Sorry about all this."

"What is going on?" Abby asked, since no one spoke.

Pepper nodded at a sheet of paper on the coffee table. He got up and put his arm around her. "It's not very good. Brace yourself."

"And don't touch it," Shipley warned. "We'll try to get fingerprints."

Abby tipped her head to read the dark-penciled words on thick white paper. The letters written crookedly, a strange mix of capitals and lowercase.

Back oFF, PePPer. If You caRe aBouT your preTTy liTTle DocTor.

Abby's stomach dropped. Her breath felt funny, shallow.

"What does it mean?" Her voice low and shocked.

"We were hoping you might know," Shipley said, "or have some ideas."

Abby shook her head, her thoughts flying, going nowhere. She stared at the note, but had no idea. Back off from what? Who could be threatening Pepper? Threatening her. Luther Lubbock remained in prison indefinitely, the deranged man Pepper testified against in a domestic violence case, the assault that left Lubbock's wife permanently brain-damaged. Abby noticed Maddie, silently terrified, sitting alone, and sat down beside her and took her hand.

"Maybe you should go to your room while we talk," Abby suggested.

"No way," Maddie exclaimed, her eyes round, white at the edges like a startled horse. She squeezed Abby's hand. "I—I was the one who found it. Stuck in the screen. I was opening the door for Uncle John after we'd been out practicing my driving—"

Maddie halted and flung Shipley a guilty look, which he either ignored or didn't notice.

Everyone felt perplexed. Pepper had not seen patients for weeks, not since his injury.

Shipley asked many questions: which patients had been unhappy lately, who complained about their bills. Mostly Abby described opiate-seekers, the ones with implausible pain syndromes who demanded large prescriptions of oxycodone, hydrocodone, or morphine. There were a few of those patients every week, sometimes every day; they never produced their medical records as she requested and they rarely returned. Then she recalled an unpleasant man both she and Pepper saw during the last four months, a hostile young patient with a minor back injury who insisted they give him a medical incapacity rating. The document would excuse him from work and award him disability payments for six months. Angry when Abby declined, when she stipulated that he first must see an orthopedic specialist, he stormed from the clinic in a rage, slamming doors and shouting at her incompetence.

But those cases hardly fit the context of the note. Abby racked her brain, unable to come up with anyone else. She mentioned the sign about the supplements, how it was missing from the lobby again, but only because it just happened and was fresh in her memory.

Pepper straightened and stared at her.

"What?" she asked.

He looked over at Maddie. "Nothing. Just thinking."

When Shipley rose to leave, Pepper gathered his crutches, darkly intense, and insisted on walking out with him. Something was up, and a queasy wave rolled up Abby's throat. She still wrestled with fright, that menacing message on the paper, but tried to push it aside for Maddie's sake. They moved into the kitchen to fix supper, but Abby intermittently looked through the front window at the men talking outside. Pepper somber and Shipley frowning deeply, almost angry. Finally Shipley departed and Pepper returned.

They played it down, kept the mood light. Nothing would happen, they assured Maddie. She shouldn't be afraid. Probably someone played a prank, or maybe a frustrated patient lashed out. It would blow over. It wasn't the first time a patient acted out, and it would likely not be the last. Rarely did anything come of such intimidations; it was usually all bluster.

Once Maddie fell asleep, they took the sleeping bag to the back deck and curled together on the lounge. The nights were warmer now, the frost gone, the stars dancing brightly across the inky heavens with a smiling slice of moon. Ridiculously cheerful, Abby thought dejectedly, as if the sky itself had no clue.

"What were you talking to Shipley about?" Abby finally asked. He had been quiet and moody during dinner and Abby chatted emptily about nothing, overly upbeat, to ease Maddie's fears. It actually seemed to help and Maddie visibly relaxed.

Pepper wrapped his arms around Abby. He felt rigid and spoke slowly.

"I'm worried that this is connected to the drugs," he finally said. "That it has something to do with the hiker heart attacks, the steroids, all those pills. Someone keeps taking down that flyer, and someone just threatened us. And so I finally told Shipley about my theory, that I didn't just fall off the trail."

Abby's heart plummeted. "What are you saying?"

"It might be all connected. Whoever it is…I think they're warning us—me—to quit investigating. To quit looking for answers. Which is pretty ridiculous since I've hardly done a thing. I mean, I think about it all the time, what's going on, but I have no idea who's responsible." He paused. "Shipley might, though. He said they have some leads, some other hikers who talked to him. New information. He thinks they're getting closer. And he was pretty upset that I hadn't told him sooner about my fall."

Abby shivered, an icy trickle down her spine. Up until now, she had suspended judgment on his impression about being pushed.

"What can we do?" she whispered.

He rubbed her shoulders, massaged her tense muscles. "This is all too disturbing. I'm not sure I can handle this, this threat to you. Maybe you should take a break. Take a vacation, until it's resolved. Go spend some time with Lucy in Phoenix, take Maddie with you."

Abby turned to look at him, met his chilly eyes, shook her head. "Maybe Maddie should go home to her parents. But I'm not leaving you here alone. Not with all this crap going on."

Pepper stared into the sky. "Even if she was my own child, I wouldn't want her here. We don't know how seriously to take this. What if something happened to her?"

"We would never forgive ourselves," Abby said quietly, unable to imagine how dreadful that would be.

"She won't take it well."

"I know." Abby felt miserable, but saw no way around it.

Pepper held Abby tightly and they lay awake half the night, jumping at small sounds, twitching at nothing, scrutinizing the dark. As if the menace might materialize any second, in unknown form, an alien presence. Something from behind a tree, something rising from the ground, something falling from the sky. Still, they refused to give in, and they spurned any temptation to abandon their favorite spot on the deck.

The quarter moon shone through the trees and seemed not to drift for a long time, as if its sharp prongs were trapped in the branches and could not move.

20

The next evening, with Abby beside him, Pepper reluctantly told Maddie she should probably return home to Illinois. He explained how he and Abby discussed it at length, and thought it was best for her safety. At least until they understood the threat better. Maybe she could return after this settled down.

Maddie went pale. Her lips compressed in a white line and her eyes turned to stone, hard blue agates.

"You can't be serious," she said.

"We just don't—" Pepper began.

"No. I cannot go home. Don't you understand anything I've been saying?" Her voice caught and she closed her eyes. "I thought you liked me. I've done everything you've said. I'm getting straight As. I help around the house, and I've been getting in shape for our hike to the river. I love being here. It's the first time I've been relaxed in months." Her eyes flew open, beseeching. "Please please *please* don't send me away."

"Of course, we like you," Abby said, her heart hurting. But she had just heard of a case in Phoenix where a disgruntled patient fatally shot his psychiatrist, and it frightened her for Maddie. "You must know how much we like you. We know how hard you've tried. But this person knows where we live. We're worried that—"

"You don't get it, do you?" Maddie spewed the words, furious. Tears stained her cheeks. "Anything—*anything*—is better than being back there. If I was killed by a lunatic, right here, right now, it would be better than being there."

She stood abruptly and rushed to her bedroom. Abby expected the door to slam, but instead Maddie eased the door shut, barely a sound. As if disappearing without a trace.

Pepper looked woeful as he crutched down the hall, where he spoke softly through the door, then went in. Abby heard their voices rise and fall, heard Maddie blow her nose. She couldn't make out the words, but they talked a long time. Abby tried to be empty. She thought about distant merging galaxies and the unplumbed depths of black holes and the mysteries of gravitational waves rippling through the stars for billions of miles, but nothing helped. Usually she found solace by fleeing into infinities, but tonight it felt contrived. *I thought you liked me* echoed across the universe.

Pepper returned and sat down heavily. Abby had rarely seen him so forlorn.

"Should I talk with her, too?" she asked.

He shrugged. "I don't know. She's incredibly upset, as if you didn't know. I hope you don't mind, but I changed the plans a little bit." Abby raised her eyebrows so he went on quickly. "I told her I would talk to her parents tomorrow. That if they're okay with all this, with an uncertain risk…if they say she can stay, then she can."

Abby felt both relieved and concerned. She wondered if it was wise, even if the parents agreed. They were selfish people, and they had not seen that sinister gut-wrenching note. Abby had no idea how to walk this tightrope. She wanted to clarify her fears better to Maddie, knowing she would hardly sleep if she didn't say something. But when she tapped on her door, the response was curt.

"Please don't bother me. I want to go to sleep."

"Sure," Abby said. "I understand."

The next morning was no better. Maddie dressed for school early and hurried through the kitchen while Abby brewed coffee. A dark dawn, heavy clouds smothering the sky, rain spattering the window off and on.

"Don't you want some breakfast?" Abby asked hopefully, trying to engage her.

Maddie turned her back. She reached into a cabinet and grabbed a protein bar.

"No thanks. This is enough." Her voice monotone, she did not turn around and headed for the door. A tight ponytail braid, wide at the top and tapering to a sharp point, hung like a dagger between her shoulder blades.

"Maddie, stop. Can we please talk about this for a minute?" Abby searched for the right words, feeling clumsy. She could usually deal with difficult patients; though she disliked it, she mostly knew what to say, how to act calm. But dealing with an agonized teen in her own kitchen swamped her.

Maddie paused, then slowly turned around, looking at the floor. Waiting.

Abby forged ahead. "Your uncle told me what you two decided. That you can stay if your parents say so. Do you feel okay about that?"

"Sure. Whatever." Still staring down.

"Maddie, please look at me." Abby resisted her impulse to reach out, to physically connect. Clearly unwelcome.

Folding her arms, Maddie flicked her eyes up, cold spears through her bangs, and Abby read the emotion loud and clear.

Betrayal.

Abby's heart sank. Low thunder crept through the clouds, and Abby said, "Can I drive you to school since it's trying to rain?"

"No thanks," Maddie mumbled. "I'm just waiting to hear what my parents say."

She turned and ducked out the door.

The clinic was a mess, filled with reckless people. People who fell off the back of pickup trucks, people with their guts racked by food poisoning when they ate unrefrigerated leftovers. People who crashed on their bicycles with helmets strapped uselessly to the handlebars. Person after person with gruesome foot blisters or bloody toes from hiking the rocky trails in flimsy loose shoes and sandals. At least it wasn't hot enough for heat injury, not yet. But it wouldn't be long.

Then she saw an injured blond woman, struck by her boyfriend at the El Tovar hotel bar. Her puffy nose, slowly leaking blood, and her blackened eyes made Abby suspect a nasal fracture, soon confirmed by x-ray. The drunken boyfriend fled, taking the car and leaving her stranded until kind strangers brought her to the clinic. Abby hoped she would press charges and left her talking with officers, and they launched a search for him as a likely DUI.

Abby sat at the counter, writing her note, when a sudden memory flashed in her brain. Rex Wrigley, last year at Yellowstone.

Maybe Wrigley wrote that threatening note. Could that be possible?

A persistent hotel manager, Wrigley pursued Abby all summer, coolly unmoved by her refusals. Inebriated, lustful, he found her alone at her farewell party and forced himself on her. Abby vividly remembered his fingers grabbing her hair, his greasy, sloppy mouth and tongue against her face. Her swollen lip and bruised breast. She shuddered to think what might have happened if she had not escaped him.

Once home from Yellowstone, Abby filed a complaint with his company, corroborated by others who were present at the party that night. After her complaint, because of previous similar grievances, Wrigley was promptly fired from his job.

How had she not thought of him? If anyone might bear a grudge, it could be him. Who knew—maybe Wrigley was having trouble getting a job, maybe his reputation followed him and he now blamed Pepper. Maybe he thought Pepper was somehow hounding him. It made more sense than anything else.

At lunch she called Pepper, listening to his phone buzz, when he unexpectedly appeared at the office door.

"Hey. That's me," Abby said as he pulled his ringing phone from his pocket.

Pepper was not convinced about Wrigley, although he promised to talk with Shipley that afternoon. But he had information from his sister, who finally returned his call.

"They don't want her. They're sure we're exaggerating about the danger. I suspect they think we're regretting this, and we're trying to dump her back on them." His face twisted.

"Why am I not surprised?" Abby felt worse than ever for Maddie. First sent away from home like some sort of nuisance, then banned from her new place, then rejected yet again by her parents who didn't care if she might be in peril.

Pepper explained how it was even more convoluted. Apparently, Maddie's parents were "experimenting" with other "arrangements" and it "might look wrong" to Maddie right now.

Abby flared. "So you mean it's not convenient? While they screw around?"

"Yeah." Pepper dropped into a chair and clumsily propped up his cast. Abby saw the familiar line of pain between his eyes and knew he'd been up too much. "Needless to say, I told Maddie none of that. I just sent her a text like she asked me to do, once I'd talked to them, telling her she could stay."

"What did she say?"

"Nothing. No response yet." He rubbed his face. "I don't think I've handled this very well."

"She wouldn't talk to me this morning. Would hardly look at me." Abby put her palm along his jaw, lightly rubbed his beard. "This parenting stuff sucks."

Pepper nodded. "I'll take her driving this afternoon. Maybe we can talk it out."

While Abby returned to work, he stayed there in the office, fiddling on the computer, checking in with staff, reading a few articles. He saw one of his patients. Between her cases, Abby caught him standing at the back door, braced on his crutches and staring darkly into the parking lot. She pulled him into the little office and shut the door.

"John. You look like your leg is hurting. What are you doing here?"

"Nothing. Just checking a few things." His expression now innocent.

"No, you're fussing. It's about that note, isn't it? You're hanging around, trying to protect me, aren't you?"

A long pause. "So what if I am?"

"Please relax. Nothing is happening—I'm perfectly safe here. Please go check on Maddie and see how she's feeling." Abby glanced at the clock. "She should be getting home soon."

Pepper gave her a long unhappy look and left.

Minutes later, Basil Taylor staggered in, supported by his frantic wife, and the already shaky day fell completely apart.

21

Abby gleaned the story from his wife, Shirley.

A year ago, Basil Taylor developed a large gastric ulcer that nearly killed him. While not his first ulcer, it was almost his last, since he loved his scotch and he always clipped his favorite cigarette between his lips, puffing away throughout the day. His stomach bled so badly back then that he needed surgery to repair the gaping ulcer, and his physicians warned him that tobacco and alcohol could trigger future ulcers. Basil tried to follow their advice, but at fifty-seven years old, he felt he should live life the way he wanted. A friendly, obese man who adored his wife and loved to tell jokes, he looked forward to retirement, and this trip to the canyon with another couple was their first celebratory journey.

Basil started vomiting blood that afternoon in their hotel room. The night before, he and Shirley and their friends spent a fine evening on the rim patio. They admired the twilight as the lowering sun burnt the clouds to red coals and the ashen sky darkened, as stars perforated the canopy over the mesas. Even though his stomach had been bothering him for several weeks, he chewed antacids and savored several glasses of scotch, enjoying his smokes, a veil of cigarette haze encircling them in the still night. They laughed and played cards and retired late.

Not feeling well the next day, he sent Shirley off on a walk with the others after lunch, which he barely ate. He insisted she enjoy the canyon even if he couldn't. Returning a few hours later, she found him sitting on the edge of the tub, blood smearing his chin and dribbling onto his shirt, while a thin stream of red ran down the drain.

Shirley did not realize the canyon had paramedics. She dragged him unsteadily to the car and rushed to the clinic, parking crookedly at the front door and running in for help. Marcus took one look at Shirley's frantic face, her clothes and hands stained red, and jumped into action. By the time they got Basil in a wheelchair and back to the treatment room, Abby and Dolores and Bessie racing to prepare IVs and oxygen and calling for emergency transport, Basil had vomited two more times, splattering blood across his belly and trailing it on the floor.

Abby managed to get two large IVs running, but Basil's pulse was one hundred seventy and his blood pressure could barely be found.

"Can we get a blood count right away?" Abby asked Bessie, scrambling to put the oxygen on and opening up the fluids, while Dolores injected potent ulcer medication intravenously. Abby turned to Shirley who stood forlornly, her face pasty with horror. "How much blood did he lose before you got here?"

"I don't know," she moaned. "I was gone an hour or two. He was sitting by the bathtub and blood was running down the drain."

"Basil?" Abby said, shaking his arm lightly to get his attention. "How are you feeling right now? Has your stomach been hurting?"

He looked at her vacantly, his skin gray as clay, and started to nod his head. Then his belly convulsed and Dolores quickly pressed a basin to his mouth. He retched heavily, spewing out a cup of bright red blood. Watching at the foot of the bed, Shirley groaned and sagged, and Abby barely caught her before she fainted.

"Marcus!" Abby cried out, easing the woman to the floor. "Come help! Take her to another room and lie her down. Bessie can come get her vitals in a second."

Abby had no time to think. Basil Taylor was rapidly bleeding to death right in front of her. He needed immediate blood transfusions, an immediate scope or surgery to find the hemorrhaging ulcer and stop the gush. But she was at the Grand Canyon in an outpatient clinic, nearly a hundred miles from help: she had no blood for transfusions, no gastroenterologist with a scope, no surgeon with a scalpel. Abby felt deeply alone and helpless.

"His hemoglobin is five," Bessie called as she hurried to check on Shirley.

"Five?" Abby echoed in disbelief. Five was a blood count barely compatible with life, and often the true hemoglobin count was actually lower than what the lab showed, at least in this kind of rapid bleeding.

Abby and Dolores shared a gasp of alarm and their eyes met with dread. Basil gagged yet again and another cup of blood bubbled up from his mouth and down his chest. His eyes were closed, his pulse over two hundred, the monitor cheeping wildly, his oxygen dropping. No blood pressure registered. Abby hung more fluids and ordered pressor medications to boost his blood pressure, but she knew with dismay there was simply not enough blood to push through his body. A person could not live with veins full of only saline.

Basil's body knew this. His pulse accelerated hysterically, paused, stuttered, and quit. All his tissues collapsed and his breathing stopped.

The desperate resuscitation did not succeed. Human organs must have oxygen to function, and blood carries oxygen to them. The lungs must breathe to pull in oxygen, the heart must beat to drive the lungs. The brain, the system's mastermind, cannot run without blood and oxygen. Nothing could work. No matter how long they pounded on his chest, no matter how long they pumped oxygen into his lungs, without enough blood there was simply no fuel, no delivery, no function. No life.

Abby thanked the stars that Shirley Taylor had friends with her—who could imagine dealing with this alone? Abby broke the news to the heartbroken woman and commiserated with her, now awake but dazed and dull, and Marcus called the friends to come get her. Then she helped Dolores clean up Basil's body while Bessie sat with Shirley. They peeled off his blood-drenched clothes, removed a pack of bloodied cigarettes from his shirt pocket and another from his pants pocket, then wiped down his blood-smeared skin. They took care because Shirley would want to see him and he needed to look presentable. Bloody footprints tracked in and out of the room, bloody handprints marked the walls and the bed and all the equipment. The paper tape from the EKG machine was sticky with red fingerprints. The place looked like a massacre and the clinic reeked of blood and vomit, even though Marcus discreetly spritzed the air with deodorizer. Priscilla came back once with a message, but she took one look at the gruesome scene and fled to her desk, where Marcus tried to distract her. They didn't need her fainting as well.

Before going home, Abby changed into clean scrubs, washed her arms and hands with alcohol and antiseptic soap several times. Fortunately, neither she nor Dolores got splattered in their faces, for there had been no time to don face shields. She entered the final diagnoses in the computer. Severe gastric hemorrhage. Exsanguination. Formal, scientific words for the revolting wreckage of a human body turned inside out. The extravasation of a life. Multisyllabic descriptions. What was that word... *sesquipedalian.* The word *sesquipedalian* was itself sesquipedalian. Did that make it an onomatopoeia? No, that was a word that sounded like a sound. A different thing.

Why was she even thinking such trivia? What was wrong with her?

Finally everything was done, and Abby sat for a moment to call Pepper.

"Maddie never came home," he answered, distraught. "I'm driving around now, trying to find her."

Abby felt stunned. It was too much.

She briefly told Pepper about the death, told him to keep looking for Maddie. She would go home right away and hopefully Maddie would be there by then. But she felt numb, unable to react.

The house was empty. Exhausted, drained, Abby sat weakly and called Maddie's phone, got no answer—it went immediately to voicemail. Of course, Pepper had undoubtedly been calling her, too. Well, what now? When did they declare her missing? Maybe Maddie hiked down the trail, maybe she decided to go all the way to the river, even though she knew better than that, because what would she do once she got down there? If she made it, if she had enough water. Maybe she stayed at school to talk with a teacher. Maybe she ran away. Overwhelmed, Abby rubbed her face with her hands and felt like crying. Over and over, she saw Basil's shocked gray face, Shirley's look of horror, smelled the metallic taint of blood. She still smelled it, even now. She wondered if she would ever not smell it again.

The door opened.

Maddie came in, wet with rain, sad and contrite. Abby hurried over to her.

"Are you all right? We've been so worried." Abby put her arm around her, then froze. Maddie's clothes and hair stank of tobacco.

"I'm sorry. I'm okay. I—"

"Have you been smoking?" Abby cried, pulling back.

"A little…" Maddie suddenly defensive.

"Are you serious?" Abby nearly shouted, couldn't seem to stop herself.

"Yes. I smoked a few cigarettes. Big deal." Maddie spoke slowly. Coldly. "So what? You told me to make new friends, so I did."

"Are you kidding? Your uncle is worried sick—he's out driving around, looking for you. With his bad leg." Abby seethed and paced. "And I will never—*never*—allow smoking in this house. Or allow anyone who smokes. I don't care who they are."

"Aunt Abby. I just—"

"Never! A man just died, right before my eyes, because he smoked. He just *died*, just like that," she snapped her fingers, "and I couldn't help him." Abby sat down, stood up, glared at her. "I couldn't do a goddamn thing."

Pepper appeared in the doorway, his face still, taking them in.

"Uncle John," Maddie began softly, "I know you've been—"

"No," interrupted Abby, throwing him a tortured look. "While you've been out driving around, driving with your broken leg and in pain and frightened for Maddie, she's been hiding out with her so-called friends and smoking cigarettes."

Maddie stared at Abby, flicked a glance at Pepper, his immobile expression. Her face puckered and her eyes flooded with tears and she threw herself on the sofa, sobbing, gasping out her words. "I'm sorry. I'm sorry. I was so scared you would send me away. Even though my parents said I could stay, I didn't believe it. But I guess you can't get rid of me, can you? Because my parents don't want me, either.

So you're just stuck with me, aren't you? I hate myself so much. And now everyone else hates me, too."

Abby closed her eyes, jolted from her outrage, filled with shame. How could she have said such things? She grimaced at Pepper and moved over to Maddie.

"Maddie," she said, easing down next to her. "No one hates you. The reason I'm so upset is because I do care about you, a whole lot. It didn't come out right, though. Not at all. I'm very sorry."

She cautiously placed her hand on Maddie's heaving back, expecting the girl to jerk away. But Maddie didn't. Instead, she threw her arms around Abby and sobbed even harder. Abby held her tightly and felt a sheen of tears on her own cheeks.

Pepper limped over.

"Can I help?" Consternation creased his face. He put his hand on the back of Abby's neck, that light grip that went to her heart. She knew from the pressure of his fingers, the slight stroke of his grasp, that he worried about what she'd endured that afternoon, acutely aware of that stress on top of this stress.

Maddie and Abby shook their heads, straightening and wiping their eyes. Pepper sat down, winced at his leg and pulled it up. He studied them and looked each one in the eye.

"Do we need to talk this out some more? Right now?" he asked.

"Probably not," said Maddie, sniffing. "Unless you want to. It's up to you."

"Not right now," Abby agreed, "unless Maddie wants to."

"All right." Pepper nodded, and they all sat silently for a while, each sorting their thoughts. Then he tilted his head at Abby and wrinkled his long nose.

"Is that blood on your shoes?"

Abby turned her foot, saw the reddish-brown stain on her sole. "Probably."

She slid off her shoes and picked them up, went outside on the porch and hosed them off, tried not to think how she was washing off part of her dead patient. She shut that notion away and came back inside, barefoot. She would pour bleach on her shoes later. Or maybe she would just throw them away.

"Please forgive me, Uncle John," Maddie was pleading.

"We're all sorry," he said. "It's a big fat mess. But we're glad you're here, with us. And I wouldn't say that if I didn't mean it. You have to believe me."

Maddie drew in a quivering breath and closed her eyes.

"I'm trying," she said.

22

Their days settled into a tenuous routine, but nothing felt ordinary or safe.

Pepper began seeing more patients. Abby knew he felt too confined at home, and anyway his pain suddenly lessened. In just a few more weeks his cast would come off. The clinic grew busier as summer approached, and Abby truthfully needed his help.

She also understood that he wanted to stay closer, watch for danger. As if he wasn't in danger himself—she thought about it constantly, but rarely gave it voice. If his perception about being pushed off the trail was accurate, which she no longer much doubted, his risk eclipsed hers. So they never relaxed, never let down their guards, always mindful of where the other walked or drove or sat, always glancing around at who stood nearby or who looked at them or frowned or stared, startling at unusual sounds, alert if someone moved suddenly or reached for something or even if they disappeared. They orbited one another like double planets, linked together by this strange gravity. Exhausted, anxious, they fumbled along and pretended to live normal lives.

Maddie dutifully reported exactly where she planned to walk after school, and returned home promptly at the arranged time. Most late afternoons now Maddie drove to the clinic, with Pepper riding alongside, to pick up Abby when she was done and bring her home. Abby slid into the backseat, missing her peaceful, transitional walks at the end of the day but tolerating Pepper's vigilance. Surely these apprehensions would fade with a little more time, if nothing more happened.

Then Pepper began talking about leaving the canyon, finding a new job. He lined up his reasons. Having worked there over five years, maybe it was time for change. He wanted to teach more, perhaps a faculty job at the medical school or at the family medicine residency in Phoenix. FirstMed remained difficult to work with, rarely valued his input and suggestions, gave them little administrative support… they truly needed an office manager, if only to free the physicians from so much paperwork. Despite Pepper's insistence, FirstMed showed no inclination to hire a manager. He grew weary of tourists, of heatstroke, and he felt like most of the time he accomplished only patchwork.

Abby was skeptical. "I'm not sure I believe all this. Don't go making such big decisions—at least, not very quickly—just to protect me. To get me away from here."

He turned his full chilly gaze on her, then a smile quirked his lips and his eyes warmed. "Why is there always someone like this, some kind of nefarious character, ever since I've met you?"

Abby smiled back. "Maybe it's you."

"I might have believed that, except for Yellowstone. You did that all on your own."

Abby could hardly deny it. What the heck.

Officer Shipley called, surprising Abby. He contacted her because Heidi's mother returned for a visit and wanted to see Abby.

"I've encouraged her to talk with you." He seemed opaque, offering little else.

"Of course," Abby agreed, and set up a meeting at lunch the next day. Abby had no idea what to expect and felt slightly anxious. Maybe the woman would accuse her of neglecting her daughter's distress. Maybe she expected Abby to explain Heidi's depression, even though Abby had not discerned it. Maybe she just wanted to vent. Maybe she just wanted to cry.

Beverly Forrest arrived early. A short round woman with short sandy hair and pink cheeks, she seemed an older, sadder version of Heidi, but she was not there to vent or cry or comprehend depression. She came in on a mission and, once they exchanged sorrows, she pulled out an orange drawing pad, several pages marked.

"I've been going through her things. Her drawings. Her writings." Beverly never smiled but she stroked the pages carefully, and Abby knew she communed with Heidi through that touch. Her worn face, her crumpled travel-weary clothes, exposed her fatigue. Not just tired from her journey right now but her exhaustion for days, weeks, months, hoping and waiting for news, for anything. Every phone call, every tap at the door, every scrap of mail, every newspaper. Abby felt hollow, knowing that she thought about Heidi less often since Maddie arrived.

"She wrote a lot," Beverly said. "Almost obsessively. About how many calories she ate every day, how much she exercised, who she met and who she talked with. What she wore, all about the weather. And she wrote about people who came into Kolb Studio to look at the art and books. Like little character descriptions, sometimes funny, sometimes sad." Beverly almost smiled. "She wrote a lot about you. You meant a great deal to her—you encouraged her. She says how kind you were."

Abby made a sympathetic murmur, but the lump in her throat kept her from speaking.

"Anyway." Beverly motioned with her hand, moving on, and turned through the papers. The thick unlined pages were filled with drawings and paragraphs of loopy writing. Some large sketches and some tiny, some made in pencil, some in watercolor, some both. "I thought we had inspected her most recent diaries and journals, but they weren't all in order, and I've found more, right up to when… Anyway, Officer Shipley said I could show you a few things, since he knew I wanted to meet you. He already made copies and let me keep the originals."

Abby now had a better relationship with Shipley, but she doubted he suggested this out of kindness. Probably he hoped Abby might react to something, remember something.

"Does it seem to you that she was depressed back then?" Abby asked gently. She had to know if she missed the clues.

Beverly's eyes jumped up, angry. "Absolutely not. That's all these men want to talk about. They want to say it's another suicidal young woman, case closed. But I've seen my girl depressed, and I've seen

SANDRA CAVALLO MILLER

her suicidal, and she was neither of those. She was trying really hard to improve, to take charge of herself, to be more assertive. To take her life by the thorns, or whatever that expression is."

"That's what I thought." Abby nodded, hoping her relief was not too visible.

"Here's what Shipley wondered about." Beverly ran her finger down a column of writing. "Apparently there was this ranger who liked to talk to her—he comes up three or four times. He'd stop by and chat about her running, ask her lots of questions. She liked him at first. Then he tried to sell her these expensive supplements, some vitamins and minerals, I guess. She told him she wasn't interested."

Abby stared at her, remembering. "She asked me about that once. I told her she didn't need pills, that she should just eat a healthy diet."

Beverly nodded, pointing at an entry. "Heidi wrote about that. But I guess he got really pushy, told her she'd never lose weight on her own."

"Pretty rude, and not true," Abby said, indignant and disturbed. It had to be the same man, the one they sought.

"She said…" Beverly paused, swallowed hard. "She told him the doctors didn't believe in his supplements. That she talked to them about his pills, that she would ask them again. He got mad and told her doctors don't know anything about nutrition…He got so aggressive that he frightened her."

Abby's hand moved to her mouth. "Did she describe him?"

Beverly turned a page. "A big ranger with dark red curly hair."

"We've heard of him before. I imagine Shipley told you, how there's no one who fits that description." Abby kept remembering Heidi's words that last day: *There's something I want to ask you.*

"Check this out." Beverly turned the pad to show Abby a rough sketch, a burly ranger in uniform, curly hair sprouting around his ears under his ranger hat. Half in shadow and without much detail, the face seemed nondescript. Vague features, the mouth a short hard line, the eyes small and generic. Heidi added dark green watercolor to his shirt and hat, a touch of rusty red to his hair. It looked unfinished.

The figure appeared familiar, but Abby could not say why. There

160

were so many similar rangers, so many strong physiques; these were fit, athletic people. Maybe he looked a bit like Jake, the ranger Abby dated when she first came to the canyon several years ago. But what did it mean? It might have nothing to do with Heidi's disappearance, or it could be the very key. While relieved that depression and suicide seemed unlikely, Abby found this all very unsettling.

Abby wished she had more for Beverly. She described how much she enjoyed Heidi's company, how Heidi always brightened her day. Beverly quieted, closing the pad and sliding it carefully into her bag. They parted with a hug and promised to stay in touch.

Abby found it difficult to change gears back to her patients, wishing Beverly had come at the end of the day.

Harry Stonewall appeared, unannounced, for his follow-up lead levels and kidney tests. He was at least a week overdue and Abby ran behind, feeling sluggish after Beverly's visit. They interacted only briefly, but it pleased Abby to see more of a spark in his eyes.

"I think I'm a smidge better," he admitted cautiously.

"Fingers crossed," Abby said. His clothes appeared recently washed. She pulled out her stethoscope to listen to his heart murmur, but he leaned back with a gnarled hand over his chest.

"There ain't no point in you telling me again to see a dang specialist," he complained. "I'm too busy. Got things to do, now that I'm feeling stronger."

"Okay." She saw no future in arguing. "But I still recommend it. And don't wait so long to come back for your lab report, all right? Because if it's not better, we need to figure out why." Abby worried less than before, especially since Marcus knew how to find him now.

"It's always something," he grumbled. His oaken eyes climbed up to her. "And can you have that Bessie woman come draw my blood? She kinda reminds me of my daughter."

"I didn't know you had a daughter," Abby remarked. Since Bessie was only a few years younger than Harry, the statement surprised her. Maybe Bessie's bright copper-dyed hair made her seem young to him. When Abby asked about his family history previously, he refused to divulge anything, saying how he and his family had parted ways, for good reasons.

"There's a lot you don't know about me," he replied, grumpy, folding his arms and ending the conversation.

The day seemed very long, partly because the lunch with Beverly was never quite out of Abby's head. She listened as Dolores and Bessie readied the rooms for tomorrow, making the routine, peaceful sounds of restocking drawers and countertops, their quiet back-and-forth talk about the day and whatever most amused or annoyed them.

Then Abby heard a new voice, an unknown woman, coming from the lobby. Marcus sounded lively, not quite like himself. Curious, Abby found a file that belonged up front and pushed through the door with it.

"Dr. Wilmore," Marcus said, a little shy, sweeping his arm toward the newcomer. "You have to meet my new golf partner. This is Mitzi Nightingale."

Mitzi studied Abby carefully, gingerly extended her hand. A fountain of chocolate brown hair sprang from a ponytail high atop her head and fell past her smooth olive skin. Petite and strong, with a wide mouth and wary dark eyes, she made Abby think of a cautious animal, on the verge of bolting.

"What brings you here?" Abby asked, wondering why this shy woman from Flagstaff would appear at the canyon late in the day. At the edge of her vision she saw Priscilla sitting rigidly, staring.

Marcus and Mitzi exchanged a look.

"Go ahead, you can tell her," Mitzi said. She looked at the floor, then slowly back up at Abby, a hint of amusement now. But only a hint. "He thinks I'll do better if I talk about it."

Marcus smoothed his shirt over his stomach, an old habit. "We met on the golf course, you know? I came up behind her where she was on the tee box, and I couldn't help but notice her because she was being sort of…loud."

Mitzi nodded, embarrassed, glanced at Marcus. "It was a par three and I missed the green by twenty feet, so I was sort of yelling at my six iron."

"There might have been a little bit of profanity," Marcus went on.

"Or maybe a lot," Mitzi admitted.

"So, long story short," Marcus continued, "I watched her play that hole, and when I caught up to her again, I suggested that she would play better if she didn't get so emotional. She has an incredible swing and you wouldn't believe the distances she can drive." Marcus nodded at her. "She could be great."

"He might be right about the anger thing." Now she truly smiled and opened up a little. "So we had this bet last week that if I could play eighteen holes with him, without losing my temper, without yelling at my clubs, or the course, or the sand traps, or myself, or anything else I've been known to cuss at, he would treat me to dinner at El Tovar." Her voice dropped, insecure again. "I hear it's quite fancy."

"It is very nice, but this is the canyon, you know. Nothing is that fancy." Abby found herself fascinated that this timid woman had such a furious, volatile side. Marcus himself never cursed, never seemed to get mad or cross—under stress he turned ever more calm and ironic.

Marcus shut off his computer and stood up, opened the front door for her, pleased as punch. "We have to hurry so we're not late for our reservation."

Abby and Priscilla gaped after him, then at each other.

"That was interesting," remarked Abby, since someone needed to say something. "She seems nice."

"I don't think she's right for him," Priscilla snapped. She displayed a golden theme today, wearing a low-cut cream-colored blouse and shiny brown capris, with layered gold chains at her throat and wrist, and honey-colored shoes. Copper eyelids and fingernails, bronze lips. Those metallic lips locked together and she patted her pale hair into place, which was not out of place. "She seems too young. Too immature."

"They're just having dinner," Abby said mildly.

Priscilla shot her an acid glare and said nothing.

That evening at supper, Abby told Pepper and Maddie about Marcus's curious new friend. Maddie listened politely, but she couldn't wait to tell Abby who she met after school. How she walked past the barn and stopped to watch the mules in the corral because they looked so cute, so sleepy and dusty standing there.

"But then I heard all this clanging and hammering in the barn and there was this woman, nailing horseshoes on a big black mule. He was sort of jumpy, like he was nervous," Maddie explained, her face shining, even more animated than usual. "She saw me watching and she asked if I would come over and keep him calm. I said I knew nothing about horses or mules and she said it didn't matter, that his name was Othello and I should just stand there quietly in front of him and talk to him and pet his nose. Isn't that weird?"

Abby smiled. "Was it Vanna Boone?"

"Yes! She was so nice. I told her I didn't know how to talk to a mule and she said I could just tell him a story, so I told him all about my book that I'm writing. And you know what? He really listened. He had these huge furry ears and the biggest brown eyes and he looked right at me, just like a person would. And his nose was so soft, like a peach, even though it was all whiskery. And when I quit talking, he sort of nudged me, like he wanted me to keep going."

"So now you're a mule whisperer?" Pepper asked.

"No, Uncle John." Maddie rolled her eyes. "Vanna says it helped because Othello can't see her while she's working on his hind feet and that makes him nervous, so he likes having someone he can see and touch. She said he hurt his hind leg once and so he gets scared, and she showed me this ugly old scar on his hock." She peered at them. "A hock is where the hind leg bends in the middle. Did you know that?"

"Not exactly," Abby admitted.

"Anyway." Maddie sat back in her chair, satisfied. "Guess what? Vanna said I can come by anytime and help her. She even let me clean out one of his hooves. And she's so strong! You should see the muscles in her arms. She said they used to call people like her black-smiths, but now the correct name is farrier."

"Well. Don't bother her too much. How long were you there?" Pepper asked.

"I don't know, but I wasn't bothering her." Maddie frowned at him, then broke into a smile. "But I was there long enough that I had to run all the way to get back home in time. You know, so you wouldn't worry about the bad guys."

They laughed awkwardly. It's not normal, Abby thought glumly, to have to worry about bad guys, and she felt sorry for Maddie. She recalled Heidi's sketchpad and wondered what Pepper would think, since there hadn't been time yet to tell him. Abby contemplated keeping it to herself, then quickly discarded that impulse. After last summer, she promised to never again hide something that might upset him. They tended to overprotect one another.

"So," Maddie cheerfully chatted on, "I've decided to put a big black mule named Othello in my book. Maybe he'll even be able to talk."

"Like the donkey in *Shrek*?" Abby asked.

"No, Auntie Ab. That donkey was silly. He was clever, but he was there for comic relief. My Othello is going to be really smart and wise, and he's going to understand what's wrong with people and how to help them get better."

"Nice," said Abby. "When do I get to read this?"

Maybe in a few weeks, Maddie suggested. Depending on how much time she found to write. Which depended on whether they got to hike to the river, she reminded Abby for the hundredth time. School would end soon and no one mentioned Maddie's approaching return to Illinois, although they all felt the inevitability, like a low ceiling over their heads. Besides scattered emails, her mother sent an occasional text to see if things were okay, which Maddie answered with two-word phrases: *Everything's fine*, or *I'm good*. Once Maddie extended herself to three words and wrote *Take your time*. She always showed these to Pepper, who nodded and rarely said much. Abby knew he didn't trust himself to act neutral.

What a disjointed day. First Heidi's mother and that disturbing sketch. If it was even disturbing at all—Abby inhabited such an odd, uneasy framework right now that the most innocent incident could be warped into a hazard. Then there were better things, Marcus with his reticent friend and Maddie with Vanna and the mules.

She made a mental note to call the backcountry office again about campground reservations at Phantom Ranch. Surely one of these days someone would cancel their plans.

23

After considerable research, Officer Derek Shipley stopped by the clinic to see Pepper and Abby. He had established that Wrigley offered no threat to them because Wrigley now lived in Mexico and managed a low-budget singles resort in Cancun.

"Looks kind of seedy," Shipley added, after investigating the place online: *Diversion Para Todos*, which translated to *Fun for Everyone*.

"That figures," Pepper commented, watching Abby's reaction.

Abby kept her face impartial and expressed relief that he dwelt so far away, and she tried not to think about who might fall prey to him there.

Shipley also disclosed they might soon arrest the man who sold the performance-enhancing drugs. More hikers and tourists complained and Shipley got better descriptions, further leads. It sounded encouraging. He still urged Abby and Pepper to avoid solitude, to always be with someone else, just in case. Abby remained vigilant but found it impossible; she needed her running, so she put up with a lurking unease and put up with Pepper's frequent calls to check on her. She did the same to him, and they both did it to Maddie. Maddie understood and tolerated it, and checked on them as well. Everyone felt neurotic, nervous, and slightly unhinged.

Abby saw Faith Waterson, a thirty-five-year-old woman with abdominal bloating. Two visits ago, they explored whether she might have lactose intolerance, or constipation, or irritable bowel syndrome. She eliminated dairy products and added fiber, but her symptoms never really fit those diagnoses and none of the treatments helped.

"Maybe I'm just getting fat," commented Faith, discouraged, rubbing the puffy mound of her abdomen. Her curly auburn hair drooped and her hazel eyes looked weary. "Fat and lazy. I've got no energy for anything."

"I don't think so." Abby sensed something wrong. "Let me examine you again, this time inside and out."

Her belly was mildly tender and a little swollen. Not enough for alarm, but too much to disregard. Abby performed a pelvic exam, felt a normal cervix, but had trouble outlining the ovaries, especially the left one. Never very accurate, a pelvic exam tried to palpate a woman's fist-sized uterus and her olive-sized ovaries through layers of muscle and fat. Abby often felt nothing but fluffy tissues between her fingers. She withdrew her gloved hand and helped Faith sit up.

"There's nothing scary, but I can't really feel your ovaries. It's a little mushy on the left, which could mean nothing." People put so much stock in exams, despite how inadequate they often were. "We need a better look, which means getting an ultrasound."

"Like when I was pregnant? That was easy."

"Yes, it's similar. They'll look at the uterus and your ovaries and anything else that might be in there."

"Anything else? Like what?"

People always knew, instinctively if not precisely, what she meant. Abby ran through the list: a cyst, a fibroid, scar tissue, or just a loop of intestine. A bubble of gas. A tumor.

Dolores arranged the ultrasound in Flagstaff the following week. Her last patient of the morning had not yet registered, so Abby went up front to check.

Priscilla stood near Marcus, hands on her hips. She wore a pink sheath dress that clung to her curves, set off by black stilettos, black nail polish, and charcoal eye shadow. She looked both girlish and grim at the same time.

"Your clothes don't fit anymore," she complained, plucking at his sleeve. "That shirt is way too big on you now and it looks sloppy. And your pants are all puckered at the waist because your belt has to pull them in. It doesn't look professional."

Marcus chuckled, catching Abby's eye. "Maybe I should just gain back the weight I lost so I don't have to buy new clothes. I could eat more cake!"

Priscilla tapped her foot impatiently. "Don't be ridiculous. You look so much better. Don't you feel better?"

"Eh." He shrugged. "I always feel good."

Priscilla saw Abby. "Can I help you, Dr. Wilmore?"

Abby agreed. "You do look good, Marcus. Have you been dieting, or is it all the exercise from golfing?"

"A little of both," he replied. "I'm getting ready for a big couples' tournament next month. I have to be in good shape so I don't let my golf buddy down."

Priscilla narrowed her eyes and wrinkled her tiny nose. "It's a competition? For men and women?"

Marcus nodded. "I'm a little bit nervous—it's been a while since I've done anything like that."

Abby turned to Priscilla. "Did you know that Marcus used to be a golf champion?"

Priscilla stiffened and glared at him, as if he had just insulted her. "No. He never told me that."

"Well, I don't talk about it much," Marcus said quietly, turning back to his computer. "It was a very stressful time for me. And by the way, Dr. Wilmore, that last patient called a few minutes ago to cancel. So we're now officially on lunchbreak."

"Excellent. Thanks." Abby felt bad, realizing she should not have mentioned Marcus's golf history without his permission. He could still be touchy about it. She would take him aside later and apologize.

The afternoon seemed long. Pepper left around three to be with Maddie, leaving Abby to finish. Ready to leave, thinking about Maddie and Pepper and bad guys and illicit drugs and everything else stressing her out, Abby overheard Bessie talking with Priscilla in the workstation. It felt odd, for Priscilla rarely came back there unless Pepper was around. Abby's door stood open a crack, and she had just hung up the phone after discussing blood sugars with a patient. She wondered how long the conversation had been going.

"So who is your boyfriend, honey?" Bessie asked Priscilla.

A pause. Abby imagined Priscilla patting her hair, lifting her chest.

"I don't have anyone right now," Priscilla finally replied. "It's hard to meet men around here, you know."

"Really?" Bessie sounded surprised. "With all these rangers and construction guys and fire crews and lumbermen? It's practically raining men. What exactly are you looking for?"

"I guess I've got certain standards," Priscilla explained. "I don't date just anyone."

"Well, I should hope not. There's lots of bums out there."

"I like someone who's tall, and slender. And I like a man who's strong, who'll take care of me. He needs to have a good job, a good career. And of course he needs to be handsome. Kind of rugged, but the quiet type." Her voice slowed, a little dreamy. "Someone romantic, who talks with his eyes as much as his words."

It might be the longest speech Abby ever heard Priscilla make.

"Ha," Bessie laughed. "That sort of sounds like you just described Dr. Pepper." Abby choked, but quickly stifled herself as Bessie went on. "Or some kind of Prince Charming. You must know that will never happen, right? Where do you get these ideas, child?"

"It could happen." Priscilla being confident.

"Honey." Bessie's voice dropped and softened. "You know that he's crazy about Dr. Wilmore, don't you?"

"Of course," Priscilla bristled. "I can't imagine why you're even saying that to me. I'm not talking about Dr. Pepper."

Abby felt acutely awkward. They must realize she sat there. Should she move, make a sound, shut the door? She coughed and picked up a book and set it down loudly, started pecking noisily on the keyboard. They seemed oblivious and she slowed her fingers as they continued.

"You should make a new list," Bessie said briskly. "Get out of your fairytale and think about what you like. Only it can't be anything physical. The best man in the world might be four feet tall and weigh three hundred pounds. He might have a giant mole in the middle of his forehead, or he might have purple skin. You know what I mean?"

Now Priscilla giggled, a fluty feminine sound. "Oh, Bessie. You're so silly. You always make me laugh."

Abby heard her footsteps recede, the quick click of heels, and the door to the front lobby snapped shut. She kept herself busy until she knew Priscilla must have gone home. When Abby finally emerged, Bessie still sat there, tapping something on her phone. She turned to Abby with a canny look, and one eyelid dropped in a long slow wink. Abby tried to suppress a smile but did not quite succeed.

Something was underway at home. Pepper and Maddie usually picked her up after work as part of the driving lesson, but Pepper texted her to be careful and to please walk home, that he and Maddie were occupied. Relieved, Abby enjoyed her little trek. The forest came alive to summer, weeds and grasses sprouting, bright green and vigorous from all the rain. Birdsong and chirps filtered through the trees. A few bees mumbled past and squirrels raced up and down, flicking their feathery tails and making her grin with anticipation, imagining new squirrel-bite reports from Marcus and Priscilla.

Should she tell Pepper about that conversation? No, not even Abby should have heard it, and it would disconcert him. She could keep a few things private, after all.

She walked up the steps to the house and heard a sharp sound, something like a yap.

"Wait, Auntie Ab!" Maddie called out. "Don't open the door till we've got him!"

Abby paused. Peculiar noises came through the screen, scrabbling and heavy breathing. Then Pepper exclaimed something unintelligible and Maddie laughed.

"Okay," Maddie said. "Come on in."

She entered cautiously. Pepper and Maddie stood side by side in front of the kitchen, rumpled, water spots dappling their shirts. Then a square dun-colored head pushed between their legs, amber eyes and a large black nose that shifted upward, whiffing Abby's scent. The head lowered and those strange yellow eyes spiked into

Abby, then the dog withdrew and faded behind them. A wet furry odor permeated the room.

"Um. Who's that?" Abby asked. "Or what?"

"This is Zeus," Maddie explained in a rush, dragging the reluctant dog forward. A large tan canine with gangly legs and a long black tail, Zeus looked exceedingly thin, ribs and hipbones tenting sharply under his skin. "Only he doesn't know his name yet. I had to give him a strong name so he would feel better about himself, because the wranglers have been calling him Loser and that's not right. He's been hanging around the mule barn for days. Vanna said he's hungry and lonely and someone should take him to a shelter or give him a home or something and I asked her if it would be okay if I took him and she said that would be fine as long as it was okay with you and Uncle John and then Uncle John said he wasn't sure and we needed to talk about it with you and so we just gave him a bath because he was super filthy and had manure stains on him because I think he's been sleeping in the stalls and he really stunk so I'm sorry if the bathroom smells bad because we tried to wash him outside but he was so scared of the hose and Uncle John said he acted like maybe someone had once hit him with a hose and so—"

"Whoa." Abby held up her hands to halt Maddie. "So no one knows anything about him? We don't know if he has any medical problems? Rabies shots? Whether he bites, or if he's housebroken, or if he chews on things?"

Pepper and Maddie shook their heads, eyes wide, as if those problems had never occurred to them.

"You're awfully quiet about this." Abby turned to Pepper, who stood uncharacteristically silent, almost helpless.

The dog took tentative steps toward Abby, toenails clicking, and thrust out his snout. He scanned her with his amber eyes, then touched his nose to her knee, ran it along her leg to her shoe, took a long sniff. He sat down before her and regarded her gravely, turning his head once to check on Maddie, then back at Abby.

"He likes you!" Maddie cried. "He just said that he thinks you're okay."

Abby looked at Pepper again. "John?"

"Well. I'm as surprised as you are. Maybe we should do this logically, make a list. Pros and cons."

Maddie ran for paper and pencils. Zeus stayed planted in front of Abby, gazing at her, as if waiting for something.

"Auntie Ab." Maddie looked sternly through her bangs. "He wants you to say hello to him."

"Does he." Abby extended her hand, let him explore it with his nose. She stroked his head and scratched behind his ears, and suddenly his tongue spilled out, a goofy grin.

He lay down under the kitchen table as they made their lists. The negatives piled up: unknown behavior and health problems, no veterinarians nearby. High maintenance with exercise, letting him in and out for elimination. Maddie insisted she could do everything, but her face fell when Abby told her that dogs were not allowed on trails into the canyon.

"Well, that's stupid." She crossed her arms and scowled. The dog groaned and put his head on her foot, making her smile. "I think he understands almost everything we say."

Abby hated to bring it up, but saw no choice. "And what happens when you go back home? Will you take him with you?"

Maddie's face turned hard. "No, my parents would never let me have a dog. He'd have to stay here with you, until I come back."

The silence stretched, and Abby felt terrible. How had this happened, their complicit silence on Maddie's trajectory? They should have been talking about it all along, but no one wanted to—it was easier to pretend Maddie's stay was not rapidly expiring. Who knew if she would ever come back? Her parents already enrolled her in a new school for next fall. Final exams approached, and after that there was no reason for her to remain. Abby's breath stuck unexpectedly in her chest.

"I don't know," Pepper said slowly, sympathetically. He looked sad for Maddie, and Abby could tell he liked the dog. "I'm not really sure how it would work out."

Maddie had no patience for this.

"Yeah, well there's something you should think about. Something really important." She circled the last word on her paper and flipped it around to show them, stabbed it with her pencil.

WATCHDOG.

"Huh," said Abby. She never considered that, and from Pepper's curious expression, neither had he.

As if cued, a bird flew into the living room window with a bang, likely confused by the sunset reflected in the glass. Zeus leaped and ran to the front door, filling the house with a ferocious roar of deep barking.

Pepper looked from Abby to Maddie, then scanned around, checking the windows and doors, calculating. The dog padded back to them, flopped down, and grinned, his job done.

Pepper nodded, somber.

"I think he stays."

24

Ten minutes later, Abby's phone rang. She stepped away to answer but quickly returned, after a short conversation, to where Maddie and Pepper sat on the couch. Zeus had crawled into Pepper's lap, his legs and tail hanging awkwardly, his head on Maddie's thigh. Pepper absently played with the dog's black ears and looked relaxed, almost young. Which made Abby long for their more carefree days.

"That's probably not a good idea," Abby said mildly.

Zeus raised his head and regarded her, reproachful, then he slipped off the couch and lay down on top of their feet.

"See? I told you he understands everything," Maddie said, also looking a little reproachful.

"Good." Abby smiled. "Then he understands that big dogs don't really belong on the furniture."

Abby gazed at Pepper, bemused. He'd gone unexpectedly soft about this lanky beast, something she would never have predicted. Maddie—of course. But cautious, reserved Pepper?

"What was that phone call?" he asked.

"Brace yourself," Abby said, turning to Maddie, "because there was a last-minute cancellation at Phantom Ranch. We can hike down the day after tomorrow and spend two nights."

Maddie leaped up and whooped with joy. "Are you serious? Really, truly? When do we pack? How much do I take? Do you have a tent? How early should we leave?"

"That's the best part," Abby said, grinning. "The cancellation is not at the campground. We'll be staying in a cabin. So we won't need to carry a tent or camping gear, and we won't take a stove. We'll eat at the canteen."

"Pretty sweet," Pepper agreed, giving Maddie a high five. "I wish I was going."

"Hey, you've got it pretty sweet, too," Maddie said earnestly. "You get to stay with Zeus."

"Wait a minute." Pepper suddenly realized what this meant, that he would be managing the dog by himself. "I'm not sure I know how to take care of a dog."

Maddie patted his knee, tolerant. "It's not rocket science, Uncle John. I'll tell you everything you need to do."

"I didn't think you ever had a dog," Abby remarked.

"I haven't." Maddie looked smug. "Some things just come natural."

Abby called the school and arranged for Maddie's absence. The principal worried about the timing, so close to final exams, but Abby sent Maddie a pointed look and assured him that she would be prepared. Maddie nodded vigorously.

Abby's main concern centered on Pepper, alone without them, curtailed by his leg. They would not be able to call him, check on him, from inside the canyon. While he managed in the clinic pretty well now, and could drive short distances with his left foot, he remained limited and vulnerable in many ways. Her stomach rolled, queasy for his safety.

By the time she and Maddie stood at the top of the South Kaibab Trail, shouldering their packs, Abby had talked to quite a few people about helping Pepper out. She felt a little bad, for last year they had promised each other transparency, but she knew he would protest if she admitted what she'd done. She planned to confess and face his displeasure when they returned, for he would certainly figure out she was behind all his unexpected visitors. Without these arrangements, though, she doubted she could have left.

Abby still felt his embrace from that morning, felt his grip one last time as he pulled her tight. He kissed her hard before letting go and caressing her cheek, his pale blue eyes searching her.

"Be careful," he cautioned. "You have to come back in one piece. You know, so you can drive me to Flag next week to get rid of this damn cast."

They hadn't noticed Maddie enter the room. They turned and she became suddenly busy rubbing the dog's ears.

Abby left him a surprise: a new cartoon. Only instead of showing stick-figure Pepper ordering people about, it showed stick-figure Maddie commanding Pepper to take care of Zeus while Pepper shrugged and looked worried. A stick-figure Zeus sat between them.

Abby knew she must let Pepper go for now, try to quit worrying and focus on the present. Maddie fizzed with anticipation, double-checking the zippers and straps on her pack, tightening her boot-laces. Abby warned her about the sharp-pitched trail, to expect aching knees as her bones slammed down for seven steep miles. In the early dawn light they surveyed the spectacle before them, this huge ruptured crack that broke into hundreds of bright chunks and dark chasms. The sky shone cobalt blue, cloudless and warm, but Abby knew it wouldn't stay that way. The forecast predicted storms for the next few days.

Taking off, they tramped over pale limestone dust from the Permian, from two hundred fifty million years ago. Dropping rapidly, speaking little, the vista spread beyond them as they moved through the wooded Toroweap slopes. Hoarse ravens rasped and fell through the sky, swooping and rising, a dizzying glide. Every downward step ticked off hundreds of years. Maybe thousands.

"So this rock was here before the dinosaurs," Maddie said with awe.

"Way before the dinosaurs disappeared, that's for sure," Abby agreed and pointed. "And now that we're down to Coconino sandstone, it's before the first dinosaurs even opened their eyes and blinked."

They studied the cliffs, the slanted cross-bed lines, hardened leftovers from deserts and windblown dunes. Eons packed into a band of minerals. Abby rubbed against it, let the prehistoric grit chafe her living cells. They all mattered so little, regardless how important most humans saw themselves. While this outrageous scope of time calmed Abby, she knew most people found her notions gloomy, and she usually kept them to herself. But Maddie watched her, so she risked sharing them.

"Okay. I get that." Maddie gazed across the canyon, the bronze and rusty towers, the ruddy broken cliffs, the sinking canyons in wine-colored shadow. "But you still have to live every day, right? You can't give up."

Abby nodded. "Absolutely. We should try to live every day as well as we can. Or else what's the point?"

"So…" Maddie went on without missing a beat, as if it was all connected. "What's the story with you and Uncle John? How come you're not married?"

Abby saw this coming for weeks. "I guess we're just not ready."

"Why not? You two seem perfect for each other. I never hear you fight."

Abby smiled. "We don't fight. We disagree, and we talk about it, but we don't fight." She was not sure how far to go. Sometimes Maddie seemed like a child, to be protected, while other times she seemed like an adult, a companion. How did parents juggle those roles? "We've both got baggage, from before we met. So I guess we're cautious. We worry that our old problems might come back to haunt us. That we could be a burden."

Both she and Pepper felt damaged, both feared they were impaired as partners. And while Pepper's story was not Abby's to tell, she realized that Maddie must already know some of it.

They drank water and shared trail mix. Maddie's eyebrows drew together.

"I know Uncle John was married before, years ago, but I hardly remember the wedding. I was too young. My mom says it didn't work out, that he was dumb and clueless. That his wife wasn't right for him. And then she died, right? She had cancer?" Maddie waited while Abby gagged on her water and nodded, startled at this version but confirming the gist. Maddie looked a little stricken. "My mom says Uncle John blames himself about her dying. She says that he missed what was going on."

Well, hell, thought Abby, unsure what to say. She knew Pepper had already filed for divorce because of her infidelities, that they were estranged when her cancer was diagnosed. No wonder he hated talking to his sister about her affairs. But Abby also knew he remained plagued by misgivings, felt he should have paid attention to her symptoms, regardless how contentious things were. Abby understood he might never forgive himself, that he doubted his fitness for marriage again.

"It's a complicated story," Abby finally said. "And it's not my place to tell you. But I will say one thing—your uncle is one of the best men I've ever met, and one of the best doctors. He's honest and kind and always tries to do his best. And that's the truth." She paused, wanting to get it right. "If he missed something, then everyone would have missed it."

Abby never saw such gratitude as in the look Maddie sent her, her cool eyes suddenly warm and satisfied.

They started down the trail again, Abby leading, ready for some silence. But Maddie wasn't done.

"So what's your baggage, Auntie Ab?"

Abby slowed and stopped, turned to scrutinize Maddie's earnest expression. Would this child never stop? Abby could not gage what to say. It felt chancy; it might help Maddie, or it might injure their relationship, the way Maddie saw her.

"That's kind of a personal question." Abby felt her face go narrow.

Maddie's features crumpled, her hand clapped to her mouth. "I didn't mean to pry. I'm just trying to figure things out. I'm really sorry. Please don't be mad at me."

"It's all right," Abby assured her quickly. Maddie could flip from curious to devastated in a nanosecond, and Abby reminded herself just how young Maddie actually was. And she reminded herself how much damage Maddie had already endured in her short life. "Listen. Everyone has baggage. Everyone has to carry their load. You just don't always want to talk about it."

"I understand. I'll never ask again," Maddie implored.

Abby looked up, where small puffy cumulus formed, spreading across the sky like lambs, clustering in herds. Friendly little herds now, until the storms began to rise.

"No, it's okay. I overreacted. Come on, let's keep walking and I'll tell you."

25

As they paced down the trail, Abby explained anxiety. She described her panic attacks, the terror that snatches the air from your lungs and hammers your heart like a maniac. The constant fear of having another panic attack, that paralyzing dread. How she started drinking alcohol every night to control it, how she lost her fiancé. Then the better part, seeking help and learning behavior management, learning relaxation techniques and visualization. That was her success, although she never quite trusted it, always worried that the anxiety lurked below her surface.

"So I worry about being a partner, and being a parent," Abby finished, matter-of-fact. "That's why I'm in no hurry to get married. I don't want to saddle Pepper with my problems, and I don't want to pass them to a child. Or make a child put up with me if I lose control."

They walked in silence a long way. Abby knew it wasn't over, sensed Maddie chewing on her words, digesting them. Before long she would pipe up. They moved deep into the canyon now, the rim no longer visible, just endless ledges of brittle stone and ruined cliffs. And the perpetual path, down and down until finally, far along, that abrupt breakthrough moment. Abby halted so suddenly that Maddie ran into her pack.

"Look." Abby pointed.

A short expanse of river gleamed below them, glimpsed through a rocky cleft.

"Oh my gosh! We're getting so close!" Maddie hopped up and down. "And it's all green and pretty. I thought you said it would be brown and muddy."

"It usually is. You got lucky."

"Let's go, let's go," Maddie urged, surging ahead, lengthening her stride. Then she twirled and walked backward, facing up at Abby and starting to talk. "But I have to tell you—"

"Stop that," Abby insisted. "Turn around before you trip and fall and get hurt."

"Okay, okay." Maddie halted, her face stern. Her eyes blazed. "But I have to say something. I've been thinking and thinking about what you said, about how you and Uncle John have all this baggage. But any kid would be happy to have you for their mom. And Uncle John, too. Well, for their dad, of course." She concentrated fiercely. "What I mean is that I think you guys should get over it and move on. No one is perfect, and never will be."

Abby felt both accused and admired. She wanted to explain how anxiety never really disappeared, done and gone, that she would contend with it all her life. Sometimes little skirmishes, sometimes bigger battles. Although so much better now, it never vanished. She opened her mouth to reply but then turned her head, distracted by a commotion coming up the trail, a mix of jingling bits and steady hooves, a male voice.

"Get along, now," the man coaxed. A mule pack train swung into view, red dust rising, hanging in the air. The wrangler touched his hat brim and spoke as he passed. "Just stand still on the inside, please. Don't move or try to touch them mules, okay?" Then he peered more closely, leaning over, and his mouth turned up in a smile. "Well, hullo there Miz Maddie. How's it going?"

"Great, Mr. Joe, just great," Maddie chirped. She and Abby stood against the cliff as the mules strained by, hauling cargo and trash up from Phantom Ranch. Packs creaked and leather squeaked, the mules blowing through wide nostrils, hides stained with sweat.

"Look, that's Peaches," said Maddie happily, introducing the mules as they passed. "She's so smart. And there's Othello—remember his scarred leg? Now stand super quiet, because here comes Jitterbug and she's always nervous. See how she's staring at us, like she's afraid? Hi there Jitterbug old girl, it's okay, you'll be fine."

Each mule seemed to look at Maddie, to nod her way, although Abby knew she must be imagining it. Long narrow faces, deep alert eyes, those extraordinary fuzzy ears that tilted their way. Then the last one clopped by, ridden by a scraggy wrangler with greasy hair and a stubbled chin, who grinned too big and stared too long at Maddie, almost a leer. Maddie took Abby's hand and went silent, seemed to shrink a little beside her.

"That's him," she whispered as the mules disappeared over the rise. "That's Roy. He's the one who picks on Vanna."

Abby flared. So this was the man who spooked the mule, injuring Vanna's shoulder. The man who complained about Vanna in front of the other wranglers. Maddie saw Abby's expression and pulled her on.

"Come on, Auntie Ab. Ignore him. Come on!"

Soon they stood on the suspension bridge, watching the Colorado slide beneath them. The water flowed green and heavy, no rapids here, an immense power coursing by, glinting and curling, bound on its long way to the coast. Her knees ached and her toes throbbed from the jarring descent, but she was pleased to see Maddie seemed strong and fresh. The canyon grew hot at the bottom, both of them rimed with dust and salt. Abby still needed to respond to Maddie's compliment, to her challenge about moving on, but she had yet to figure out what to say.

Maddie stared at the river, mesmerized, her mouth gaped in awe.

Built to accommodate four, their cabin felt downright luxurious for just two. They settled in quickly and followed a simple afternoon of reading and relaxing, walking and chatting. Abby focused on Maddie, tried to create a deep experience for her, although she never completely shed her unease, thinking of Pepper alone. Every few hours she checked her cellphone, and every few hours it denied her a signal.

That night they gazed up at the inky swath of sky, the sugar-sprinkle of stars, the impossible distances beyond them.

Abby checked her phone one last time.

"He'll be okay," Maddie said, sympathetic. "Besides, Zeus will guard him."

"I know." Abby pocketed the phone. A dog couldn't do everything.

"He'll be with Marcus tonight. They're watching *Vampires vs. Zombies*, and I told Marcus to sleep over with Uncle John. He'll make up some reason."

"That silly show." Abby made a face. "And I asked Marcus the same thing. He must think we're nuts."

"No, he doesn't. And it's actually a pretty good show. I've watched it a few times, and there's some nice themes about loyalty. You should try watching it."

Abby shook her head. "Zombies give me the creeps."

Maddie laughed, then sobered. She looked at the glittering sky, then down at her feet. "Are things really okay with you and Uncle John? I mean, it seems like it. But I'm a little bit worried—don't you guys ever have sex?"

Abby choked for the second or third time that day. "Maddie, really. First of all, that's none of your business. And second, you're too young to be thinking about that sort of thing. Why on earth would you say that?"

Maddie scowled. "I'm not that young. People my age have sex, you know." She saw the alarm on Abby's face and hurried along. "Not me, don't worry. Gross. But I know it's really a big deal because my parents always talk about it, how important it is, and that's why they can't decide about staying together. I'm not a baby—I've read *Lolita*, you know. And trust me, I know when my parents do it because they're kind of noisy. They don't think I hear them, because my mom asks me and I say no, but I do."

Ridiculous. Abby felt furious that Maddie was forced to sift through this, these confusing, perverted messages. As if any parent should say such things.

"It's not all about sex, for heaven's sake. It's more about respect, and having the same values, and enjoying each other's company. It's about sharing and caring—really caring—what happens to the other person. About how you would never, ever, want to hurt them." Abby hadn't imagined she would be addressing sex with Maddie on this trip, but she could not let that stand. "Sex is great, if it's with the right person, someone that you care about. But the caring comes first." Abby paused, scowled. "And just so you know, *Lolita* is not exactly a guidebook to life. It's deviant."

Maddie pursed her lips, not quite ready to let go. "So you're saying you guys have quiet sex?"

"Maddie! Listen to what I'm saying and quit worrying about our sex. We're fine. Besides, your Uncle John has a broken leg, in case you forgot. That kind of makes it more difficult."

Abby could hardly tell her about their intimacy, how rousing it became since Maddie arrived. How they had to keep shushing each other as they heated up, had to linger for control. The need for silence prolonged their foreplay with delicious pauses, until she ached and shivered. He would bring her to the brink until she began to moan, then stop and wait, barely moving, until her panting subsided. Then start again. It created the longest, most intense lovemaking. One time she forgot, lost restraint, and he suddenly planted his hand on her mouth, without stopping, which sent her right over the edge.

The next day, their middle day, started sunny and hot, but by afternoon a fleet of heavy clouds trooped across the sky, bumping against each other, moving in. Abby and Maddie hiked a few miles up the North Kaibab Trail and back. They played in the clear water of Bright Angel Creek as it bounced over rocks, until it finally joined the Colorado. They roamed along the edge of the river where it lapped at the stones, stuck their bare feet in the cold water. Finally they sat under a tree, Abby reading and occasionally checking her uncooperative phone, Maddie writing in her notebook, serious and absorbed. The river glistened and dimmed as sunlight came and went, the water making small slaps, gurgles, and glugs against the stones and sand and cliffs as it muscled by.

Maddie looked up, thoughtful. "I love that quiet sound. This river is so strong—I mean, look what it's done—" she swept her hand at the canyon, "but it's not making a big deal. Like it's saying *Yeah, I did that*, but it's kind of humble about it. I like that...that's how I want to be."

Abby smiled and marked her page, closed the book, and leaned back against the tree. "Well. This river may be calm here, but it's also got some massive wicked rapids, and they're so loud that you have to shout to talk."

"That's okay. It has a complicated personality." Maddie watched the water, glanced back at Abby. "What do you think it says?"

This was Abby's favorite theme, the measure of stone and space, the incandescence of stars and the caged molecules of earth beneath her feet. She thought of the Precambrian silt suspended in the water, traveling to new shores, of the empty universe and its secrets, of the castled cumulus, tall and foreboding yet made of nothing but vapor.

"That time never stops. That everything keeps moving and changing. Just like each of us." Abby made a wry face. "On a very tiny scale. I mean, we barely count."

Maddie stared at her. "You count to me."

Abby stared back, grasping how much she cared for this young woman, this raw soul. As if Abby had been digging through dirt, just ordinary soil, and struck hard iron. Strong, ringing metal. And she realized how much she would miss her when she left, felt an unfamiliar hollowness in her core.

Maddie walked over and handed Abby her notebook, brushed grit from the page. "Anyway, I wrote a new haiku about our hike."

Humans, mules, we all
Trudge uphill, our weighty loads
Lightened next to friends.

Abby stood and embraced her, wondering again how a sensitive, thoughtful person could emerge from that tainted environment.

"That's amazing. I love it."

26

Pepper seemed fine when they returned, at least physically. But a gloomy mood shadowed him, justifiably, considering what happened while they were gone.

Abby fretted the entire way out of the canyon. Her imagination ran wild with visions of Pepper injured, or worse. She worried whether anyone would find her, contact her, if something happened.

The canyon itself turned temperamental as Abby and Maddie hiked up, shifting from a splendid morning, exuberant with light and shadow, to an afternoon where surly low clouds lobbed wind and rain against them. Wet and muddy, exhausted and aching, Abby and Maddie clambered up the porch and through the door, thankful to be home. Pepper helped as much as he could, bringing towels and hobbling to drape their dripping gear on the back porch while Zeus gamboled between them, wiggling and barking and smearing water all over the floor.

In dry clothes now, they sat in the kitchen enjoying hot tea and the sugar cookies that Pepper made. Abby noticed he seemed uneasy, that something felt off, but she waited.

"You made cookies?" she said instead. He had never baked before, and Abby sensed a papa-bear sort of keenness that made him want to feed Maddie.

"Well, not really," Pepper said humbly. "I sliced them off a roll of dough that came from the store, and then I baked them. But I had to find the cookie sheets and read the instructions. So yes, practically from scratch."

SANDRA CAVALLO MILLER

Weary, Maddie soon announced she might need a nap and left for her room. Zeus scrambled up and padded after her. Abby waited until Maddie had time to settle, then leaned to Pepper, speaking quietly.

"What's wrong?"

"Is it that obvious?" He rubbed his face, looking drained.

Abby smiled faintly. "The dangers of a close relationship, right?"

"Mm." He took her hands, caressed them a moment then gripped them tightly. "I sure missed you."

Abby nodded, stroking his long fingers, waiting.

He briefly closed his eyes. "There were two cases while you were gone. A forty-year-old man with a heart attack, and a thirty-two-year-old woman with a stroke. The man died before they got him to the clinic, and the woman can't even talk now because of the stroke. She may spend the rest of her life in a wheelchair...too soon to tell. Both of them were strong, fit hikers. Both had crazy high blood pressure. And both of them carried those pills."

"No," Abby breathed, dismayed.

"It was awful. Sometimes I can't get them out of my head."

"Have you talked to Shipley?"

"Yeah, he was beside himself. I've never seen him so upset." Pepper frowned. "He claims he's got it narrowed down to a few suspects."

"I'm so sorry you had to handle it by yourself." Abby remembered how helpless she felt when Basil Taylor died, how alone.

"Everyone helped. People kept coming by." His face changed, and his blue eyes knifed over at her. "People came over who normally wouldn't stop by. Almost as if they were checking on me. What do you suppose that was about?"

Abby flushed. Part of her wanted to make light of it, but she didn't dare. "I don't know. I might have mentioned to a few people that you would be here alone. You know, when I was just making conversation."

"Right." He started to say more, then let it go. Instead, he rapped his knuckles against his cast. "Two more days. I've arranged the clinic schedule so we can leave early, so we can get to the orthopedic office before it closes. I should just do it myself, just saw the damn thing off."

186

"Don't you dare. He'll need to take an X-ray, anyway."

"Something else I could do myself," Pepper pointed out.

"John. Just try to be a compliant patient and listen to your doctor. He'll need to give you a rehab program, an exercise schedule, all of that. You know your leg will be weak and stiff. It's going to take weeks—months—to get back to normal."

"Are you lecturing me?"

"Maybe a little." Abby smiled and leaned to him, kissed him. "Come on. Let's go to bed."

"It's pretty early to go to bed," he protested. "I don't think I can sleep right now. I might go out back and work on the deck some more."

A corner of the back deck sank that winter, the wood black and rotting. Abby noticed signs of his labor when she hung out her wet jacket, some new beams stacked under the roof, a shovel and pickaxe propped against a post. He shouldn't be doing such work in his cast, but this was not the time to complain.

"I said we should go to bed. I didn't say we should go to sleep," she said, pulling him up.

Pepper grinned, back to being himself, and quickly followed her.

Appointments crammed her clinic the next day. While Pepper tried to handle most of her work while she was gone, his efforts were ambushed by the two disasters, which put him far behind. Abby first saw two puking infants with ear infections, their cute onesies stained with curdled vomit. She saw a fevered teenager with huge crimson tonsils coated in pus, certain to be mononucleosis. There were sprained wrists and cracked fingers and mangled toes, sour stomachs and toothaches. One man stood on the brink of divorce, a divorce he badly wanted but felt guilty about. Abby bounced back and forth between her roles as a counselor, an orthopedist, a gastroenterologist, and an otolaryngologist. Welcome to family medicine, she thought. Then her favorite kinds of preventive visits, three patients who sought advice on losing weight, or controlling their cholesterol, or stopping tobacco.

Because the season was warming up, more people arrived with heat injury: dehydration, severe sunburn, heat exhaustion. Shaky, crusted in salt, bright red, nauseated, stumbling. They needed fluids, rest, food, and common sense.

The day wound down. Finally, just one patient left, Marietta Appleby, concerned about a sharp sticking pain in her right chest that poked her a few times a day, whenever she bent over to fasten her shoe or pick something up. Wilbur sat as usual in his corner on his phone, studying something about squirrel populations in northern Arizona.

"You should talk to Marcus and Priscilla." Half teasing, Abby told him about the squirrel bite reports. "They can tell you some great stories."

"Ahem," coughed Marietta, pointing at her chest. She wore her usual flowered shift and sensible thick shoes, her white braid pinned securely to her skull in a tight spiral.

Certain that Marietta had pulled a muscle between her ribs, Abby tried to talk the woman out of an electrocardiogram. The more persuasive she grew, though, the deeper Marietta dug in, fearful of her heart and citing friend after friend who had unexpected heart attacks after similar symptoms. Abby finally ordered the test, tired of arguing.

She sent Wilbur to the lobby while Marietta undressed for the EKG. Abby sat in the exam room, typing her note while Dolores hooked up the wires.

"What's that scrape on your hand?" Marietta asked sharply, pointing at a short red scratch on Abby's wrist.

"Please hold your arm still," Dolores instructed calmly, pulling it back to the table.

Abby smiled. "Just one of the joys of having a new dog. A big rambunctious new dog."

Marietta lay silent as Dolores pasted the EKG leads to her chest; from the corner of her eye, Abby saw Marietta scrunch up her face. Probably thinking how much she hates dogs, Abby suspected, bracing for a caustic comment. The woman struck her as a cat person.

"I still miss my dog." Marietta said. The corners of her mouth tugged down.

"I'm sorry," Abby offered, thinking *so much for my insight.* "How long has it been?"

The woman's chin trembled. "Six years, but I still miss him. He was my family. Well, Wilbur too."

She actually rolled her eyes, realizing how that might sound, and a little chuckle broke from her throat. Caught off guard, Abby and Dolores laughed too, and in a moment all three were giggling together. Eventually they composed themselves and wiped their eyes, and Abby took a long look at the EKG.

"Normal," she pronounced. "But Mrs. Appleby, why don't you get another dog?"

"I don't know. It won't be the same. And I hate to do that to Wilbur. It would mean more chores for him, walking the dog and all, and he already works so hard."

Abby gathered her laptop while Dolores cleaned the sticky patches off Marietta's skin.

"You should think about it," Abby said. "A dog would be nice company. And I'll send Wilbur back in, as soon as you're dressed."

"Don't you tell him what I said. About family."

"Not a word," Abby promised.

She found Wilbur leaning on the front counter, talking with Priscilla, a lively exchange about squirrel bites. Priscilla pointed her pen at the clipboard, her shoulders turned toward him, thrusting out her chest. She wore a sky-blue fifties-style shirtdress with a deep neckline, her waist cinched by a wide belt, the skirt standing out. She looked like she belonged at a sock hop. Marcus was gone, taking the day off to practice with Mitzi.

"See this one?" Priscilla said coyly. Abby saw him glance down her cleavage, then skip back up to her face. Cherry-red lipstick highlighted her smile and blue eyeshadow matched the dress. "This patient said the squirrel looked old and gray, and it raised up on its haunches and stood there like royalty, like it must have been a squirrel king. Like it expected people to wait on him. You know about wildlife, Wilbur—are there really squirrel kings? The patient said that's why it bit him, because he was too slow when he offered his cracker."

"This is awesome stuff," Wilbur said, scanning down the page. "Why, you could write such a funny book from these reports. Did you do all of them yourself?"

"Well, not all of them," Priscilla remarked, seeing Abby come through the door. "My coworker Marcus did a few."

"Your mom is ready," Abby announced, thinking that Marcus had probably written about 98 percent of the reports. "And her EKG was fine."

Wilbur moved reluctantly from Priscilla, his eyes large, still taking her in. "I know I have to go now, but do you think you could show me more someday? I've hardly seen anything."

Priscilla stared at him and Abby turned away to control herself. His double meaning had to be unintended. Didn't it?

"Well, of course, Wilbur," Priscilla said slowly, giving him the full force of her mascara-fringed eyes. "I'd be happy for you to come anytime. After work might be best, at the end of the day, so we wouldn't have to hurry. Or be interrupted."

I can't be hearing this, Abby thought.

The front door banged open and Hatch Carpenter strode in, his face tight and upset. He seemed barely clothed, wearing a khaki tank top and skimpy cutoff denim shorts, muscles bulging everywhere. He craned his neck to look past Abby and scowl down the back hall, as if searching for someone.

"Hey, Doc Wilmore," he said brusquely. "Is Doc Pepper here? I've got to talk to him."

"Can I help you?" she asked formally, put off.

"No, I need to talk to him. Now." His normally gelled hair stood out at odd angles, mussed up, his face flinty and a little belligerent.

"He's not here. And I'm afraid he won't be here tomorrow, either. He has to go to Flagstaff." It wasn't entirely true, for Pepper would see patients in the morning. Abby wasn't entirely sure why she said that, except that he was being rude and annoying.

"Hey, I'll be in Flag tomorrow. I bet I could meet up with him there." He looked almost crafty.

"No, he can't. I'll be with him." Abby paused. Maybe this had something to do with the supplements, maybe a new clue. She remembered how much Hatch wanted to collaborate with Pepper. Probably a male thing, proving himself. "Can't you give me a message for him?"

Hatch stared hard at her, as if calculating. Then his gaze coasted across her figure and back up. "No. I'll have to catch him later."

He turned on his heel and walked out. What the hell, Abby thought.

Abby turned to Priscilla, to see if she had witnessed that exchange and ask what she thought, but Priscilla was no longer there. Did she follow Wilbur to the back? No, here she came, carrying her bag, ready to leave. A tiny smile curved her cherry lips.

"Did you and Wilbur have a nice conversation?" Abby asked, trying to get Hatch out of her brain. Was he being a jerk, or was she overreacting? Maybe it was the way he looked at her, made her feel undressed.

"Yes, we did," Priscilla said. Prim, slightly flushed.

Abby noticed that her hair was a little out of place, the bangs on her forehead rumpled and flying awry. As if she had thoughtlessly, impetuously, pushed it back.

27

They simply had to address the obvious. Maddie needed a plane ticket home.

But Maddie refused to bring it up to her parents. They talked every other week, a short call from them to see if she needed anything, her dad in the background, her mom saccharine. Maddie shared everything with Pepper. And her mom flung emails her way every few days, professing how much she missed Maddie. Those mom-missives gushed on and on, filled with the trivia of her daily life, how she triumphed, who treated her unfairly, gossiping about people Maddie barely knew. Her dad sent one email, short and generic: *Hey kid, just not the same here without you.* That's open for interpretation, Maddie remarked.

This left Pepper to deal with the travel. He waited until Abby and Maddie went to walk Zeus, then took his phone to the back deck. They heard his voice as they strode away, and he did not sound happy. Their eyes met, and the misgiving Abby saw in Maddie's face made her heart ache.

The slate sky darkened over them, the forest rustling with small sounds that made Zeus stop and stare. Once he stood in front of them, a barricade, and woofed into the gloom.

"Probably a coyote," Abby guessed, peering into deep shadow, seeing nothing. "Maybe a racoon or skunk?"

"It's okay, Zeus," Maddie said, petting his head. "Thanks for protecting us."

The dog wagged once and let them proceed. Maddie kicked pebbles and twigs along, disconsolate.

"Look," said Abby, pointing at the sky. She ran her finger across the star-strung vault. "Mars, Saturn, Jupiter, Venus. Four planets all at once, all in a row. Add in Earth, and that's over half our solar system."

Maddie gazed up, scanning those distant worlds. "Thanks, Auntie Ab. That helps put things in perspective. Which is a little scary, because that means I'm starting to think like you. How I'm just a dot in the universe." Her mouth switched back and forth. "I guess I can survive three more years at home before I go to college. Right?"

Abby nodded firmly. "I think you can. You're pretty tough—just stay focused. And you can come visit us quite a bit."

Maddie shot her a determined look. "Just try and stop me."

Pepper was off the phone when they returned.

"There's been a change of plans. In a few weeks, your parents are taking a trip to Tahiti." He spoke carefully, neutrally, clearly unsure how Maddie would react. "They say it's their last chance to make their marriage work."

"Do you know how many so-called last chances they've taken?" Maddie complained. Then her expression brightened as she got it. "Wait. Are you saying I can't go home yet because they'll be gone? That I'll have to stay here longer? Because they'll be in Tahiti, getting drunk?"

Pepper went stern. "Don't talk about your parents like that."

Maddie barely heard him. She pulled up Zeus, held his front paws and waltzed him around in a little dance, ears flopping and head bobbing, his tail wagging madly.

Abby exchanged a look with Pepper, then turned to Maddie. "We haven't had a chance to discuss this, but I don't see any way around it. This means you'll have to go with us, when we go visit Gem and William. When we meet them in Yellowstone."

Maddie let loose a loud whoop and Zeus began howling.

Later that night, Pepper told Abby how his sister could not afford the trip, but they were determined to go regardless. Abby knew his sister owed him money, although she would never bring that up.

And Pepper discovered that they had not yet settled on her high school, either. They wondered if maybe she should be farther away from her taunting classmates. Pepper smelled something fishy after his sister mentioned a distant boarding school.

"I thought they couldn't afford it," Abby said.

"I guess they'll just get a few more credit cards." He looked troubled. "I worry most about Maddie's reaction—this could feel like another rejection."

"But it might actually be better. For Maddie." Abby smoothed out his forehead with her fingers. "You'll get a headache if you keep frowning like that."

Pepper lay silent, then cut his eyes at Abby. "I didn't see this coming. I didn't mean to get so close to her…I don't want her to go. Especially not back to them."

She settled against his shoulder. "I don't either. I thought she would be a mess, that we'd be so relieved when she was gone. But it's just the opposite. And she should be a mess after all this nonsense, but she's not. I can't even imagine why."

As they fell asleep, Abby remembered that she meant to tell him about Hatch Carpenter, how insistent he acted. But talking about Hatch was the last thing she wanted right then, and she put it off till the following day.

The next morning, Harry Stonewall finally reappeared. Concerned once again by his absence, Marcus stopped by Harry's campground the previous week. He found Harry spryly energetic, busy sorting rocks, reorganizing his workspace. His battered ice cooler had been replaced with a miniature refrigerator, and a jaunty Arizona flag fluttered atop his tent. Harry seemed surprised at how long overdue he was for an appointment, and promised to come right in. Which for Harry meant in a week or two.

"I ain't felt this good in years," Harry chortled to Abby. His eyes gleamed under his bushy brows, his wild rooster-comb hair lay neatly brushed, and he wore clothes she had never seen before, a striped shirt and leather vest instead of mended denim. Even his eyeglasses looked cleaner, not smeary, and a chain glinted from his vest, suggesting a pocket watch. "I plumb forgot to come back and check those tests. That Marcus, he keeps me in line."

"You look like you feel well," Abby agreed, pleased.

"You ain't seen half of it. Wait till we're done, and I'll have you take a gander out the window at my new wheels." His chin rose, proud.

"You bought a new car?" Abby remembered his rusted VW Beetle.

A sly smile. "I guess you could say I've had a good month."

Abby leaned forward, lowered her voice. "Not gold? Don't tell me you found gold?"

Harry sat back and laughed his wheezy chuckle. "Why, I can't imagine what you're talking about, young lady. There's no gold in these parts."

He revealed nothing more. After Bessie drew his blood, complimenting his stylish outfit, they all looked out the front window to admire his shiny red Jeep. Before he left the clinic, and most remarkable to Abby, Harry scheduled an appointment to have her remove his two skin cancers.

"He's a new man," Marcus commented.

"Thanks to you," she pointed out. "Do you think he actually found any gold?"

"Maybe, but not likely," he laughed. "But he sure wants everyone to think so. What I think is that he finally got some inheritance money, from when his brother died last year. You know, his older brother Maxwell, who had liver damage from drinking so much booze? He and Harry were never close, mostly because Harry always nagged him about his whiskey. But Harry is the last sibling left."

"You're incredible." Abby was endlessly amazed at what Marcus elicited from people. Which made her wonder. "Hey, what can you tell me about Hatch Carpenter? I can't figure him out. He was really pushy yesterday, kind of rude."

Marcus's face pinched up. "He's a pill. He won't talk to me."

"That's a first." Calling someone a pill was pretty coarse for mild-spoken Marcus.

The front door swung open and Marcus looked past Abby, beaming. Mitzi entered, a large silver trophy balanced in her arms. Depositing it carefully on the counter, lustrous in the light, she used her sleeve to polish off a smudge. Mitzi glanced shyly at Abby, then back at Marcus and grinned. Deeply tanned, she wore a long skirt and her chocolate hair hung down, falling in soft waves. A hint of color touched her lips, a trace of smoke to her eyelids.

"We had another bet," Marcus said playfully, seeing Abby's astonishment.

"Does this mean you two won that golf tournament? Why didn't you tell us? I thought it wasn't until next weekend." Abby looked back and forth between them, Marcus smug and Mitzi's eyes on the floor, a smile playing on her face.

"I didn't want to make a big deal about it, in case we didn't do very well," he explained. "I didn't want everyone asking me about it. You know."

Abby nodded. Marcus still struggled with his nervous putts. "But it looks like you managed pretty well."

Mitzi raised her head. "I made the bet this time. I bet him that if he could keep me from getting mad, and I could keep him from being anxious, then I would treat him to dinner. So this time I'm taking him out to El Tovar."

"Very impressive." Abby admired the gleaming trophy, their names engraved on the plate. Two small silver golfers adorned the top, male and female, raising clubs high in victory. "Congrats."

Pepper appeared and joined in with his praise.

Then Abby saw the clock and realized they needed to get on the road to Flagstaff for Pepper's cast removal. And first they had to pick up Maddie, who insisted on going, too.

"I want to hear what the doctor says," Maddie said.

"Who's in charge here, anyway?" Pepper complained.

Maddie looked at him and grinned.

28

Pepper's leg looked frail without the cast—a pale, sickly shadow compared to its strapping partner. He took his first step and nearly buckled over, the limb too stiff and weak to support him. Maddie listened intently to the orthopedist's instructions and quizzed her uncle about his rehab regimen during the drive back, making sure he remembered all his exercises and how far he could walk and how much to use the crutches. Pepper acted a bit testy, feeling like an invalid again. Abby could tell from his tense mouth that his leg felt sensitive and sore.

"You'll be back to normal in no time," Abby assured him, arranging him on the couch with pillows in a scene that felt oddly like the first time he returned after surgery.

"I feel like I'm starting over," he grumbled. "I want to be done with crutches."

"Just give your poor skinny leg a day or two to get used to daylight, Uncle John," Maddie said sternly. She studied the surgical scars, the shriveled muscle, the dead white skin. Then her face turned impish. "If you'd rather, we can probably go get you that walker from the clinic. You could use that instead of crutches. We used walkers a lot when I worked at hospice—I can show you how to use one."

"I don't need a walker," he complained. "I'm not that unsteady. Or that old. And please remember, I'm not dying."

Maddie laughed and went to help Abby fix supper. Abby took a moment to draw Pepper a new cartoon, where Maddie pointed at him with his crutches and Pepper exclaimed *Remember, I'm not dying.*

Abby had one more task she wanted to accomplish before the string of upcoming events engulfed her. If she stopped to think about all of it—Maddie's finals, then the trip to Yellowstone, then Maddie leaving for home—she felt overwhelmed, especially as summer visitors arrived in droves and clogged the clinic. Many brought their medical problems along with their luggage, and many created new issues once they arrived.

"Let's take a walk," Abby suggested to Maddie, late the next afternoon. They left Pepper home, working on his exercises with grim determination. He longed to be more mobile at Yellowstone. "There's someone Zeus should meet."

Earlier, Abby located the Appleby address in the clinic chart. Maddie looked puzzled but went along, seeing that Abby had something up her sleeve.

Marietta answered the door, clad in a lumpy gray shift and black stockings, her shoulders wrapped in a black cardigan despite the warm day. Her long white braid hung down her back instead of curling tightly around her head, making her look softer and younger. Relatively younger, Abby corrected her thoughts, since the woman was approaching ninety.

Marietta squinted suspiciously. "Are you selling something?"

"Hello, Mrs. Appleby," Abby said. "It's me, Dr. Wilmore. Abby. And this is my niece, Maddie. And her dog, Zeus."

"Pleased to meet you," Maddie said formally, sticking out her hand. Marietta paused before cautiously taking it, staring at Maddie as if she hadn't seen a young person in years, while Maddie continued. "And no, we're not selling anything."

"Wilbur! Dr. Wilmore is here," Marietta shouted back into the house. "Did you call her?"

"No, Mrs. Appleby," Abby forged on. "This is a social visit. I remembered how you missed your dog, so I thought you might like to meet Zeus."

Hearing his name, Zeus stepped up and thrust his nose toward Marietta, huffing a few investigative sniffs. Satisfied, he sat down in front of her and lowered his square head, as if waiting for a pat. Marietta almost reluctantly reached down and rubbed his ears. As she withdrew, he leaned forward and nudged her for more.

"Well, aren't you something," Marietta said.

"Come on in," Wilbur said, edging up beside her and opening the door wider. "We don't get much company."

"Can Zeus come in, too?" Maddie asked respectfully.

"Of course, child." The old woman beckoned them in, as if the question was ridiculous.

Immaculate, the house had everything in its place, not a speck of dust. Furniture crowded the living room, a mix of modern and vintage. Abby worried that her strategy might not work out after all; Marietta kept a fastidious household.

They started chatting politely, but Maddie's natural curiosity took over and soon she and Wilbur were delving into the canyon's water supply problems. And the challenges of regulating the river's flow from the dam without impacting ecosystems. And the success of the California condor program. Wilbur lit up and Maddie devoured his words. Meanwhile, Zeus edged up to Marietta and slid his head on her lap. When Marietta talked with Abby and went too long without stroking him, he plopped his large paw up on her leg to remind her.

Eventually Abby confessed the purpose of their visit. She worried about Zeus during the day, with everyone busy at work or school, and she worried what to do if they were gone for a few days. Would Marietta consider watching Zeus during the day? They would bring him over each morning and pick him up in the afternoon. And would they be willing to caretake him while they went to Yellowstone? Abby would pay them, of course.

"I've heard of doing that," Wilbur said. "A sort of dog-sharing agreement."

Maddie piped in, immediately onboard. "And it will be really important when I go back to Illinois for a little while. I mean, Uncle John and Auntie Ab take good care of him, but he gets lonely when he's home all day by himself."

Abby nodded, watching Marietta. It felt like it could go either way, and no one wanted to say too much or too little. Except Maddie, who barely hesitated.

"Could you please try it, Mrs. Appleby?" she pleaded. "It would be so helpful. I don't know exactly when I'll be back, and I would feel so much better if you could."

Distracted, Marietta looked back and forth between Maddie and Zeus. She realized something was off.

"Why, where are your parents, child?" she asked.

Maddie composed herself. "They're having problems. They're kind of messed up. So I'm here to be out of the way, and I wish I could stay here forever."

Abby put her arm around Maddie, a little hug. Marietta scowled and stiffly stood up, put out her hand to Maddie, and led her to the kitchen as if she was three years old.

"Come on, honey. Let's go get some cookies. And Zeus can have one, too—it won't hurt a big dog like him to eat just one cookie. I guess we'll need to buy some doggie treats, won't we?"

Abby and Wilbur looked at each other. She saw how his scrawny moustache was trimmed neater than it used to be, that he'd had a recent haircut. His eyes glowed warmly behind his black-rimmed glasses.

He put his hands together and mouthed "thank you" to Abby.

29

Pepper cautioned Maddie not to linger at the mule barn that day after school. She needed to get home to study for final exams, and powerful thunderstorms were predicted for late afternoon. The forecast, in fact, looked ominous, with a 100 percent chance of rain. Abby wondered if this summer would be like last year, besieged day after day with angry tempests.

Maddie agreed, but she just had to stop by to see Vanna, for it might be her last chance this season. Pepper pointed at Maddie's skin, asked about three or four scattered white scars, like little snowflakes on her forearms.

"Vanna's been letting me hammer out some shoes," Maddie explained enthusiastically. "Sometimes little bits of hot metal fly up and land on your arms. It sort of hurts, but not too much. Don't worry, though—Vanna always makes me wear goggles and gloves."

Pepper sighed. Abby could tell he was trying to decide whether to draw a line, wanting to protect her from possible injury. "Your parents might not approve."

"Like they would notice."

There had been no more cardiac cases, no more strokes, no patients with illicit pills. According to friends of the last two cases, those hikers likely bought their pills months ago. No one removed the warning sign from the clinic wall, no more threats appeared, and Shipley had not dropped by in a while. Maybe the perpetrator had moved on; Abby began to hope it would all fade away.

When Abby and Pepper left the clinic that day, they stopped to stare at the boiling sky. A vast thunderhead overwhelmed the northern atmosphere, growing and spreading as they watched. The crown shone creamy white while the insides roiled, curdling and flexing, an uneasy churn. No thunder yet, too far away, but it wouldn't be long since it seemed headed straight for them. Bands of purple clouds streamed before it and the underbelly blackened, dark as doom. Quick legs of lightning danced and jittered below.

"Yikes," said Pepper, "it looks like a nuclear explosion."

"That's terrifying." Abby kept looking over her shoulder, as if it was dangerous to turn her back.

He hurried them into the car. Although his leg slowly improved, he still limped and could not yet walk home. Abby could see his discomfort after a long day seeing patients and suspected he would have trouble sleeping that night.

Maddie was not yet home. Abby kept standing on the front porch, studying the sky, looking down the road. The cloud mass still rose, the top fanning out, the internal knuckles edged with orange and gold, a tricky alchemy. Dusk would gather soon, hastened by thick gray shrouds of vapor rapidly filling the sky.

"Maybe you should call her," Pepper suggested when Abby came back inside.

"Maybe…" Abby never knew how protective to behave. She wanted to foster independence, but felt like a mother hen at the same time. Too little, too much, impossible to gauge.

A faint murmur of thunder stole through the air. Abby made herself do a few things, cleaned off the table, hung up a jacket. She went out back to pick up the pillows and bring them inside, saw Pepper's shovel and made a mental note to bring it in next. Zeus followed behind her, panting, anxious about the thunder. Abby stepped out front again and reached for her phone, when suddenly here Maddie came, jogging down the road, her dark hair flying out in the freshening wind.

"Sorry it took me so long. But you're not going to believe what just happened!" Maddie's faced flushed with excitement and exertion.

She turned her head to look out the window. "Have you seen those clouds? It looks like Mordor out there."

"What happened?" Pepper and Abby asked together.

Wound up, Maddie paced back and forth, and took a few breaths to settle down.

Maddie wanted to say goodbye to Vanna just in case she missed her, since Vanna's schedule was often erratic. Maddie arrived at the barn after school, chatting and helping Vanna with small tasks, fetching water or adjusting a halter rope. Some wranglers stood around as usual at the end of the day…a good deal of teasing and good-natured joshing, everyone laughing. Maddie and Vanna chipped in now and then.

Vanna was shoeing a handsome gray mule called Majesty. She crouched over, bent double with his hoof between her knees, reaching over for a tool, when Roy wandered up behind her. Vanna couldn't see him, but Maddie could. Maddie saw a sly grin spread across his face as he edged closer, cocking his head and pointing at Vanna's butt.

"Nice ass!" he crowed.

One wrangler briefly guffawed. Everyone else froze where they stood, staring at Vanna and Roy. Maddie was pretty sure she quit breathing.

Vanna kept working on the hoof between her knees, taking her time, methodically finishing her task. The silence stretched except for the rasping and tapping sounds of her work. Then she slowly lowered the hoof and straightened, turning to Roy with a deadpan face. She ran her palm along Majesty's hindquarters, patted him firmly.

"Yes, he is a magnificent ass." She put her hands on her hips, stared at him coldly. "But now we're all waiting."

Roy kept smiling, a little awkward, a little disconcerted at the lack of reaction from the wranglers.

"Waiting for what?" he sneered, his eyes shifting.

"You just said something inappropriate in front of a minor here." Vanna glanced at Maddie, who wanted to shrink and disappear.

"While you're at work. I thought you might like an opportunity to apologize."

"Naw, I don't hardly think so," he retorted, backing up a step. "The hell with that."

The men shuffled. Several moved aside to reveal that the head wrangler Pete Collins sat behind them on a bench, working on a bridle. Only now he stood up, setting the broken bridle aside. He strolled forward and touched his hat brim toward Maddie.

"Begging your pardon, Miz Maddie," he said politely, then turned to Vanna. "Miz Vanna."

He advanced until he stood two feet from Roy, his old face like granite, his eyes slits.

"You can gather up your gear and get out of here. You're fired, as of right this minute."

Roy's face sagged with disbelief. "Aw, Pete. You can't—"

"Yeah, I can. And I just did. You got any problems, you can take it up with the personnel department. I'm done with you. Now get out." Pete stiffened and his fists clenched, and his droopy moustache rose and bristled.

Roy's expression transformed into an ugly contortion, furious and hateful. He tried to say something, sputtering and spitting. Instead, he threw a vicious glare at Vanna and Maddie, started to raise his hand in Vanna's direction. Then he spun on his heel and stomped away into the tack room. A moment later he emerged with a saddle over his arm and, without another look back, he disappeared out the end of the barn. The rag he kept in his hip pocket for wiping his boots hung partly out, waving back and forth.

Done with her story, Maddie slumped back in her chair, her eyes wide. Her face shone with admiration.

"Wow," said Abby.

"Quite a story," said Pepper.

They talked about harassment and support. About the benefits of staying calm and collected like Vanna, coolly logical, instead of reacting with anger and heat. Outside, the low thunder picked up, and a sudden loud boom made them jump.

"You'd better get over to Marcus's place if you're going to watch your creepy show," Abby said to Pepper, "before it starts pouring." Pepper nodded. Maddie planned to spend the evening studying for finals, now just two days away, and Abby would help quiz her. Lightning flared and another crash of thunder shook the house. "Do you want me to stay?" he asked, looking out at the trees, flailing in the wind. "It looks bad."

"No, just hurry so you don't get drenched. We'll be fine. You don't want to miss your last precious episode of *Vampires vs. Zombies.*" Abby made a face and Maddie laughed.

Pepper grabbed his rain jacket and hurried out the door, limping down the steps to his car. Marcus lived only a few blocks away, but Abby knew his leg ached after his day at work. And he would be glad to have the car with the weather deteriorating. The storm smothered the evening sky now, slinging lightning barbs all around them, illuminating an agitated miasma of tortured cloud.

"Yikes," Abby said, echoing Pepper's favorite exclamation.

She and Maddie settled in on the couch with notebooks and pencils, trying to ignore the rising commotion outside. A nearly continuous growl of thunder rumbled between the brighter outbursts. Abby tried counting the seconds between lightning and thunder, but gave up after two minutes of endless muttering from the sky. Then in quick succession, two blinding bolts lit up the world, one after the next, and the immediate, deafening bangs of thunder stunned them, hands over their ears. Zeus barked and jumped into their laps, trembling, which broke the spell and made them laugh as they petted and consoled him.

"It's kind of hard to study," Maddie complained good-naturedly. "Maybe we should take a break until this is over."

"We just got started, and this storm could go on for hours," Abby said, standing. "But that lightning was so close—I want to make sure nothing nearby got hit."

She looked out the front door. Except for the thrashing trees, bark and leaves flying through the air, everything seemed intact. She checked that her car windows were up tight. Then she moved to the back deck, a little more protected from the gale, and peered out into the woods for a splintered tree or any signs of smoke or fire, a burning snag.

Something pale moved through the trees, off at the edge of her vision. Abby stared into the night, nearly dark now. Was that smoke? She sniffed for a burnt odor but the wind was too strong; it would blow away any scent.

Lightning flicked and she saw it again. Not smoke. Her breath caught and her heart leaped. A shirt, a man. Someone slipping behind a tree.

No one would be behind their house. The land sloped up into the forest, rocky and dense—no one ever walked there. Her heart bounded in her ears as she strained to see and hear. Tree branches whipped back and forth and the air moaned with the wail of pines. Then again, between trees. Then nothing.

A wave of fear slammed against her. She could not have imagined it. Could she? She backed up to the door, afraid to take her eyes off the woods, flooded with fright. What if it was Roy, come for revenge against Maddie? Or the pill pusher, come to fulfill his threat? Abby glanced hastily about and, with a dreadful jolt, she saw that the shovel was gone. Gone. The shovel she meant to bring back and put away. Someone took it. Someone had been on the deck, maybe looking in the window. Why would anyone take the shovel? As a weapon, you idiot, a completely different part of her brain screeched at her.

Galvanized, Abby rushed inside and shut the door hard, locked it.

"Everything okay?" Maddie asked, not looking up from her book.

Abby could hardly talk. She grabbed up her phone to call for help.

"Don't bother," Maddie said, not yet seeing Abby's face. "That big lightning must have knocked out the towers. The internet's down and there's no phone service at all."

"Get up," Abby cried, grabbing Maddie's arm. Her book thumped to the floor. "We have to get out of here."

All she could think was to get Maddie safe, get her away. It could be nothing; maybe she was overreacting, maybe even losing her mind. But she had to get Maddie out of there.

Maddie saw Abby's terror and her eyes opened wide. "What's happening?"

"I don't know," Abby said frantically, pulling her through the room. She snatched up her car keys. "I saw someone in the woods. I don't know who, but it might be bad. We have to leave. We have to get help."

"I don't understand!" Maddie howled, resisting as Abby hustled her out the door and down to the car.

"I think someone's out there, watching us," Abby jerked the passenger door open, pushed Maddie inside. Zeus followed them, dashing about as if it was a game, then he vaulted over Maddie and scrambled into the backseat.

Abby rushed around the car, looking fiercely back and forth, then jumped into the driver's seat and jammed the key into the ignition. She couldn't think straight. Should she go warn Pepper first? Or go for help first? Marcus lived in the opposite direction from the main highway, a few blocks away at the end of their road. What if she went there and someone followed? They might be trapped—she couldn't take Maddie there.

"Where are we going?" Maddie screeched.

"We have to go to the ranger station and get help." Abby backed out recklessly, nearly clipping a tree. She cranked the wheel and tramped the accelerator, the car lurching forward. Maddie cried out, gripping the dash. Then Abby realized, like a blow to her mind, that whoever it was might know Pepper's car. If he knew where they lived, he would know what they drove. What if he saw Pepper's car at Marcus's house? She had to warn them.

Abby slammed on the brakes and threw open the door, clambered out.

"Now what?" Maddie shouted.

"I have to warn Pepper—I'll run back down the road. You drive to the ranger station, okay?" Abby jerked Maddie's door open, pulled her out, pulled her around the car, and shoved her into the driver's seat. "Tell them to go to Marcus's house. Do you understand?"

"Come with me!" Maddie's face went white, filled with panic.

"No, I have to go. You can do it." Abby stared feverishly down the road, into the keening pines. A strange gleam caught her eye, deep in the gloom, but when she tried to fix on it she couldn't find it again.

"I've never driven at night. I've never driven your car," Maddie wailed, gripping the wheel, starting to cry. "I'm too scared."

Abby leaned in and flipped on the upper beams. Zeus leaped into the front and sat up stiffly beside Maddie, avidly looking about, as if he grasped the situation.

"Zeus will protect you—you know he will. You'll be fine. Now lock the doors and don't stop for anyone, anywhere. Don't even slow down, no matter what. Hurry! Go!"

Abby slammed the door and Maddie found the button, clicking the locks shut. She looked up at Abby again through the glass, beseeching and strained, but Abby shouted once more, *Hurry! Go!* Maddie shifted and gingerly pressed the pedal, slowly pulled away, glancing back over her shoulder as Abby motioned her on. The car crept down the road like a turtle, brake lights glowing frequently, making Abby want to run after her and shout at her to speed up.

She whirled and scanned the road. No one. Should she run along the pavement or go through the woods? There was no path, but it wasn't far and she would be extremely visible on the road. Lightning seared the sky and everything flashed white, making her feel utterly exposed. Abby gulped and dove into the forest, a peal of thunder chasing her. Everything was in motion, the trees swaying and bending, groaning and grinding.

Abby stumbled along, over stones and deadfall branches. Her cheeks stung from lashing switches as she pushed through the growth, her heart galloping like a great beast. What if it really was Roy? Would Maddie keep going if he ran in front of the car, threw himself on the hood? She imagined him smashing the windshield with the shovel, the splintering glass. Fear nearly overwhelmed her and she could hardly catch her breath. Then she heard something out of place even in that turbulence, felt a presence behind her. She twisted and crouched down to look.

Nothing.

Maybe there never was anyone. Maybe she had truly gone off the deep end. All these months of worry and exhaustion, so little sleep. Heidi. Pepper's fractured leg. The threats, the missing sign in the clinic. And now Roy, losing his job because of Vanna and Maddie, another possible menace. Maybe the stress was just too much and she had finally cracked.

There stood Marcus's house, the windows shining yellow and warm. Abby dashed up, wondering why she only saw Pepper's car. Where had Marcus left his car? She pushed the door open in back—Marcus never used his front door—and hastened through the kitchen, past the pantry, his golf clubs leaning against the wall.

A flood of relief. Pepper sat on the couch, watching the news, his leg propped on the coffee table. The television newsman droned on about a heatwave in Phoenix, the temperature up to one hundred eighteen, and a story about an older woman who died when her air conditioner broke. Pepper looked up leisurely, clearly expecting Marcus, startled at seeing Abby and her wild expression.

"What are you doing here? What's wrong?" he asked.

"Where's Marcus?" Abby said quickly, not even sure why.

Pepper frowned. "He had some snacks for us, but he forgot and left them at the clinic, so he just went back to get them. Why aren't you home with Maddie?"

"Someone—something—in the woods," Abby stammered. She felt breathless and incoherent, unsure of herself. "I saw someone. We couldn't call. The lightning—"

Pepper jerked his head over, looking behind her.

"Hey!" he exclaimed, awkwardly pushing himself up. "What the hell are you doing here?"

Abby felt a hand circle her left upper arm and a soft growl in her ear told her to stand very still.

30

Pepper lurched up, but the man behind Abby moved faster. Still gripping her arm, he pushed past her and shoved his right arm against Pepper. Pepper staggered crookedly on his weak leg and fell back into the couch.

Abby cried out in alarm, turning to look. Stiff almond hair, small brittle eyes, thick ropy forearms.

"Hatch? What are you—"

"I said to hold still. You should both listen to me." He adjusted his hold on her and pointed a blunt finger at Pepper. "If you move at all, Pepper, just one more inch, I swear I will break her neck. And don't think I won't."

Pepper had started to rise, livid. Now he froze.

Hatch's hand clenched her arm, an iron grasp just below Abby's shoulder, his thumb wedged deep into her armpit against the bone. He jabbed and an electric bolt of nerve shot down into her fingers. She flinched and Pepper's face jerked, but he did not move.

"You just couldn't let it go, could you?" Hatch sneered.

He bent over her, a hulk of muscle and heat, his head just above hers. Part of her mind kept thinking *Really, Hatch, please stop this*—as if that piece of her brain could not comprehend what was happening.

"You just had to keep poking, keep prodding," Hatch went on. He sighed loudly, dramatically. "Putting up signs, trying to warn everyone. Talking with that goon Shipley, giving him ideas."

"I never told—" Pepper started.

"Shut up. You must have told him. Why else did he pull me in yesterday, ask me all those questions? I know it was you." His thumb stabbed again and the nerve jangled through Abby's arm, taking her breath. She forced herself to not react, to not incite Pepper. Hatch's other hand now rested lightly on her right shoulder, beside her neck. His fingers strayed along her clavicle, barely touching, as if playing with it. Back and forth, softly, as her skin prickled and stung, as if the flesh itself was appalled.

"No. Not me." Pepper's face a mask of fury. "There were others, other hikers, who talked to him. He told me—"

"Others like who? That chubby woman, that artist? The one who worked at Kolb? She wasn't very smart, but suddenly she started asking me all these medical questions, acting really suspicious. Do you think I'm stupid? She must have gotten those ideas from you. I saw her there, hanging around the clinic. So I had to get rid of her."

Heidi.

Abby recoiled inside. She felt herself go rigid, every cell turn to stone. Impenetrable, unbelieving. Her muscles and organs and brain solidified, chunks of igneous rock. Her lungs locked and her heart clogged, her joints congealed. She felt like she would never move again.

"Do you know what you've cost me?" Hatch kept going and she heard his teeth grind. "You don't have a clue. I was making a fortune here, selling those pills. And now I have to leave, get out of here fast, before they arrest me. Start over somewhere else. New disguises, new identity, all that crap. All because of you."

Something tumbled loose. Abby took a breath and opened her mouth to explain, to protest that it wasn't Pepper, that she was actually the one who told Heidi not to buy the pills. As if telling him that would fix everything. But he felt her inhale to speak and he crammed his thumb against her. He twanged that rich brachial plexus of nerves and the buzzing pain leaped down her arm and ripped into her fingers. Unbidden, Abby thought of anatomy charts, nerves drawn in yellow. That braided river of nerves streaming down the limb. Dizzy, she stifled a gasp.

"I thought I'd eliminated you that night." Hatch's voice silky, venomous. "I couldn't believe my luck, seeing you walk up that trail. So close—I still can't believe I didn't finish the job."

A new rage rose inside her, threatened to overtake her. Her stony rigidity loosened, began to melt and seethe.

Where was Hatch going with this?

Pepper's eyes were dark, desperate.

And where was Maddie? Abby became aware of the storm, still blowing and flashing outside, rushes of rain. She realized she hadn't shown Maddie the switch for the windshield wipers. Fresh fears swamped her, that Maddie got lost, had an accident, got accosted. No, it wasn't Roy—it was Hatch, so Maddie should be safe. But shouldn't someone be here by now? Abby had no idea how much time had elapsed since she watched the car creep down the road with Maddie at the wheel, Zeus attentively riding shotgun. It seemed hours ago. Days.

"What do you want?" Pepper rasped. Abby knew Pepper was trying to engage him, create a dialogue, shift the point.

"I don't know yet. I just hate you and want you to pay for this."

His hand on her felt hot and harsh. He kept thumbing across her nerves every five or ten seconds, kept zapping out voltage. She couldn't concentrate, could hardly think straight, bracing against it over and over. But she grasped the danger. Hatch just admitted so much. From Pepper's dire expression he understood, too.

"Maybe I'll just take this little piece of sugar with me," Hatch purred. His right hand rose, and he dragged his finger across her mouth. "I could use a sweet little pet like her. For a while."

He pressed his lips against her temple, a lingering kiss. Then he murmured something and licked her cheek, a long slow swipe.

Abby snarled, wrenching her face away, unable to control her revulsion. Pepper went gray and his lips curled back, feral.

"Don't do that, pet," Hatch said quietly in her ear. His fingers on her clavicle again, stroking. He shifted back to Pepper. "Don't worry. She'll learn to be a good little pet—it won't take me long to tame her. I can teach her tricks."

He was accelerating, taunting Pepper into action. Tormenting Pepper until he moved, tried to intervene, so Pepper would have to blame himself when Hatch did something to her. Abby grasped with certainty that Hatch would never take her with him—it was too risky. She would slow him down too much.

She must do something. Now. Break away, throw him off balance, before it was too late. Her mind raced, sorting options. Jab her finger in his face, fall to the floor kicking, leap for the door. Something, anything, was better than just standing here. Her heart quickened crazily and she gathered her muscles.

"Abby!" Pepper glared at her, his eyes a blue burn. "Abby. Look at me. Listen to me."

She glanced back and forth, planning her move.

"Be quiet," Hatch ordered Pepper. His head remained alongside hers; she felt his jaw move when he talked, his breath on her forehead.

"Abby!" Pepper said again, fierce. His eyes snared and held her. His face altered, vivid. "Listen to me. Don't move. I mean it. Just look at me. Right at me."

"I said shut up," Hatch shouted, angry. He too sensed something changing.

"Don't. Move." Pepper projected a searing stare at her.

"If you think you can—" Hatch began.

Abby felt it, a whirr of air, a draft.

A loud crack, a crunch, by her ear.

Hatch's hand clamped and a fiery jolt whizzed to her fingertips. Then reprieve…the hand released, sliding off. Hatch leaned heavily against her, making her stumble, then he slowly toppled away.

Pepper was suddenly with her, catching her up, drawing her away.

"Don't look," he commanded, pulling her harder.

But of course she looked.

Hatch lay twisted on the floor, unconscious, a deep rutted wound above his ear spilling blood.

Marcus stood over him, a darkly stained golf club clutched in both hands, his knuckles white. His face unrecognizable, warped with rage, as he stared ferociously down at Hatch.

"She's not your pet, you fucking monster," he said.

31

Pepper hauled Abby away, out of the room, out through the never-used front door, which creaked and groaned when he shoved it open. They stood braced against each other in the yard under a soft rainfall, the drops illuminated from the window, a dreamlike silver mist in the coal-black night. Pale and distraught, Pepper kept running his hands over her, as if searching for defects, as if he must assure himself of her existence again and again.

"I'm all right," Abby said, capturing his hands with hers. Her left fingers acted clumsy, tingling. She felt blank, detached, struck almost dumb. Now and then the sky briefly lit, a glimpse of tattered cloud, but the storm stalked away, grumbling and cranky.

"What was he doing?" Pepper insisted, again touching her face, her hair, moving his hands down her arms, her back. "I couldn't tell. I thought I would go insane."

Abby shook out her hand, her arm, the tingle diminishing. But most language had abandoned her. "I'm all right, I'm all right," was all she could say. They seemed the only words she knew.

He kissed her forehead, then leaned back, his eyes hunting her once more.

"Oh, no," she cried, suddenly alert, reaching up and touching his beard, his cheek. "Why is there blood on you? How did you get hurt?"

He made a sound between a laugh and a sob. "That's not me. That's you. I mean, that's his blood. On you, on your face. And now on my face, from kissing you."

"Well, goddammit," Abby said severely, swiping at her cheek. The rain wet her face and her palm came off watery red.

"It doesn't matter," he said and enclosed her in his arms.

That's how they stood when seconds later headlights came bouncing up the road, blinding beams that probed the night, a roar of diesel and a flash of emergency lights as rangers piled out, some coming up to Abby and Pepper, some dashing inside. Then a truck door slammed and a high voice shrieked, a loud bark. Maddie flew up to them and stopped short, staring horrified at Abby. Zeus ran into her from behind. Pepper grabbed her.

"It's okay. She's not hurt," he said, carefully slow and clear.

Maddie nodded and gulped, seizing his arm as the paramedic Paul stepped in and led Abby back under the porch, out of the rain. He sat Abby down and quickly examined her head and face.

Abby shook her head and pointed backward with her thumb. She shivered all over but her words were coming back.

"He needs you, in there. That's his blood, not mine."

Someone put a blanket over her shoulders, someone offered her a towel. Pepper sat and blotted her face with the towel while Maddie clung to his side as if glued there. Vanna appeared—why on earth was she there?—and peeled Maddie off, led her a few steps away, talking quietly. Maddie nodded and watched Abby fearfully, as if she didn't dare look away. As if Abby might disappear.

"Marcus!" Abby said abruptly, suddenly remembering him.

She and Pepper twisted around, looked through the front window where he stood inside, still immobile, his round face wild-eyed and his teeth bared. A ranger attempted to gently pry the golf club from his locked hands, telling him to let go now. Behind them on the floor, others bent over Hatch.

Abby broke her gaze from Hatch and looked at Marcus. Their eyes met and his mouth moved. Some sort of response.

It took forever to piece it all together. To explain what happened, to answer all the questions, then answer them again. Taking photos, writing in notebooks. At some point, Shipley appeared, and they had to start all over. Shipley fumed and paced, blaming himself for not acting sooner. Waiting for a search warrant, he planned to arrest Hatch the next day.

Once Hatch was gone in the ambulance, everyone moved back inside, and Vanna eventually left. Shipley shifted back and forth, bringing Abby a glass of water, asking Maddie if she felt okay, clapping Pepper on the back. Abby smiled a little, surprised to see this tender side. He didn't know Marcus very well so he shook his hand and thanked him.

Then Shipley turned official again, scrutinizing the scene, although there wasn't much to see. He asked Pepper why a shovel lay on the hood of his car; Pepper looked perplexed and Abby startled, remembering the missing shovel from their backyard. Hatch must have carried it with him when he followed her, then left it outside. If she had known he was chasing her through the woods with that shovel, she thought, she probably would have died of terror.

Shipley bent over to peer at the floor, the congealed pool of blood, the stained golf club lying next to it. He stepped around the club, studied it without touching it. Then he looked up at Marcus with a funny expression.

"Really? A two iron?" he asked dryly. "You *must* be good."

Marcus's face twitched and Pepper snorted.

"What am I missing?" Abby asked, confused.

Marcus finally spoke, found his voice. He needed to talk, to say something or anything, and words tumbled from him like water from a broken dam. As if explaining about the two iron became somehow important. He concentrated on Abby, his eyes still shocked, showing white. His fists opened and closed repeatedly.

"It's an old golf joke. A two iron is a difficult club and no one almost ever uses it because it's really hard to hit because it's so long and the loft of the head is shallow." His words piled together, barely discernible. "So the joke goes that this golfer doesn't want to get hit by lightning, so he holds up his two iron toward the sky, and the lightning hits a nearby tree instead. And then the golfer says 'See? Not even god can hit a two iron!'"

Marcus pulled in a long shaky breath.

"Okay, then," Abby said, forgetting herself, seeing how he looked on the edge of hysteria. "So why did you pick the two iron? If it's so hard to hit?"

A reckless laugh burst from him. "As if I even noticed. I came in and I saw…I saw…I saw what was happening, and I just blindly reached into the bag. I just tried to be so quiet. I just—"

Abby finally got it, turning to Pepper. "That's why you kept telling me not to move. Because our heads were so close together. Hatch and me. You saw Marcus behind me, and you knew that if I moved, if Marcus missed, he might hit me instead."

Pepper closed his eyes and nodded.

Marcus let go a little more. "I didn't have enough room to take a full swing—the wall was too close. I was so scared. And so angry. I felt like I could rip him apart with my bare hands."

"If you'd taken a full swing, he'd probably be dead." Shipley nudged the club with his toe, then looked sharply at Marcus. "You were pretty damn accurate, even with all that adrenalin. I mean, he was right next to her, right? What was the margin of error—an inch or two?"

Marcus breathed deeply again, his hands no longer clasping, his eyes less frenzied. He murmured humbly, "Well, I can be pretty good, on the right day. A golf ball is a pretty small target, so you sort of *have* to be accurate."

They turned to Maddie for her story. She sat wedged between Abby and Pepper, clutching them to her, her face pale but lively. Zeus lay on their feet.

Maddie told how she drove away from Abby and immediately became lost, a wrong turn in the dark, then missed the main road. She had to reverse and find it. Zeus kept peering out the windows and woofing, scaring her to death. Once on the main road, cars began honking because she drove too slowly, so she sped up and kept her eyes so intently on the pavement that she never saw the ranger station. Muddled, terrified, confounded by the night and the wind and storm, Maddie couldn't tell if she had missed it or hadn't passed it yet, so she forged onward to the one place she knew she could find—the mule barn. She arrived to find Vanna climbing into her farrier's truck to leave.

Panicked and incoherent, flailing with anguish, it took Maddie a few minutes to make Vanna understand. With the phones still down, Vanna piled Maddie and Zeus into her truck and took off to alert the rangers. Then they all came upon Abby and Pepper, standing there in the rain.

"Nice work," Pepper remarked, holding Maddie close. "That was incredibly brave."

"Wait," Abby said. "So my car is at the barn?"

"Um, I guess so," Maddie replied, suddenly uncertain. "I mean, I think I turned it off. I probably shut the doors. And locked it. Maybe."

Shipley put his hand on Maddie's head and fondly rocked it, a gentle thing. "I'll go check on it right now. You folks just go home. We'll finish sorting this out tomorrow. I didn't even think you were old enough to drive."

Maddie glanced at Pepper and they both said nothing.

Other personnel had completed their tasks—photos and reports. The golf club was taken for evidence and a large towel now covered the blood on the floor.

Abby went to Marcus. She felt edgy and weak, relieved and fidgety. She could only imagine his state of mind.

"Do you want to spend the night at our place?" she asked him with concern. "You can have the couch. You shouldn't stay here alone tonight."

"Nope." Marcus seemed back to himself, poised and organized. At least on the surface. "I'll never be able to sleep tonight. Maybe never again in my life. So I just called Mitzi—the phones are back up. I'm driving to Flagstaff, right now. I'll spend the night with her."

They all stared at him.

"Oh, come on," he said, rolling his eyes. "As if you didn't all know by now that we're dating each other."

Pepper gave him a look. "We all knew it, Marcus. We just weren't quite sure that you knew it."

Then Pepper took Abby and Maddie to his car as Shipley left for the mule barn. Shipley promised to retrieve the car keys and bring them to Abby the next day. Hopefully, he added, since Maddie had no recollection of where they might be. Just to be sure, Shipley had her check her pockets before he left.

They arrived home. Abby wanted to collapse in the kitchen, make some tea, find herself. She had gone dull again, withdrawn, her thoughts slipping between those unspeakable threats, that he would take her with him.

"No, not yet." Pepper took charge, guiding her to the bathroom. She knew he saw her darkness. "You have to shower because there's still blood on you, and it's in your hair. I'll help. Maddie, please bring us fresh towels."

He shed his shoes and briskly stripped off her clothes, left them in a pile. Then he ran the water as hot as she could stand and stepped into the shower with her, still dressed in his shirt and jeans. He lathered her hair twice and scrubbed her skin while Maddie delivered the towels. Abby stood passively, closed her eyes and let him take over, let the soap and scalding water rinse over her like a river and cleanse her as he scoured every molecule of Hatch from her skin and hair. It felt like a baptism, an induction back to normalcy. At least some kind of normalcy.

Pepper wrapped her in towels and turned her over to Maddie to help dry her hair, while he dripped in his sodden clothes and began to unbutton his shirt, waiting for Maddie and Abby to leave the bathroom so he could undress.

"You know, Uncle John," Maddie said, glancing at him as she went, "you didn't have to leave your clothes on just because of me."

"Excuse me?" he said.

"I mean, I've seen naked men before."

"*Excuse me?*" he said with force.

"Don't forget, I worked at hospice. One of my jobs was to help patients take baths."

Pepper glared and shut the door. "Just remember. I'm not dying."

The shower did Abby wonders. She unwound and let Maddie wield the hairdryer, recognizing she needed something to do.

No one had an appetite for supper. They all ended up on the master bed, Maddie propped between them. They talked for hours, exploring their thoughts, sometimes deep, sometimes worthless and silly. They discussed what makes a good person good and what makes another person go bad, why some people are kind and others turn mean. About the value of possessions, and the worth of friendships. And they delved into fantasy, about whether there ever were unicorns, and if fairies or giants still existed, maybe somewhere on a lost island. Finally around one o'clock in the morning they got hungry, and Abby brought a plate of cheese and crackers and sliced apples to the bed, where they devoured it.

"This has to be the last time," Pepper lamented. He reached over Maddie and held his palm along Abby's cheek, searched her eyes. He stroked her eyebrow, that crooked step, that old scar. "Can we please go a year without some sort of disaster? It doesn't seem too much to ask. This never happened before you came along."

Abby smiled faintly. "I think I should point out that it never happened to me until you came along. Who's the real catalyst here?"

Maddie sighed, appreciative. "Do you know how amazing it is to be in a conversation with people who use words like *catalyst* in a sentence?" She patted each of them on the arm. "It's surreal."

Zeus, who sprawled asleep at the foot of the bed until the food appeared, inched his way to the plate and pleaded for a share with his wide amber eyes.

"I thought there was a policy of no dogs on the bed," Pepper pointed out mildly.

"Not tonight," Abby and Maddie said together.

Eventually they extinguished the light and tried to sleep. Maddie succumbed first, then Pepper. The storm disappeared. A full moon stood high in the sky, brazenly claiming the night. The bedroom shone with that milky light, and Abby thought of all the moons embracing their planets. She thought first of Mercury and Venus, bereft of moonly companions, having to orbit the sun alone. Of Earth with its one glowing friend, called simply "the moon," in a singular lack of imagination. Mars with its two small jagged moons, Phobos and Deimos, barely moons at all…Phobos zooming around Mars three times a day, drawing closer and closer, spiraling in, doomed by Mars' gravity to someday perish. Then the huge planets farther out, tugging dozens of moons and moonlets into orbit for themselves, as if greedy…as if they couldn't get enough moons, all shapes and sizes, all speeds. Some moons even running backwards, whimsically circling the other way, just because they could. Jupiter with its giant

Ganymede…Saturn with its Titan…a rare moon cloaked in true atmosphere. By the time Abby reached Uranus, she finally drifted off. Near dawn, she awoke when someone next to her twitched, a faint groan. Barely conscious, Abby reached out to touch Maddie, to soothe her back into slumber. Instead, her fingers contacted a furry head, and Zeus rolled over and slopped a wet kiss on her nose. Maddie lay between Zeus and Pepper, deeply asleep, while Pepper lightly snored.

Wide awake, knowing she would not sleep more, Abby slid out of bed and went to make coffee.

32

The Yellowstone trip did not disappoint.

They met Gem and William at Old Faithful after driving seven hundred miles north, across cracked flaking deserts and endless jumbled canyons, gold and ginger and buff. The roads skirted purple hills and indigo mountains, flying beneath a pale blue sun-washed heaven. They played trivia games, listened to audio books, talked about things important and things frivolous, and watched the timeless terrain unfold.

Maddie claimed the backseat, settling herself in a nest of books and papers. She read her novel to them aloud, after a careful disclaimer that it needed more work, especially the parts about Othello the black mule, who saved the day by discovering the villain and trapping him in a ravine for wolves to destroy. At one low point in the plot, a weary Othello and the heroine trekked into a deep prehistoric valley where they drank from an enchanted green river and restored themselves for the battles ahead. Abby and Pepper proclaimed it to be the most promising story they had read in years, and hoped the movie would do it justice. Maddie rolled her eyes, thrilled.

Yellowstone was not a great place for dogs. Zeus stayed with Marietta, after many goodbyes from Maddie. In exchange, Marietta gave them a crunch-topped homemade berry pie, which they demolished before reaching Wyoming.

"Best trade I've ever made," commented Pepper, his lips slightly purple, crumbs on his shirt.

Maddie howled. "Zeus is worth more than a pie, Uncle John!"

Abby avoided the crowds by rising early, when dawn was hardly a suggestion. That minimal lightness of sky where night bends toward a hope, but not yet a certainty, of morning. With few people about, she paced the boardwalks across the Upper Geyser Basin, shrouded in brimstone vapors. She moved through steams from simmering pools and gibbering pots, some waters barely gulping, others hissing frantically. She thought about the last time Yellowstone burst, over half a million years ago, thought of this unsteady world beneath her feet with its colliding plates and shuffling continents, the deep stirring magma. Then she sat with Old Faithful in the pale peach daylight and watched it erupt, send its boiling water far into the sky, that massive feathered plume.

Pepper and Maddie found her there. The scalding water bubbled and trickled away down the blasted hill, the ruined slopes.

Pepper stood behind her and rubbed her shoulders, while Maddie moved off a way, giving them room.

"You good?" he asked.

Abby nodded. "I'm good. Better than you'd think. There's nothing like the canyon, nothing like Yellowstone, to restore your perspective. It's a big, old, complicated planet. Here we are, there we go. Blink, blink."

"Well, that's reassuring," he said, a little hesitant. "If you say so."

Abby laughed and pulled him down next to her, called Maddie over. "I think we're supposed to be meeting Gem and William for breakfast in about ten minutes. Are you hungry?"

"Of course," Maddie said.

For the last three summers, William worked at Yellowstone as a seasonal interpretive ranger. They could hardly have a better guide. Now, just graduated from his PHD geology program, they officially called him Dr. Bridges, much to his annoyance. Hardly five minutes passed without someone tapping his knowledge, Maddie most of all, diving at every concept with unquenchable curiosity.

"Are you always so exhausting?" William asked Maddie. She had just insisted he look up another relentless question when he didn't immediately know the answer.

"Yes," said Abby and Pepper together.

Maddie looked pleased.

Gem and Maddie bonded instantly. When everyone else tired in the afternoon, they went hiking instead of napping. At night, while Pepper and William had a beer in the bar, they pulled a drowsy Abby from her book and made her explain the dark dome, all the lights that glimmered or winked or burned from trillions of miles away.

Twice, Gem and William took Maddie with them on some pursuit, leaving Abby and Pepper alone. Abby suspected Pepper put them up to it, but didn't care. She knew he felt lively, his leg rapidly gaining muscle as he walked longer and even jogged a little. As he improved, Abby started to fathom just how truly abnormal their last few months had been, Maddie notwithstanding.

"I think I've been depressed," he confessed, pulling her against him after the others left. He administered a long, slow kiss that warmed her inside out, a deep flush. Then he sat on the bed, arranging her on his lap, nuzzling her throat. "More depressed than I realized, with my leg and all. And I was so preoccupied with those heart attacks. Now that I'm better, now that everything's resolved, I feel like maybe I need to make up for lost time."

"Mm." Abby brushed his beard, ran her fingers through his dense brown hair, grown longer than usual, trailing down his neck. She remembered that weekend in Jerome, right before Heidi disappeared, when they seemed so carefree and spontaneous. How long ago was that—four months? Five?

Now his eyes danced, boyish, a blue sparkle she hadn't seen in a very long time.

"Is that a thing? Catching up?" she asked.

His mouth twisted, a roguish smile. "Maybe."

"Wait. What if Maddie comes back?"

"I locked the door."

Abby was about to point out that Maddie had a key. But he turned suddenly hungry, ravenous, and nearly overcame her... so different from their cautious, slow lovemaking since Maddie arrived. His hands mouth tongue consumed her, demanding, everywhere at once, coaxing each nerve alive until she was nothing but a hot smoldering wick, ready to burst into flame. He surged and she ignited, and every nerve unraveled and sprang apart.

They were so wrung out that they could only cling weakly to each other, wrecked, for a long time.

"Wow," Abby said finally. "That might have done it."

"Done what?" He flopped on his back.

"You know. Caught us up."

He moved his head a fraction and looked sideways at her. His hair messed, his beard unruly, his eyes soft.

"I hope not," he said, wiggling his eyebrows. "Because I want to do that again. Well, not right this minute."

Abby groaned. "You almost killed me."

"But what a way to go, right?"

She opened her eyes and they grinned together.

"I think maybe I just fell in love with you," she said, reaching over, smoothing his rowdy hair from his forehead.

"Just now? You weren't already?" He acted wounded.

"I thought I was. But now I see I wasn't, because this is even better."

He rolled over and wrapped himself around her.

———

Then their trip to Yellowstone was over.

Then Maddie left.

Pepper planned to drive her to the Phoenix airport, but Maddie declined. Instead, she took the shuttles again. Grand Canyon to Flagstaff. Flagstaff to Phoenix Sky Harbor. That long downhill dive, seeing the pines shrink from Ponderosa to pinyon to scrub, watching the saguaros arise. She wanted to reverse her arrival journey, to retreat the way she had entered. To ease herself back to Illinois, to her parents, in a long empty voyage. She said she needed the space to prepare herself.

Summer work at the clinic took on its hectic pace. Tourists poured in by the thousands, the millions. Cars crashed and the sun beat down, burning and blistering skin. There were no more heart attacks in young people, but hikers broke ankles and hit their heads. They carried too little water, suffered dehydration and heatstroke, and one of them died, deep in the canyon on the wrong trail on the wrong day, when the temperature struck one hundred ten degrees at the river. Diabetics forgot their pills and asthmatics lost their inhalers. Fetuses miscarried and would-be parents cried, while other couples hooked up without condoms and their urine burned, whirling with chlamydia. One man shot another man in a fight at the bar, and a woman stumbled and fell off the rim. Gone.

Abby and Pepper worked long hours, took care of the locals and visitors. Their lives settled back into a routine. They worked, they walked and hiked. Abby ran and Pepper resumed drawing, and they lounged on the deck with morning coffee and evening books. The sky revolved above them and the colors transformed, aching blue to deep purple, delicate yellow and orange to burnt black. They laughed, cooked dinners, made love, worried about their patients.

Everything seemed back to normal.

Except it wasn't.

Zeus often paced. Late afternoons, after Abby or Pepper picked him up from Marietta's, he stood staring out the screen door, waiting. At night he slept in Maddie's old room. If someone accidentally closed the bedroom door during the day, Zeus plopped outside in the hall until one of them opened it. Abby pitied the plight of waiting dogs: they grieved without understanding, without knowing from minute to minute when it would end. Maybe right now. Maybe in a few minutes. Maybe tomorrow. Maybe next week. Maybe never. Abby played with him more and took him running with her, which made him bark and cavort with joy. Pepper walked alone less into the canyon, taking the rim trails instead, where a dog was welcome.

Once, when Abby retrieved Zeus from Marietta and Wilbur, she pulled away as Priscilla arrived in her car. Priscilla pretended not to see her.

They tried not to talk about Hatch. Shipley told them Hatch moved from the hospital to a prison rehab unit; his speech was broken and he could barely walk, a shambling, uneven gait. They hadn't found Heidi, for Hatch's thoughts were too scrambled to recall. There were small signs of memory improvement, though, so maybe someday. Every now and then, Abby and Beverly Forrest sent notes back and forth.

Marcus and Mitzi talked about moving in together, either her coming to the canyon or him going to Flagstaff. Neither idea seemed practical, and for now things stayed the same. He carried a haunted look at times, and Abby offered him the number for her telephone counselor, which he wrote down.

Maddie, of course, was not really gone from their lives. The texts and emails sailed back and forth, and they talked frequently. Her parents engineered a bonding event, a forced family vacation to New York City, and her comments arrived often:

They sleep till noon, so I go walking and eat bagels. New York is kind of cool.

I sit in the park with nannies and old men until my parents wake up, and then we spend two hours over lunch, reading the paper and not talking.

We could do this at home.

The nannies and old men are kind of funny. Some talk to me.

Everyone is walking dogs and making me sad. Missing Zeus.

I made them take me to the natural history museum. They lasted an hour.

I think they're doing things to each other in their bed. I'm hiding under my pillow.

So do you think you two will ever have kids?

Was that too personal? I'm just saying, maybe you should talk about it.

I could use a cousin, that's all. Don't be mad, okay?

We saw a musical. Mom loved it and I did not. *Cats.* I hate cats. I miss Zeus.

Back home. At least I have my own space again.

I finished my book, will email to you. Othello is my hero.

I miss good Mexican food.

Tell Marcus my dad got bit by a squirrel that made a nest in our garage. My dad said the squirrel had mean little eyes and fluffy blond fur on top and looked like Trump.

We're checking out boarding schools. What do you think of that idea?

I think they're getting a divorce.

Abby and Pepper debated the wisdom of boarding school. Maybe it would free her from the endless drama at home and allow her to thrive. Or maybe it would leave her feeling abandoned, lost. Abby thought fondly of that night after Hatch, the four of them tightly together, supporting each other.

"It's bizarre," Pepper said. "I know they can't afford it. For some reason, though, the banks keep giving them loans. Or credit cards. Or maybe they've been robbing convenience stores."

Abby felt grim. "It's so impersonal, a school like that. But it might be better than at home with her parents, especially if they split up. I can't imagine that they restrain themselves. I'm sure they say terrible things about each other."

"There's no good answer here." Pepper sighed. "We'll do what we can. Maybe we should go visit her before classes start, before she moves to that new school."

Abby blinked, surprised she hadn't thought of that. It certainly might boost Maddie's morale. "But we wouldn't stay with them, would we? At their home?"

"Heaven forbid," Pepper said. "Why do you think motels were invented?"

"Do we even have to see them?" Abby knew that was unrealistic. Although she had never met them, she could hardly imagine sitting with those people, making small talk, pretending not to disdain them. Usually Abby tried hard not to judge, gave everyone a second chance, but she felt stubbornly shut on this front.

Pepper laughed. "Well, I don't imagine we can just pull up in front of their house and honk the horn. Have her come running out, wave as we leave." He paused, contemplating. "Although the idea is definitely appealing."

"We can go to the museums in Chicago," said Abby, warming more to the idea. "Go to the lakefront, go to a concert. See a play. What fun would that be, to do all that with her."

Pepper promised to start making calls, to see what arrangements could be made. They had to do something.

33

On the highway to Flagstaff, a serious accident halted traffic in both directions. By the time they edged past the wreckage, the paramedics and ambulances were gone and mangled remnants of twisted cars littered the shoulders, bent metal and broken glass, glittering along the road like confetti in the warm August sun. It oddly made Abby think of her work, just cars instead of humans, reduced to rubble by poor decisions and reckless whims. At least, some days felt like that, and today her mood seemed fragile, too raw.

"We're going to be really late," Abby fretted as they finally picked up speed again.

"Check the airline on your phone," Pepper suggested. "Maybe the plane will be delayed."

The plane was on schedule. Naturally.

"Well, it will work out, just not quite how we planned," Pepper assured her. "We can roll with it."

Abby leaned back and watched the sky. Flexibility was not her strength. But he was right, of course. The sun blazed across northern Arizona, now enduring a summer of drought, an eccentric contrast to last year's storms. The sapphire sky, so bright it nearly gleamed, felt soothing and timeless, and small woolly clouds floated above, white tufts of cotton. Abby picked up his hand and kissed the back of it.

"You know how I am…I like everything to go smoothly. I just want it to work out best for her."

He smiled. "We should be doing this, right?"

"Are you kidding?"

He pulled into the Flagstaff airport, an understated place, small and simple. Cars shuttled in and out, places to go, and they impatiently waited their turn at a corner.

"Do we have time to park?" Pepper asked.

"I don't think so. Just pull up to the terminal, up to the curb, and we'll figure it out then."

"There!" Pepper pointed.

Maddie stood waiting next to her bags and boxes, standing on tiptoe, craning to look at the approaching cars. She seemed a little taller, her raven hair a little shorter, curving like a shiny wing beneath her chin. Her bangs were too long, but those blue eyes pierced through and caught them like a beacon.

Her face lit up.

Acknowledgements

I remain indebted to Cheryl Pagel MD, physician at the Grand Canyon for years, who has helped keep everything accurate and authentic.

No writer gets by without help. Thanks many times over for my dedicated first-draft readers: Ted Cavallo, Cheryl Pagel MD, Kelly Luba DO, and Cindy Alt. And to fellow author Patricia Cox for her final read and valuable suggestions—and so much support.

Much thanks to Sara Depert Ferguson, my role model for Vanna, an extraordinary farrier who helped me with horseshoeing terminology and equipment. And for tackling and excelling in an unusual and demanding profession with determination and grace.

Thanks to my favorite radiologist, Katherine Cavallo Hom MD, for the phrase "gravity got mad."

Appreciation to authors Thomas Myers and Michael Ghiglieri for *Over the Edge: Death in Grand Canyon*, Puma Press, Flagstaff, Arizona, 2001.

Thanks to Steven Curry MD, toxicologist, for his guidance about heavy metal toxicities.

And for the hospitality and magnificent breakfast at The Surgeon's House Bed & Breakfast in Jerome.

Thanks also to all the helpful publishing experts at the University of Nevada Press: especially Sara Hendricksen because, without her enthusiasm and support from the beginning, I never would have had this opportunity; to project editor Sara Vélez Mallea; marketing maven Iris Saltus, copyeditor Luke Torn, and JoAnne Banducci for their hard work.

And I am endlessly grateful for all the others, and the resources at my fingertips that helped keep the science and medicine accurate, especially the CDC and AAFP websites.

On anorexia:
https://www.aafp.org/afp/2015/0101/p46.html

About those moons:
https://solarsystem.nasa.gov/moons/in-depth/
https://www.space.com/20413-phobos-deimos-mars-moons.html

On Jerome:
https://en.wikipedia.org/wiki/Jerome,_Arizona
http://jeromechamber.com/history-of-jerome-arizona/

On performance-enhancing drugs:
http://www.mayoclinic.org/healthy-lifestyle/fitness/in-depth
    /performance-enhancing-drugs/art-20046134?pg=2
https://www.drweil.com/vitamins-supplements-herbs
    /supplements-remedies/can-performance-enhancing
    -supplements-kill/

On kidney disease:
https://www.niddk.nih.gov/

On the Orphan Mine site and uranium:
https://www.nps.gov/grca/learn/historyculture/miners.htm
http://www.azcentral.com/story/news/local/arizona-best-reads
    /2017/03/08/uranium-mining-near-grand-canyon-safe-answer
    -may-water/98816536/
http://www.grandcanyontreks.org/orphan.htm
https://www.atsdr.cdc.gov/csem/csem.asp?csem=16&po=9

About gold at the canyon:
http://www.roadtoroota.com/public/181.cfm

Thundersnow:
https://weather.com/science/news/what-thundersnow-and-why
   -does-it-happen-20140218
http://news.nationalgeographic.com/news/2009/03/090303
   -thunder-snow-storm.html

Lightning:
http://www.lightningsafety.noaa.gov/struck.shtml
https://www.nytimes.com/2017/07/18/us/hit-by-lightning-tales
   -from-survivors.html
https://en.wikipedia.org/wiki/Lichtenberg_figure

Lead toxicity:
https://www.ncbi.nlm.nih.gov/pmc/articles/PMC5135532/
https://www.cdc.gov/mmwr/preview/mmwrhtml/00000164.htm

About the Author

SANDRA CAVALLO MILLER is a retired family physician in Phoenix who spent most of her career in academic medicine, but she was always a writer in her secret heart. Little fiction has been written about women physicians and modern primary care, and she enjoys showing the personal and medical challenges in an entertaining way. You are likely to find her hiking or on a horse, or off somewhere under a tree reading about volcanology and astronomy.

Check out her website at www.skepticalword.com, and you can contact her at skepticalword@gmail.com.